"What can I do? The  something."

Mark reached through the narrow gap and touched Charlotte's fingers, the closest they could come to holding hands with his still handcuffed. "This." He sighed. "This helps. Knowing I'm not alone."

"You're not alone," Charlotte whispered.

"That's the best part of a SEAL team. Someone has your back."

"I'll help you any way I can."

"You've made that clear. At this point, I think it's best if we let things play out."

"How much can you take?"

"The SEAL training drummed all the quit out of me years ago."

"I'm serious."

"So am I. I know you're scared. I'm sorry. We just have to stay tough. This is a performance. An attempt to prove he can best a navy SEAL, that's all."

"Well, it's not even B-movie material."

He sputtered a small laugh. "Let him have his fifteen minutes of fame. I can take whatever he dishes out."

"How?"

"Mind over matter. When I get an opening, I'll jump on it no matter how bad I look right now."

"*We'll* jump on it," she said.

* * *

Dear Reader,

Mark Riley has been making waves almost since birth. The older twin, he was known for being outrageous and outspoken. He even went so far as to buck the Riley family tradition of serving in the US Army by joining the Navy and becoming a SEAL.

Reputation and military rivalries aside, Mark's notorious curiosity ignites when he sees an old family friend, Charlotte Hanover, in a new light as a woman and a rising star in the art world.

But the man who has been tormenting the Riley family interrupts Mark's attempts to reconnect with Charlotte, and Mark must rely on all of his skills and training to protect her.

This wild adventure was a joy to write. I loved discovering the balance between Charlotte and Mark as they worked to escape an unimaginable crisis. I hope you come to love these two characters and the rest of the Riley family as much as I do.

Live the adventure!

Regan

ESCAPE WITH THE NAVY SEAL

Regan Black

HARLEQUIN

ROMANTIC
SUSPENSE

Recycling programs
for this product may
not exist in your area.

ISBN-13: 978-1-335-62683-7

Escape with the Navy SEAL

This edition published by arrangement with Harlequin Books S.A.

For questions and comments about the quality of this book, please contact us at CustomerService@Harlequin.com.

Harlequin Enterprises ULC
22 Adelaide St. West, 40th Floor
Toronto, Ontario M5H 4E3, Canada
www.Harlequin.com

Printed in U.S.A.

Regan Black, a *USA TODAY* bestselling author, writes award-winning action-packed novels featuring kick-butt heroines and the sexy heroes who fall in love with them. Raised in the Midwest and California, she and her family, along with their adopted greyhound, two arrogant cats and a quirky finch, reside in the South Carolina Lowcountry, where the rich blend of legend, romance and history fuels her imagination.

Visit the Author Profile page at Harlequin.com for more titles.

For Melanie and her mother, Patty, two amazing women who exemplify everything beautiful about what family means. I am thankful every day for your friendship, laughter, wisdom and guidance.
The world is a better place because you've shared your joy of art through the color, perspective, light and shadow that creates the unique canvas of a life well lived and well loved.

Chapter 1

Alone in the central room of the art gallery, Charlotte Hanover turned a slow circle, surrounded by her canvases. A year's worth of work about to go on display for anyone with eyes and an opinion to critique. She closed her eyes, breathing deeply through her nose. If she ignored the murmur of voices from the side rooms, it was almost like being in the peaceful, muted light of her studio at home.

In minutes, the gallery doors would open to the VIP guests for her first solo showing. Approximately an hour after that, any interested art lover in Virginia Beach would be welcome to wander in and take a closer look, as well.

She pressed a hand to her belly to smother another wave of jitters and felt the rich silk of her dress under her palm.

Almost like home. Almost like home.

She almost believed it. In her studio, she'd be in a soft T-shirt and her favorite jeans that were held together with more paint than denim after all these years. She imagined the light pouring through the skylight and windows of her cabin at the edge of an inlet north of town while her heart rate settled.

There. She could hold that feeling close and let that sweet security buoy her through the night ahead. Although the next few hours would be a challenge, her agent promised it would absolutely be worth the energy drain. She opened her eyes.

"Oh, aren't you a vision!" Charlotte's agent, Marisol Collins, swept into the space and the air vibrated in a happy response. She was a petite powerhouse in an expertly tailored black suit and glossy black heels. Her dark hair was swept up and back in a perfect twist and her porcelain skin glowed. She wore onyx drops at her ears and an intricate onyx ring on her right hand. The overall effect was pure feminine elegance.

Marisol had never met an objection she couldn't overcome or a situation she couldn't fix to her client's advantage. As opposite as they were in both appearance and personality, Charlotte was perpetually grateful to have signed with her.

Marisol fluttered her hands, urging Charlotte to turn, despite the fact that she'd already danced at least one circle around Charlotte. "Lovely." She gave a decisive nod. "I knew this was the right look for tonight."

Charlotte's dress was deceptively simple, a soft sheath falling from a network of thin straps that crossed in the back. The silky fabric rippled with color and movement from the neckline to the hem in shades of pale seafoam to deep aqua. Marisol slipped her arm around Charlotte and took her on another tour of the gallery, chattering about each of the bar and food stations. The effort should have put her at ease; instead, those jitters climbed to new heights.

"We're ready, sweet girl," Marisol said, giving her a squeeze. "On my signal, they'll open the doors to the VIPs and you're *on*."

That's what she was afraid of. Being *on* required grace and charm and enduring the same questions over and over with only mild variations thrown in. Tonight she must keep up the full-watt smile until her cheeks ached and then some, pretending she knew how to excel at social events.

She understood people wanted to feel a connection to the person behind the art that moved them. Was it so much to ask to connect from a respectable distance? A continent between her and this gathering felt about right.

"Any changes to the VIP list?" Charlotte asked, quickly doing a mental rundown of the coaching Marisol had provided about each of the elite guests who were eager to meet her and, with luck, be inspired to purchase the paintings on display tonight.

Normally, she didn't mind selling her work. Part of the joy of her art was sharing it with others. Turning a profit was the practical side of the miracle of making a career from her view of the world. The private sales seemed more personal than a gallery show, as if she was sending her work to a good home. A nonsensical feeling really, since she had no idea how, where or *if* her paintings were displayed when they reached the buyer.

More than one pragmatic art instructor through the years encouraged her to find the balance between creative joy and creating marketable work. "Da Vinci never starved and neither should you!" Marisol had preached a similar motto from their first introduction. "How can you create to your true potential when you're worried about bills, overhead or even groceries?"

Truly, Charlotte had never worried about food, having been raised by practical parents with a strong work ethic. They'd led by example, teaching her to budget, save and invest wisely in the present to secure a future. Still, believing Marisol's predictions about the evening meant Charlotte's bank accounts were about to get a serious infusion of cash.

"And miraculously, all before I'm dead," she muttered under her breath. Like so many creatives before them, she and her fellow students had often joked that artists and poets made for rich soil, having little value until they were six feet under and could no longer create.

"Here now, you're still nervous." Marisol drew her attention back to the present and pressed a filled champagne flute into her hand. Taking one for herself, she raised her glass for a toast. "To your first solo show." She tapped Charlotte's glass, the crystal ringing with a merry chime. "You just slay them with that smile." She arranged a loose wave of Charlotte's hair over her shoulder. "I'll take care of the sales."

Taking a sip of champagne, she braced herself as the gallery doors opened to the VIPs.

It wasn't all strangers who surged in with smiles ranging from reserved to enthusiastic. Her parents and older brother were here to lend their support. Several close friends had also been invited to help ease the pressure. Many of her friends who lived within driving distance were happy to come out for her, as well. Marisol's office had handled the official invitations and responses so Charlotte wouldn't stress over the numbers.

The friendly faces muted a bit of the immediate overwhelming feeling she encountered with the press of people swirling around, each seeking a moment to ask a question or offer congratulations. Hopefully that steadying sensation would hold her when the doors opened for the next wave of curious gallery patrons.

Already she was counting down the minutes until she could duck out for a break and a breath of fresh air. She checked her wrist and remembered too late her watch had been ruled out by Marisol.

"People want to believe you have all the time in the world for them. It's just one night," she'd added when Charlotte had argued. "Only a few hours of one night. I promise you'll have the breaks you need."

Charlotte dutifully kept up the smile, the answers that had her feeling like a broken record and the litany of thanks. All the while, her quiet-loving soul clamored for an expansive view of a sunrise over the Atlantic Ocean.

"Congratulations," a mellow baritone voice said from just behind her.

She turned, baffled enough that her smile faltered as the man attached to the voice exchanged her empty champagne flute for a full one. "Mark?"

What on earth had brought Mark Riley here tonight?

Adult Charlotte was sure she was hallucinating, while the love-struck teenager she'd once been now danced in happy pirouettes to see his handsome face. His perfectly tailored dark blue suit emphasized his breathtaking physique from his broad shoulders to his trim hips. The ivory shirt was open at the collar, giving her a tantalizing view of his tanned skin. Surely he should be doing something dangerously heroic on the other side of the world. Navy SEALs were too tough and far too busy to visit old friends at art galleries, weren't they?

He smiled and her knees turned weak at the mischievous sparkle in his light brown eyes and the single dimple winking in his cheek. "You've come a long way, Lottie." He used her childhood nickname as he raised his champagne glass, saluting her. "It looks good on you."

She had no idea if her reply was even remotely coherent or if the smile she attempted resulted in a pleasant expression or an off-putting grimace. She lifted her glass in response and he politely moved on before she melted into a puddle of longing and wishful thinking at his feet.

Having done his self-appointed duty of refreshing Charlotte's champagne glass, Mark wandered through the gallery, studying the paintings on display. The range and variety of her work surprised him, from wild to wistful, vivid landscapes and subtle skylines, works large and small. From the time she could hold a crayon, she'd been drawing, filling notebooks and sketch pads with her take on the world around her. Sometimes as accurate as a photograph, other times otherworldly. He'd never given a thought to what she might do with her talent and creative energy. Art and Charlotte simply went hand in hand.

From the far side of the room, he looked back, studying the artist. Her strawberry blond hair was styled in loose waves, lending an untamed, carefree vibe to the colorful curve-hugging dress that reminded him of the Caribbean Sea. The presentation probably fooled the people who weren't as observant, but he recognized the flash of nerves in her big blue eyes when he'd said hello. She'd been shy with strangers as a kid, quieter than any of the Riley siblings, but she was holding up under the pressure tonight.

He turned away to admire a haunting painting of a valley blurred by fog. The Blue Ridge Mountains in the fall, if he had to guess at the location she'd used for inspiration. It was impressive how well she'd grown into herself, her career. The last time he'd seen her in person she'd been in college, bright and happy and discovering where her art would take her. And the pictures of her college graduation, the family Christmas cards in the years that followed hadn't done justice to the woman she'd become.

When his mother had invited him to join the family for Lottie's first solo showing, he'd prayed for a diversion. He would have welcomed the chance to grab a high-value target and help end violence in one corner of the world. A pirate takeover of a cargo vessel in international waters would have sufficed. He would have eagerly accepted the chance to observe a training exercise on the West Coast. Better than all of those options would have been the news that investigators needed his help taking down the man who'd been pestering his family with one manufactured attack after another.

In short, he'd thought *anything* would've been more entertaining than spending hours staring at art, even art created by a dear family friend. How wrong he'd been.

The paintings, as well as the beautiful woman behind them, were actually a fascinating diversion. Good entertainment had been sorely lacking from his life while he was stuck working on administrative tasks due to an ongoing vendetta against his father, which left the entire Riley family on edge.

For several months, a man dubbed the Riley Hunter had been hiring mercenaries to put Mark's older siblings, Matt and Grace Ann, in dreadful, life-threatening situations. He'd caused all kinds of havoc for Matt until Matt survived a death trap. Then he'd abruptly shifted his focus to Grace Ann. She too had survived a series of events designed to break her mentally and physically. Since the hunter seemed to be attacking in birth order, all of the precautions were now cast over Mark, temporarily removing him from his team for the safety of the group.

All of the Riley children remained under a protective watch. Although investigators were working overtime, they'd only learned his name, John Eaton. They had yet to pin down his location and were only beginning to understand how he hired and paid the men who carried out his orders. Whenever they got close, a lead dried up or died—often literally.

Everything indicated that Eaton was bent on revenge and torment more than outright murder, seeking to inflict as much suffering as possible on their father, Ben. While the men had been serving in the army overseas, General Riley had been forced to bust Eaton for a criminal act during an operation. Eaton blamed the general, rather than accept responsibility for attacking civilians. He'd lost his career and his family in the fallout. Apparently the man's wife divorced him and took his daughter away, changing their names in an attempt to find peace and a normal life.

Eaton's tendency to shift focus didn't make him or his mercenaries any less of a threat. The whole situation made Mark's shoulders itch. As a navy SEAL, he preferred to meet danger head-on and would do anything to flush out Eaton once and for all.

Setting his unfinished champagne on a tray, Mark shoved the Riley Hunter out of his mind, refusing to allow the specter of the vengeful madman to undermine a happy occasion.

Finished cruising through the gallery rooms on the main level, Mark wandered up the stairs, a clever, curving design that perfectly showcased the displays in the central gallery, as well as the artist of the evening. Watching Charlotte, Mark struggled to reconcile his memories of the introverted little girl with the woman deftly managing the crowd gathered to celebrate her work.

He remembered *meeting* Charlotte when she was a baby. Her mother and his were best friends, having met through their army-officer husbands. Back then the Hanovers lived just down the block. As a five-year-old, he'd been unimpressed by the strange squirmy face peeking out from a cocoon of blankets. He didn't see much benefit in having a baby around, until the Riley boys and her older brother realized she was an effective distraction, giving them all more leeway in their never-ending quest for trouble.

Upstairs, his mother joined him near the balcony railing. Side by side, they silently admired an enormous canvas on the floor below. He couldn't speak with authority to the style or interpretation, but he saw a storm raging on the sea, slamming into a rocky coastline with great force that he could practically feel. Somewhere in the Pacific, he thought. He couldn't decide if the painting left him feeling empowered or cowed.

In his layman's opinion, a painting with that much life and power would only fit in a library or museum setting. Or maybe the house he'd once imagined owning, a place with clean, modern lines, soaring ceilings and windows that let in tons of natural light where he and his wife would raise their kids. He really needed to let that vision go, at least while he was on active duty.

His gaze drifted back to Charlotte. It was far more enjoyable to study the artist rather than review the way his career had tanked his past relationships.

"No," his mother said, low enough that she wouldn't be overheard.

"No what?" he asked.

"Do you think I've forgotten your face?" she queried.

Unsure what that meant, Mark gave her his most innocent expression. "I think you've thought I was Luke more than once, whether you're mom-enough to admit it or not." The long-standing family joke referencing his twin was the best diversion he could offer with his mind on the stormy scene.

Patricia Riley had left her career in the army nursing corps to raise her five children and keep house and home while her husband moved up through the ranks to become one of the army's most admired generals. She had bright eyes, a wicked sense of humor and a smile that could slice to the bone or soothe any heartache. Never once had her husband or children doubted her devotion, wisdom or courage. Her standards were high and, in Mark's mind, disappointing her was the worst consequence a kid could suffer for a mistake or poor choices.

"You look nice tonight," he added for good measure. Since his father retired, she'd sworn off dressing up and fancy occasions. For Charlotte, she'd made an exception. In a trim black dress and classic pearls, she didn't look like the mother of five adults with intense military careers.

Standing shoulder to shoulder, Patricia angled away from the gallery below to pin him with an unflinching gaze that cut straight to the point. "I am mom-enough to speak candidly to my son, a young man I admire and respect. And whom I love dearly," she added after a brief pause.

"Young?" He cocked an eyebrow. He supposed thirty was young if you were looking at it from the parental side of the equation. In his line of work, he'd passed *young* several years ago. These days, he was almost to the top of the hill, and occasionally peering over the edge.

He'd noticed the changes in recent years. It required more discipline and effort, extra reps and fewer beers to stay in peak mental and physical condition for himself and his team. His experience was valued, but a SEAL who couldn't keep up with the demands was quickly shuffled into a less active role. Just when he'd thought a change was right, he'd been sidelined against his will thanks to the recent attacks on his family. The situation had had the unexpected benefit of revealing he wasn't ready to make that shift yet.

"*You* are too jaded for Charlotte," she said baldly.

What did that mean? She was a family friend. He wasn't here to stalk through the gallery and carry Lottie off, her long, silky strawberry blond curls trailing over his arm. The notion was far more appealing than it should've been. And recognizing the tension in Charlotte earlier, he wondered if she wouldn't appreciate the gesture. Once she got over the heavy-handed approach.

"Mark."

"Mom," he said, mimicking her exasperated tone.

She wasn't impressed. "Promise me you won't do something foolish."

He supposed he'd earned that, having embraced his role as the gregarious son, always happy to flirt outrageously or crack a joke, often at his own expense to put others at ease. On top of that, he was the only Riley child to buck his army upbringing and join the navy. Still, he gave her an arch look on principle. "Being expertly trained in a variety of subjects, I find myself offended."

She aimed her eyes heavenward in that way she'd developed whenever he and his twin brother, Luke, gave her grief. "Stop it. Stuffy and overblown doesn't suit you."

"Good. Interfering and nosy doesn't suit you," he countered.

"It does too." Grinning, she patted his cheek. "Expertly trained mother at your service."

She was, that was true. Always there to celebrate, soothe or redirect them as needed. "Well, no need to worry. I don't have any romantic designs on Lottie."

"*Hmm.* Is that an attempt at reverse psychology? I know you have too much free time right now and the two of you are in the same city."

"Make up your mind, Mom." Laughing, he slipped an arm around her shoulders and gave her a gentle squeeze. "I thought you wanted me to find an intelligent, caring and pretty girl to settle me down." He'd been close to succeeding once. Now he wasn't so sure all three traits existed in the same woman. "Isn't Lottie all of those things?"

"Are you implying you're ready to settle down? *That* would be music to my ears." She rubbed his back as she'd done countless times throughout his life. Here he was, part of an elite team of operators and he still appreciated that sweet maternal affection.

He hadn't missed the way she dodged *his* question. Obviously, Charlotte was pretty and she was definitely intelligent. Caring? That wasn't an easy one to answer. Who knew what made a woman start or stop caring about a man?

His mom was right; he was jaded, and being the wife of a career army officer, she understood the risks he'd overcome better than most. But those experiences piled up, putting much more than a five-year age difference between him and the sunny, vibrant Charlotte. While he couldn't deny he found her attractive, she wasn't a woman to flirt with lightly.

"I'm closer," he admitted, giving his mom a winning smile. "But there isn't anyone in particular on my radar. Not even Lottie."

Hope, concern and disappointment rippled across his mother's face in rapid succession. He had no idea how to interpret or respond to any of those reactions. It all came from love, he supposed. And he knew she only wanted the best for him.

For Charlotte too. The Hanovers, Sue Ellen and Ron and their children, were as much a part of the Riley family as any of his blood relations. So it stung a little that his mother seemed to think he wasn't good enough for her honorary niece. He battled back a surge of irritability, the result of being off the active operations team for too long.

"I should get going. Early PT," he lied.

"We'll see you at the beach house soon?" she asked.

"Sure." There wasn't anything better to do with his weekends now that he was riding a desk and running training simulations thanks to the Riley Hunter. "I'll definitely come down for the Fourth of July."

"Great." She beamed. "Caleb will be thrilled to hear it."

Mark scanned the crowd milling about on the main floor, searching for his nephew. "I'll let him know on my way out." It was a good way to reassure his mom he wouldn't back out of the promised visit.

"Love you." She kissed his cheek. "Be safe." The final words chased him as he strode away. She'd made that particular farewell a habit when he and his siblings started driving on their own. These days she'd put it back into use because of the ever-present threat hanging over the family.

By leaving, he was probably increasing the safety factor at the gallery. There was no telling when Eaton would make another attempt to embarrass, undermine or flat-out kill one of the Riley children. Though Mark hadn't received any overt threats like Grace Ann and Matt, everyone involved believed he'd be the next target, since he was next in the birth order. Even if he wanted to settle down, this would be the worst time to bring a woman into his life. Catching sight of Charlotte, her hair glowing under the perfect lighting, he was grateful for the protective detail hovering inside and out.

Mark had read through the security plan earlier. A patrol team was posted on the rooftops of neighboring buildings and another team cycled through the gallery with the guests. If anyone stepped a toe out of line, they'd be subdued and questioned, with the primary goal of gathering information on Eaton's location.

Restless and uncharacteristically grumpy after his conversation with his mom, Mark decided on a little recon of his own.

Charlotte had never been entirely comfortable in the spotlight, but having Mark in the gallery made her big night a thousand times worse. She was too aware of him, always had been. She couldn't recall a time when she hadn't been charmed by his quick wit or the laughter lurking in his eyes. And that dimple when he smiled… It made her melt.

The man was a serious threat to her peace of mind. Inwardly, she scolded herself for giving only half an ear to her conversation with a lovely couple, longtime clients of the gallery, while keeping tabs on Mark. Her gaze seemed drawn to him when he was upstairs, when he paused to pick up a beer at the bar, when he circled through the smaller gallery rooms. It was like being in the throes of her crush as a teenager all over again.

Long before her first real kiss, she'd daydreamed about kissing Mark, holding his hand on vague romantic dates. Outrageous fantasies, considering the age gap, but her young heart was stuck on him. Back then, five years might as well have been a century. Eventually, he drifted out of her life and into his career. She grew up and gained a more realistic framework of dating and relationships, though none of her boyfriends had completely exorcised her image of Mark as the perfect guy.

And being the target of his charming smile was all it took to bring that image back to the top of her mind. What awful timing.

For weeks, she'd been envisioning this night the way an athlete might visualize a critical performance or important game. Tonight had the potential to change everything. These connections could propel her name into the right circles, open more doors and launch her career as an independent artist. She loved working as an art therapist, but taking this past year to stretch herself had revealed a new facet of her passion. What she wanted more than anything was to develop a retreat for artists and creatives, maybe even hold camps for students. Tonight could be the first step on that path.

To prepare, Marisol had employed role-playing conversations and drilled Charlotte in the art of graciously accepting compliments. None of her practice scenarios included an appearance by Mark. Naturally, her agent wouldn't have thought about the possibility because she didn't know about Charlotte's lifelong infatuation with the man. It hadn't crossed her mind that he would even be available to attend.

Having him here threw everything off-kilter. She wanted to put the world on pause or hide in the back room until she could adjust to being in the same vicinity as his perfect body and devilish grin again.

She hadn't seen him in person since a summer party a few years ago when the families had rented cottages in Cape May. Mark had brought his girlfriend on that trip. In the Riley family, that kind of move indicated a serious commitment. Charlotte had done her best to be a supportive extra sister, ignoring the last of her teenage heartbreak. She'd vowed to be happy when the wedding announcement arrived, but it never had. She hadn't asked for any details, too worried that her crush would be revealed.

He hadn't brought a date tonight.

As he strolled by, for what must have been the third time, she felt like a shipwrecked sailor, helpless against the circling of a hungry shark. Every time her gaze landed on him, temptation swelled through her. This wasn't good, couldn't be healthy.

If she asked, would he kiss her? An experiment between friends was all she needed. If he agreed, she could finally stop wondering and *know* what his lips felt like against hers. Then she could put an end to this fixation.

Losing track of yet another conversation, she covered the gaffe with a smile. "Please excuse me." She apologized for interrupting the older gentleman quizzing her about a painting and stepped into Mark's wake. Hopefully her intent to catch up with him wasn't too obvious.

She found him chatting with a teenage boy she didn't recognize. "Pardon me—"

"Perfect timing," Mark interrupted her. "Caleb, this is the artist of the evening, Charlotte Hanover." He winked at her over the boy's head. "Charlotte, my nephew, Caleb."

The relationship raised a dozen questions, but she kept them to herself. How and why had her mother never mentioned the next generation of Rileys was in the works?

"He's Matt's oldest," Mark said cheerfully, his warm brown eyes alight with mischief. "It's a great story."

"I'm sure it is." Charlotte could see the Riley genes in the boy's eyes and smile. Better to keep her nose out of it than ask the wrong question. "Is this your first art show, Caleb?"

He nodded. "Other than school or museums."

"I'm honored you're here," Charlotte replied. She enjoyed talking with kids more than adults. Younger people were typically more direct and willing to share an honest opinion once they warmed to the topic. Or her.

"They said it was a family event." He shrugged one shoulder, his cheeks coloring a little. "Not that it isn't great."

She liked him immediately and she got the sense that he didn't mind *family things* as much as he let on. "Are you bored?"

Caleb's gaze brightened. "I thought I would be, but it's actually cool."

High praise, she thought, and more sincere than some of the conversations she'd had this evening. As she and Caleb walked toward one of the smaller rooms, he candidly shared his opinion on various pieces. Following a hunch, she mentioned comic books. He jumped at the topic and they discussed pros, cons and his favorite comic book characters and artists. By the time they met up with Caleb's mom, Bethany, and Matt, Charlotte felt as if she'd made a new friend. Possibly created a new fan of art, in general.

"Well, he's hooked for life," Mark said from just behind her. "Nice job."

She managed to keep all the fluttery tremors on the inside. "Thank you," she replied in the same friendly tone she'd practiced in the mirror for the past month. "Some lucky girl down the line will be grateful that such a cutie can talk about something other than sports or pizza."

Mark tilted his head. "Is that some kind of jab at my lousy conversational skills at fifteen?"

"Not at all. If memory serves, you could talk bark off a tree at his age."

"Someone had to be the chatty twin," he pointed out.

She laughed, hoping the sound came out more like an amused, accomplished woman than a giggly, bubble-headed girl. That was forever her trouble with Mark. He was approachable, friendly and though he teased her on occasion, he was never unkind. The hang-up had always been on *her* side, in her heart and mind where hormones and daydreams twisted up the friendly signals, weaving them into a delectable, impossible world that revolved around that handsome face.

"Actually Luke was chatty enough with me earlier," she said.

Mark's dark eyebrows snapped together. "About what?"

"*Hmm?* Oh, Italy. He vacationed in the same region where I studied abroad for a semester." What was it about Mark that got her all wound up while his twin easily fit into the brotherly category? It made zero sense to her when they looked so much alike.

She made an effort to study Mark objectively. He currently wore a close-trimmed beard that flattered his strong jaw and highlighted the lone dimple. His dark suit was typical of those worn by the majority of the men in attendance. But to her, he wasn't typical at all.

Mark inquired about Italy, then asked her how she'd prepared for this show. She found herself inexplicably at ease as the party swirled around them, a blur of color, light and sound. Thank goodness. It was high time adult Charlotte showed up for these interactions.

While they chatted, she caught Mark scanning the room, his gaze occasionally settling on one person or another. Was he expecting someone? *Please, not a date.* Before she could ask what or whom he might be looking for, Marisol appeared and tugged her away to speak with an interested patron and a gallery owner visiting from the West Coast.

She didn't recall invitations going that far out of the area, but there was no time to ask for clarification. Marisol made introductions and Charlotte smiled through the poorly veiled condescension as the two men grilled her about her alma mater, her mentors both here and abroad and her brush techniques. Marisol abandoned her to the not-quite-polite interrogation with a bolstering thumbs-up behind their backs as she darted away to sweet-talk someone else on Charlotte's behalf.

To her immense relief, Patricia Riley drew her away from the men a few minutes later. "How are you holding up?"

"Better now," she replied. Mark's mother had a knack for seeing right to the heart of any person or issue. "Thanks for the save, Aunt Patricia."

"They sounded like a couple of jerks." Patricia cast a glance over her shoulder.

"To paraphrase my agent, jerks with money must not be ignored," Charlotte whispered.

"Maybe they should be. On a case-by-case basis, of course." She aimed a subtle glare at the pair. "Earlier, that snobby gallery owner overheard Caleb talking about your redwood landscapes and had the nerve to correct his opinion," she said. "It's art and he's a kid." Patricia shook her head. "Ben kept me from putting the snob in his place."

Charlotte smothered a snort. "That would have been fun to watch."

"That's what *I* said." Patricia winked. "My overprotective mother-bear mode only seems to intensify with age." She waved the observation aside. "You're handling this evening with amazing grace and patience. We're all so proud of you."

"Thanks. That campground by the lake in Florida is my happy place," Charlotte confessed. "I think about it when I'm stuck in the more challenging conversations." Her current challenge was how to casually inquire if Mark was seeing anyone. She wanted a kiss—to get over him—but she wouldn't ask if he was currently involved with someone.

Patricia beamed. "Those weeks with your family were some of my favorite summer vacations. We're planning a big bash for the Fourth of July at the beach house. Everyone is coming. Why don't you join us?"

"Oh." *Yes! Yes! Yes!* Teenager Charlotte was doing back handsprings; adult Charlotte wasn't so sure. As much as she loved the Rileys, more time around Mark could undermine her efforts to leave her crush in the dust. Especially if he agreed to her fantasy-ending kiss tonight. "I don't know…"

"No entitled jerks with more money than taste, just the family, I promise," she added, making Charlotte grin. "It's an ocean view rather than the lake, but we have plenty of room and a decent stretch of the beach all to ourselves. And no one will hassle you about your inspiration and influences."

It sounded like the most wonderful adult version of the best parts of her summer memories. "Are my parents going down?" A much safer question than inquiring about Mark's love life.

"They will if I have my way about it," Patricia replied with a conspiratorial grin. "There's plenty of time between now and then. Even if you can't make it for the holiday, you're welcome anytime. We're a relatively short road trip from here."

"Thanks." A tide of sincerity and gratitude washed over her.

They'd managed to find a small gap in the crowded gallery and Charlotte caught a whiff of fresh air coming in from the rear doors. Her body instantly relaxed.

"Go take a break," Patricia urged. "You've earned it. I'll tell Marisol you went upstairs to mingle."

"You're the best." She gave the woman who'd been her second mother a quick hug and then dashed for the back room and outside.

The night air, salted with the nearby Atlantic Ocean, brushed away the odor mash-up of people and perfumes, wines and hors d'oeuvres. Closing her eyes, she breathed deeply, the tension flowing out of her shoulders.

Out here, no one asked her the same question in forty different ways. No one pressed her for an educated opinion on masters like Picasso or the potential of their first grader's latest finger painting. The solitude was marvelous, restorative bliss.

Until she noticed she wasn't alone.

Chapter 2

Mark had been headed back inside the gallery after speaking with the security team monitoring the perimeter when he heard the back door open into the alley. He stopped short, holding his breath until Charlotte emerged. She'd always craved quiet and solitude, needing more of both than anyone else he'd known. Not wanting to disturb her hard-earned break, he paused, unmoving, in the shadows.

The way she tipped back her head and lifted her arms as she stretched back put him in mind of the legends of beautiful sirens that lured sailors to their deaths. Fanciful but true. And yet more proof he needed to get back to doing the real work with his team.

She shook back those lush waves of her golden red hair and he immediately felt guilty for lying to his mother. No, he didn't want to settle down, but he suddenly had Charlotte on his radar. He tried to shove the foolish thought away, but there was something different about her tonight. Less quiet kid and more enticing woman.

His mother thought his hard experiences made him all wrong for Charlotte. She saw the beauty in the world; he saw the violence. But maybe, if she was amenable, they could have some fun before those differences caught up with them. Just thinking of how to phrase that suggestion left him feeling like a jerk. She deserved better than a friends-with-benefits fling to pass the time.

He cleared his throat, cringing when she whirled around. "Easy. It's just me. Mark," he added, when she squinted at him.

"What are you doing out here?" she queried.

"Same as you," he said. "Enjoying the extra elbow room."

"Bliss, isn't it? Your mom is covering for me." She gathered her hair up in her hands, lifting it off her neck and sighing a little.

His pulse stuttered and he couldn't seem to pull in enough air. It was like the drowning drills in SEAL training, but way more rewarding. Her purely casual move wasn't a deliberate temptation, yet the way her dress gathered and dipped across her sumptuous curves made it an alluring display.

The devil dancing on his shoulder taunted him, dared him to reach over and caress that vulnerable nape of her neck. He shoved his hands into his pockets. Hell, he didn't even know if she was seeing anyone. Which was irrelevant. He couldn't give into this strange, amped-up attraction. He liked her, respected her. She deserved more than a temporary fling with him, a man whose only art was war.

"From what I hear, that kind of crush is a good problem to have," he said.

"Crush?" she echoed. "Oh, sure. My agent is thrilled by the turnout." She let her hair tumble down, her hands falling limp at her sides. "What I wouldn't give to get out of here early."

"Why?" He was genuinely curious. "You're the star. Even the snobs are praising you."

She plucked at the front of her dress, fanning herself. "You know I've never liked being the center of attention."

No, she hadn't. Her tendency to avoid attention had been a foreign concept to him when they were young. He and Luke had always been striving to keep up with or outdo their older siblings. "After tonight, I think you'd better get used to it. You're a celebrity waiting to happen."

"Maybe," she said with more than a little regret. "I might be the only person desperate to avoid my fifteen minutes of fame." Her gaze locked with his. "If you tell Marisol or anyone else I said that, I'll deny it to my dying breath."

He laughed. Charlotte was definitely a habitual good girl. "Anything I can do to help?" He'd step up and be her buffer—as a friend.

She tipped her head back again, her hands on her hips as she studied the inky sky above. "Yes."

He took a step closer. "Name it."

"Buy out the gallery so I can go home and get some sleep?"

Her warm smile dazzled him. The urge to agree was on the tip of his tongue and it had nothing to do with helping a family friend. He had a crazy, primal motive to please her, body and soul. Mark mentally took a step back, rattled by this sudden, pressing response. How had a few random thoughts led him here?

"Relax, I'm kidding." She smoothed her hands over her dress. "It's good to have your support. Good to see you," she said, pacing away. When she turned back, she was nibbling on her lip. "Did you see a painting you liked? Wait." She waved her hands as if she could erase the words. "Don't answer. It's not a fair question."

Her nerves were climbing, giving Mark pause. She wasn't the type to fish for compliments, though he was flattered she might want his opinion of her work. How to answer without gushing and embarrassing them both? "You have one with the view of the ocean from a cliff," he began. "Several, actually," he added. "But I'm talking about the smaller one in the series." He held his hands about a yard apart. "That would—"

"You saw a whole series?" she interrupted.

"Yes." The way she stared at him, as if she didn't quite recognize him, raised a prickle along the back of his neck. Maybe he'd been wrong and the biggest canvas and the smaller paintings weren't all variations from the same setting. He barreled on anyway. "The painting I mentioned reminds me of sunsets in Monterrey," he explained.

"Most people don't realize that's the same setting," she said. "They take one look at my headshot and decide my wild mermaid hair is the origin of an ocean fixation."

Mermaid hair. He liked that. The description suited her. "You shouldn't trust people who don't like the ocean."

"Says the navy SEAL who started out as an army brat." She laughed, the merry sound washing over him as sweet and light as the stars winking overhead.

It would've been nice to kiss her, to taste the bright energy surging through her. Charlotte was oh, so tempting, but his mother was right. He *was* all wrong for her. All he could offer any woman at this point was a fling with an eventual end date. His career came with serious pressures and so far, he couldn't seem to hold a woman's loyalty and trust.

Kissing Charlotte would only twist things up within the family. This burst of attraction would pass. Tonight was an anomaly, something wonderfully intriguing about seeing her as an accomplished woman. She was familiar to him and yet brand-new. He wanted desperately to take her hand, to feel the strength and tenderness that must be an integral part of how she transferred those dynamic scenes to the canvas. "We should get you back inside."

Her lips parted, but the reply was cut off by the noisy rumble of a heavy engine approaching. Immediately, he went on alert. Who would be coming down this alley at this hour at that speed? Something wasn't right.

He turned, blocking Charlotte from view as two men jumped from the rear door of a cargo van at the end of the alley. Both were dressed in black from head to toe, with black ball caps pulled low, shielding their faces.

"Mark Riley?" the man in the lead asked. He was lean compared to his barrel-chested partner.

To Charlotte, Mark whispered, "Go back inside." To the slim man coming toward him, he said, "Who's asking?"

"Come with us." Slim approached while the second man remained with the vehicle, a handgun visible in a tactical holster at his belt. "There's a security issue at the base and we need your assistance."

That was a load of crap. He wasn't active on any team right now. If there had been real trouble, his commander would've called him. "Show me an ID," he demanded.

The leader reached into his jacket and pulled out a gun instead of a badge. Eaton's men. Had to be. He started calculating how to get out of this without putting Charlotte in danger. She hadn't moved.

"How can I help?" she whispered from behind him.

"Go find Dad or Matt," he replied.

He kept his gaze on the leader's gun while her high heels clicked rapid-fire against the pavement. She'd be clear in a few seconds. Instead of the door, he heard a startled scream. He swiveled around to see a man dressed in the catering uniform blocking the door to the gallery and holding a gun aimed at Charlotte.

Where in the hell was the security team?

Jumping forward, Mark caught Charlotte around the waist and twisted, shielding her before the waiter could take an accurate shot. "Stay close to me," he ordered.

She tucked up behind him, her hands on his waist as he angled his body, putting her between him and the brick wall of the building. The odds favored the three armed men, but they couldn't possibly want to open fire and draw more attention. The security patrol must have noticed the van. He expected backup any second now.

"Walk away while you can," Mark said evenly to the

aggressors. "Walk away and there won't be anything to charge you with."

The waiter and Slim advanced.

Mark swore under his breath. Charlotte couldn't escape in either direction without going through at least one of the men who'd come for him. "Whatever Eaton's paying you, I'll double it if you leave now," Mark offered, just to test the reactions.

None of the men reacted to the mention of Eaton's name or the money—but who else would know his name and pull this kind of stunt? Being outnumbered didn't faze him. Alone he'd take them down fast, but if Charlotte got hurt simply for being in the wrong place at the wrong time, he'd never forgive himself.

"Mark?" she queried.

"Trust me?"

"Yes."

That single confident syllable empowered him. Solutions rolled through his mind. He had to get her safely away.

"Into the van." Slim motioned with his gun. "Both of you."

"No," Mark said. "I'll come without a fight, as soon as you let her go back inside," he countered.

Behind him, Charlotte gasped a denial.

"Come on." He spread his hands. "She's irrelevant and it's her first solo showing. Have a heart."

"Cooperate and we won't kill her," the waiter said, closing in from the side. "That's heart."

"I'd like to see you try," Charlotte snapped, and brandished one of her high heels as a weapon.

Both the waiter and the leader closed in on them. Mark sized up his opponents and options. The fact that they'd not fired a shot told him they were afraid of drawing attention to themselves. They must have just figured he'd go along with their thin ruse. He would use their poor planning against them. Taking out the waiter gave Charlotte a path to escape. He lunged, grasping the waiter's shirt. Hauling him close, he shoved him hard into the leader. The momentum knocked the gun from the waiter's hand and blocked any shot the leader had.

"Run!" Mark barked at Charlotte, driving the men toward the alley opening to give her time to safely reach the gallery door.

The waiter recovered and came at Mark with lightning-fast punches and kicks. He recognized the type—a martial arts enthusiast with more confidence than sense. Blocking most of the blows, Mark lost his breath when a kick connected with his ribs. He had to twist under another flurry of flying limbs, and took a kick to the shoulder that would have knocked him out cold if it had landed on his jaw. He had to get on the offensive or he'd take a severe beating.

Where was the perimeter team? He wasn't fighting off kidnappers in stealth mode out here. Mark now assumed the lack of response meant this crew had taken them out somehow. At least Charlotte would raise the alarm inside.

Seeing an opening, Mark shot out his leg and tripped the waiter, following the man to the ground as he fell. He used his size advantage, driving his knee into the man's rib cage. The leader shouted and the waiter groaned, curling into himself protectively. Mark bounded to his feet to deal with the man in charge.

"Get in the van or I kill her right now," Slim said in a snarl.

Mark spun around to see the man guarding the van

had caught Charlotte while Mark was preoccupied with the fight. The guard had her pinned against the wall of the building with a meaty fist around her throat, the pressure clear by the pain etched on her face. Mark's vision hazed red around the edges.

Charlotte's eyes were brimming with tears. "Sorry," she rasped. Barefoot, her toes reached for the ground while her fingers scraped at the man's arm in her struggle to breathe.

Good grief. She'd gone on the attack, tried to help him fight, rather than run for safety. He could sort out why later. Right now, he had to make sure she didn't suffer any further pain or humiliation.

"Move," the leader demanded.

Mark held his ground. "Let her go."

The leader fired once, the bullet slamming into the brick inches from Charlotte's head. The blood iced in Mark's veins. "We're *all* going." The man raised his gun again. "Will she be riding along dead or alive?"

Mark raised his hands, surrendering. He couldn't win here without risking Charlotte. "Lead the way." The man holding Charlotte hurried her into the van and Mark obediently followed.

She was shoved to the end of a bench and the guard cuffed her hands to a long chain looped around a bar bolted to the panel behind the bench. Mark was led farther down the bench and handcuffed the same way beside her. It was uncomfortable, but both of them could move the length of the bench and almost rest their hands in their laps.

The leader hauled the groaning waiter to his feet and dumped him in the back of the van, as well. Sliding the cargo door shut, he then climbed into the passenger's seat up front while the guard took the driver's seat. Moments later, they were speeding away from the gallery.

A clock started in Mark's head as he gauged distance and direction. He had to bide his time. Mentally, he tallied every rough gesture or rude word Charlotte had endured, vowing to make each man pay.

From his place on the van's floor, the waiter sat up, glaring at them as he recovered from Mark's brutal tactics.

Next to him, Mark felt Charlotte's body trembling, though her eyes were dry now and her jaw was set. "You wanted a way out of the evening," he said to Charlotte, trying to distract her.

"This wasn't exactly what I had in mind," she murmured. "I'll be more specific in the future."

"Clarity is best," he agreed, giving her a confident smile. "I'm betting our limo was once an ambulance. Maybe they'll wind up the siren." He wasn't counting on it. As he scanned the vehicle, he also noted the interior door handles had been removed.

"Why are you so calm?" she wondered aloud, easing back to study his face.

He wished he could put his arm around her, give her real reassurance. "Because it's too soon to panic," he said breezily. "Would it help if I broke his nose?" He tipped his head toward the waiter.

"Shut up." The man's command held zero authority.

The driver jerked around a corner and Charlotte was tossed into him, landing on his battered shoulder. The cuffs jerked against her wrists and she cried out.

"You okay?" he asked, gritting his teeth against the spike of pain.

His anger was mounting over failing her and allowing the waiter to land some solid blows. He could score his lousy performance later; the pressing issue was finding a chance to get her out of here.

"Sorry," she whispered.

"No worries," he replied. He used his body to leverage her back into place so the cuffs wouldn't tug on her hands. On the plus side, her supple body had been a warm and sweet distraction, if only for an instant. Under the silky dress, there had been strength to match the warrior-like spirit that compelled her to fight off gunmen with a shoe. He had to take the positives where he found them.

Mark waited for the next swerve and used the momentum to slam a foot into the waiter's shin. "Whoops."

He slid out of Mark's reach. "Do it again and I'll shoot you."

"Yeah? With what gun?" Mark sneered. "Oh, that's right. It's back in the alley." He gave Charlotte a smile. "Someone will find it soon. Marisol noticed you were gone ages ago. This crew is amateur hour. I'm sure security is already scouring the surveillance video." Assuming the security team wasn't incapacitated.

"I'll take your word," she said, her blue eyes full of worry.

Mark had to believe help wouldn't be far behind. "You're the star tonight, Lottie. They miscalculated when they brought you along." He caught the waiter's cringing reaction to that and pressed his point. "We can hang tough until the cavalry arrives."

She snorted at his joke. "A SEAL rescued by the cavalry. I like it."

"You would." He was glad she saw the humor. There was a certain Riley pride in army service that he'd bucked by joining the navy. His twin, an army ranger, would never stop gloating about the best branch of Special Forces operators if Mark didn't find a way out of this predicament.

Charlotte took great comfort in Mark's steady presence and persistent humor. He wasn't nearly as blithe about this situation as he seemed, but he wasn't posturing or giving her useless platitudes either. Without him, she'd be panicking or dead. Her throat was tender from the grip of the guard who'd caught her and her cheek stung in several places where the brick had splintered when the leader had fired his gun in her direction. At least her ears had stopped ringing from that blast.

Mark was right that Marisol would miss her. On more than one occasion at past appearances, her agent had tracked down Charlotte when she'd shied from the spotlight. She latched on to that ray of hope and refused to let it go.

She was more than scared, but she had to find her courage, find a way to be more than a weakness Mark had to worry about. Catching the waiter glaring at her again, her fingers twitched as she imagined sketching him in various vignettes and pieces.

"Easy," Mark murmured.

She glanced up at him. "What?"

"I can almost hear you plotting his demise," Mark said, loud enough to be heard. "I'm sure it's a creative ending."

He was far too observant. "Positively gory," she admitted. Turning her attention toward more appealing topics, she studied the precise line of Mark's short beard.

She'd drawn his profile and face countless times through the years. Though he'd caught her at it a time or two, he'd never said a word or given any indication of his thoughts. He'd be appalled if he knew how many sketchbooks she'd devoted to him. She found it fascinating the way he'd changed and matured from those sharp angles of his teens to the powerful elegance he sported this evening.

Mark and his twin brother, Luke, were identical, except for the location of the dimple, and the boys had used it to their advantage more than once. She'd never understood how they'd fooled anyone. Even as a girl, she had an innate tendency to focus on the details that made faces, even identical faces, different.

"Keep staring at me like that and I might catch fire," he said. "You're not thinking of my demise now?"

"Never." She might not understand the full scope of what was happening, other than she seemed to have terrible timing tonight, but she knew she wouldn't get out of this without him.

"Then what were you thinking about?"

Meeting his gaze, she saw the spark of humor in his brown eyes and the flicker of that dimple in his cheek. This was the flirtatious side of him that typically brought women in for a closer look. She understood the draw and thought again of that kiss she'd been hoping for.

"Luke," she answered. It wasn't a complete lie.

"Liar."

How did he know? Heat flooded up from her neck, into her cheeks, and she was grateful for the poor lighting in the back of the van. Various colors from traffic signals and street lamps strobed across them from the cab windshield, hiding her ridiculous blush.

Except he was so observant and he'd known her all her life. He'd been around in those moments when she got flustered because her mother gushed over her prize-winning artwork or her brother teased her about something going on at school. Thinking back, she recalled the way he'd crack a joke with his brother or stir up a diversion that she'd use to escape the unwanted attention. Was it possible he'd done it on purpose?

"I *was* thinking of Luke," she protested a little too late. "His jaw is heavier than yours on the right. He could hide it if he wore a beard."

"He'd look silly with a beard," Mark joked. "His dimple's on the other side too."

"True." Despite the dire circumstances, she grinned. "No one remembers that detail."

"It's shocking," he agreed. "If I'd been thinking, I would've told them I was Luke."

"Shut up!" The waiter pulled a small revolver from a holster at his ankle.

The tremors Mark had soothed returned with a vengeance. She'd been around guns all her life, mostly at firing ranges. Target practice wasn't as calming for her as a nice long hike, but she enjoyed shooting. The first lesson her father had taught her was never to point a firearm at another person. Until tonight, she'd never been on the business end of a loaded gun.

Every instinct said to hide, but there was no escape

back here. Her heart pounded and the chain linking her handcuffs rattled across the bar as fear took hold.

"Quit scaring her, you jerk." Mark blocked her with his body as much as his handcuffs allowed.

The snub-nosed barrel of the gun was now aimed squarely at Mark's chest. No surprise that only terrified her more. In the confined space, the odds of the bullet missing were nil. At this man's whim or a bump in the road, either of them could wind up seriously wounded or worse.

"You're slow, aren't you, buddy?" The waiter spoke with obnoxious deliberation. "I'm in charge. You behave." He stood up and yanked her away from Mark's shelter, pressing the cold barrel of the gun to her skin, just under her collarbone. "Are we clear?"

Mark changed before her eyes. Gone was the carefree, good-natured guy she knew from their family vacations. His jaw set into a hard line and his warm brown eyes went flat. Cold. She was almost glad he was out of reach, afraid that any touch would set all that coiled strength into action.

The entertainment industry loved portraying navy SEALs as invincible. She knew they were trained to *believe* they were invincible. As much as she wanted to embrace the myth and believe Mark could overcome any obstacle, how could he take down three armed men while handcuffed to the van?

From the moment these men appeared in the alley, he hadn't shown an ounce of fear. In fact, if the guard had any sense of self-preservation, he'd stop goading Mark right now. Belatedly, she realized she was the only reason he was holding back. Whatever was going on, she refused to be a pawn they used against him.

"Back off," she demanded. The pressure of the gun against her skin eased abruptly as the man compensated for the driver's acceleration. "What's your name?"

"John Doe." Standing over her, the waiter's gaze dropped to leer at the low neckline of her dress. "You ever paint nudes?"

She'd heard the same sleazy question all through college. Every guy thought they were the first to ask. "Did you see any nudes on display in the gallery?"

"I wasn't really looking," he said.

"Of course you weren't."

Mark bumped her knee with his foot. "Don't let him get under your skin."

"We have what we came for." He lowered the gun and twirled a finger through a loose curl of Charlotte's hair.

Bile rose up into her throat.

"That makes you a bonus." The man licked his lips. "Maybe he'll let us share you like we're gonna share the ransom money."

Her stomach clenched and she struggled to hold his gaze against a new wave of fear. But the waiter smiled, and she hated herself for being so transparent.

"That will not happen." The tone, low and lethal, wasn't one she'd ever heard out of Mark.

Abruptly, the man was down, his feet kicking the air and the gun he held clattering on the metal floor of the van. Thankfully no bullets erupted. Beside her, Mark simply shifted in his seat, compensating for the next turn as the leader swiveled around in the passenger's seat.

"What the hell is going on?" he demanded.

"Your guy lost his balance," Mark said with laughable innocence. To Charlotte he added in a whisper, "The hammer wasn't cocked."

She dipped her chin in acknowledgment, not trusting her voice. He'd taken down an armed man with his hands cuffed. She hadn't even seen him twitch, just a slight movement of his leg.

"I never would've taken the risk otherwise," he added earnestly.

She believed him, she did. Unfortunately the awareness did nothing to slow her thundering pulse or erase the tears rolling down her cheeks. She didn't want to have this meltdown, not when he needed her to be strong.

At their feet, the waiter groaned as he came around. Reclaiming his revolver and shoving it back into the ankle holster, he retreated to the opposite side of the van, embarrassment and fury rolling off him in waves. Blood dripped from a wound on his chin, staining his white uniform shirt.

"You might need stitches," she observed.

Mark made a weird snorting noise that she assumed was suppressed laughter. The waiter didn't even acknowledge her. That was fine by her. More than fine. It would be a long time before she forgot the feel of that cold gun barrel digging into her skin.

As the driver took the next turn, she grabbed the chain of her cuffs to keep from sliding into Mark's side again.

"Don't worry about hurting me," Mark said. "Just stay tough. I'll figure this out."

Fear surged anew and all she could do was ride it out as the van approached a nondescript warehouse. As the driver inched forward, a black metal door rolled up to grant them access. The warehouse interior was shrouded in darkness and shadow. Charlotte caught a whiff of the ocean under more abrasive notes of grease and metal and…

"Tires," Mark said, as if he could read her mind.

Yes, that was it.

He leaned forward, trying to get a better look or blocking her view, she wasn't sure.

The waiter, on his feet again, shoved him back. "You're awful eager to meet your maker."

"It'll be a pleasure to take you with me," Mark snarled.

The van doors parted and she winced under the assault of a bright light. As her eyes adjusted and lights came on in the warehouse, she took stock of the man holding the flashlight on them. He was average height, almost skinny, with unremarkable short brown hair going gray at the temples. His eyes were also brown, but his cold-blooded gaze left her shivering as he looked her over, head to toe.

He turned his back on them. "What the hell is this? I sent you for Riley."

She stared at the blood on the floor of the van. The tread of the waiter's shoe had tracked through the mess, creating an abstract. As a kid, she'd searched for shapes in the clouds; tonight, she searched for shapes in the blood smears to keep her mind away from the terror of dying.

She'd expected to have more time. There were a thousand things she might never get to do. She wanted to travel to Africa, take an Alaskan cruise and build a retreat for artists. She'd never fallen madly in love. Crushing on Mark didn't count. At least her artwork would increase in value after this. How often did an artist get kidnapped from her first solo showing?

"Your men can't tell the difference between a famous artist and a SEAL?" Mark tsked. "Good help is *so* hard to find."

"We had to bring her along or she would've blown our escape," said the leader, who'd done all the talking in the alley.

Damn right she would have.

"An artist?" The man in charge studied her for several long moments before speaking to Mark. "How is she related to you?"

"She isn't." Mark dismissed her as easily as swatting away a buzzing gnat. "I was trying to get lucky when your brilliant team grabbed both of us."

Was she supposed to play along? She had no idea how to help him so she kept quiet. The man in charge eyed her again and she started to sweat. She swallowed an automatic, pitiful plea for mercy, certain that anything she said to this man would be twisted and used against her.

"Come on. Let her go," Mark said. "You've scared the poor woman enough for a lifetime."

The man held up a cell phone, snapped a picture of Charlotte and slammed the doors. A small amount of light filtered through the windshield. She heard footsteps fading and then the lights went out, plunging them into darkness.

All she could hear was Mark's slow, even breathing. All she could feel was the hard seat beneath her, the cool metal circling her wrists. Though Mark was at the other end of the bench, he seemed a hundred miles away.

Tears threatened again, but this time she kept them at bay. Mark was here. He'd get them out of this mess.

There was a scraping sound of metal on metal, followed by a loud bang and the van shook.

Mark cursed, a colorful combination she could almost visualize on a canvas as a stream of angry red and muddy purples flowing into a black horizon, as he pounded his fists against the side panel. It took her a minute to make sense of his ranting.

"You know who that was?" she asked.

"Yes." Another slam of some hard body part against the unyielding van. "That was John Eaton." He swore again. "Now that you've seen his face, it'll be harder than ever to get you out of here tonight."

That was the name he'd mentioned in the alley. "What does he want with you?"

"He's the man out to destroy Dad, one kid at a time."

She told herself he couldn't mean that, hoped he was exaggerating, yet here they were, prisoners in a van. Whoever Eaton was, he had resources and manpower. They had…a navy SEAL. She curled her bare toes into the ridges of the van floor. Mark would come up with an escape plan. Her fingers gripped the chain the cuffs were linked to and she pressed her knees together, trying to quell the tremors so he wouldn't feel her fear. "What do we do?"

She had to believe in him, had to stay positive. Every problem had a solution. Every single one. Mark would get them out of this; she had absolute faith in him.

Mark subsided. "We bide our time," he said, his voice flat. "And then we leave."

She bit her lip, not liking step one so far. She patiently waited for him to explain the rest of his plan, her unease growing with every beat of silence that followed.

Chapter 3

Mark didn't need good lighting or an outright admission to know Charlotte was terrified. And who could blame her? It was common sense of course, but he could also hear the fear in her shallow breaths, the slight rattle of the handcuffs.

In a matter of minutes, she'd gone from lovely artist in the spotlight to threatened prisoner in the dark, thanks to him. It would've been bad enough if she'd been a stranger, a woman he only wanted to flirt with or possibly hook up with, but she wasn't. Charlotte was special. Not just to their families, but to him.

When they were kids, the uniquely quiet way she soaked up the world, as if she could bring everything she wanted closer to her, had fascinated him. She was a direct counterpoint to his tendency to charge into the fray, be it a friendly game of tag football or a counterterrorism mission. Having her in harm's way went against everything he believed, against all of his training.

Yes, logically, Eaton was to blame. He'd come after Mark, and Charlotte had just been in the wrong place. But Mark had let down his guard in the alley, been distracted, and now she could pay the price. He should have pushed her through the gallery door, not just told her to go, before any of the action started. He should have forced her out of the way.

He slammed his good shoulder into the rail. Where was a loose bolt when he needed one?

"Don't hurt yourself," Charlotte warned. "Please. You said we had to bide our time."

He admired her effort to hide her fear. "I've said a lot of things," he muttered. "Every restraint has a weakness," he said. "If there's a way to get out, I'll find it."

"Then what?"

"One step at a time." If he was free when that van door opened again, surprise would be on his side. "Do you have a hair pin or something I could use to pick the cuffs?"

"I don't. Sorry," she replied. "Marisol wanted my hair all loose and crazy tonight. She rambled on about Bohemian chic or something along those lines."

He twisted around on the bench, leaning back as far as the cuffs would allow. "She made the right call on the hair and the dress," he said. "Everyone was falling in love with you."

Finding the point where the bar was bolted to the side panel, he kicked and stomped and nothing budged. Whoever made dress shoes for James Bond deserved a medal. His shoes were completely useless. He swore again. "Sorry."

"For the salty language?" she asked.

He heard the smile, wished he could see it. "Yes." He was apologizing for the language, along with everything else he'd done wrong, though he'd rather not itemize his every failing of the evening.

"Please. I heard worse on our family vacations."

He shushed her quickly. "Someone might be listening. I don't want Eaton to know you're connected to the family."

"Okay," she murmured.

"Please, don't be afraid." He scooted close to her now, keeping his voice low. "With a little luck, I can convince him to let you go. I think you'd be an excellent ransom-delivery messenger."

"Every artist needs a fallback."

He appreciated the attempt at levity. "That's the spirit."

Mark stood and tested the full limits of the cuffs. The sound of the chain sliding back and forth across the bar made him feel like a restless ghost in the dark. "Would it help to know this isn't the worst predicament I've been in?" he asked.

"Not really."

"If my fast talking doesn't work, be ready to follow my lead when an opportunity presents itself. This isn't over until we're safe." Or at least until she was safe.

"I believe in you."

Her declaration of faith nearly did him in. It was exactly the reply he'd hoped for, yet the pressure mounted like never before. His career demanded the best of the best at every position. He'd been in tight spots before, in situations that felt insurmountable at the time. In those cases, his team had been in his ear on the comm link, watching his back, talking him around or through any glitches.

This was different, so far removed from the controlled chaos of those operations that his confidence kept flickering like a light bulb about to blow. He knew how far he could push himself. He didn't know how far he could push Charlotte.

"When you seize an opportunity, don't expect me to go alone," she said. "We get out of here together or not at all."

"That's the ultimate goal," he replied. He refused to open a debate with her by explaining why she might have to leave without him.

"I mean it, Mark."

"Understood." The sound of approaching footsteps cut off any further discussion. The lights in the warehouse brightened, filtering through the windshield. "Be ready," he whispered.

They heard a key slide into a lock and then the doors were flung wide. Eaton smiled, and a man at his side aimed an assault rifle at Mark's chest.

"Mark Riley," Eaton said. "Your service record is impressive. You are here because you're a son of General Riley, US Army–retired. I give you credit for bucking the old man and going into the navy, but that doesn't exempt you from my plans."

Mark stared at his enemy, unflinching. It took tremendous willpower to remain equally unmoved as Eaton's calculating gaze shifted to Charlotte.

"And you are Charlotte Hanover."

Inwardly Mark winced.

"An acclaimed artist and dear, dear friend to the Rileys," Eaton continued. "He didn't mention you when I served with him, but a quick perusal of your background and recent publicity makes me believe he'll be very distressed that you've gone missing." His lips curled into a cruel smile. "I *am* going to enjoy getting to know you better."

"Let her go," Mark said. "This isn't about her."

"Isn't it?" Eaton asked, studying Charlotte. "She means something to your family." He reached out and caught a lock of her hair between his fingers. "Beware, young lady, the Rileys will always let you down."

Mark's pulse thundered. He would rip Eaton apart for touching her, for scaring her, for interfering with her big night. Only the threat of the gun kept him still. He couldn't help Charlotte if he were dead.

Eaton leaned closer to her. "General Riley, your honorary uncle, took everything from me. *Everything.*" He put a razor-sharp edge on each syllable. "Now his children will do penance for his betrayal. So far two have been tested and passed. I *let* them live because I am the *better* man."

Was Eaton implying he'd shown restraint? "No," Mark argued. "They outwitted your traps and survived." He had to draw Eaton away from Charlotte. He wouldn't let this bastard's ugly words tarnish her opinion of his father. "And I will too, no matter what you've cooked up this time."

Eaton's gaze finally shifted to Mark. "Your father ruined my career, crushed my reputation and destroyed my family. My wife and daughter are *gone!*" he shouted. "I'll never see them again. You think these men at my back are friends?"

"Friends or enemies, they're a pack of idiots to stand behind you," Mark said.

Eaton snorted. "Hardly. They're skilled soldiers and *loyal* to me, the source of their money."

"We'll see how loyal they are when the authorities get here." He stretched as far as the cuffs allowed so Eaton's men could hear him clearly. "Did he tell you that we're all under surveillance? Before long, they'll swarm this warehouse and round up everyone who helped your fearlessly delusional leader."

The only faces he could see were Eaton's and the gunman's and neither man flinched. Didn't matter. Eaton might pay well for his private army, but when the crazy started to show, a mercenary's survival meant walking away. Quickly.

"I expected better." Eaton shook his head. "You didn't follow blindly in his footsteps. I'm hoping you'll provide a more devastating kind of trouble for your father." He stepped back, reaching to close the doors.

"Wait!" Mark said. "Let her go. An act of good faith." He pitched his voice so it sounded more like a plea than an order. "She's not military. She isn't even a Riley," he added, feeling like a jerk. "It's not like Dad raised her."

Of course, she had the mettle to be a Riley. His parents and hers had been inseparable, and they'd brought up the kids as if they were all cousins. But he was trying to use Eaton's definition for revenge to get her out of here.

Eaton studied him. "They told me you were together when they found you. She stays."

"Together? No. Not like that." The idea of *together* with Charlotte stuck in his head. He could see her art on the wall in the house of his dreams where a little girl with strawberry blond curls and a sweet dimple in her cheek danced in a bright sunbeam. "No," he said again, as a chill slid through him. Eaton had proven he didn't mind putting innocent lives at risk in his sick games.

Eaton's gaze slid from Mark to Charlotte and back again. A knowing smirk creased his weathered face. "She stays."

The door slammed and the lock turned.

"I'll go ahead to make room for her," Eaton said to his men. "I want this place cleared within the hour. No trace…" His voiced faded as he and his men trooped off.

Charlotte's breath hitched. Damn it. He had to do something. "Charlotte—"

"I hate this dress," she said, wrestling with the neckline. "This is the worst time to feel like a girl."

"You are a girl," he pointed out.

"A frilly, useless girl," she amended. "Vulnerable."

"Hardly," he argued. "You're strong. And the dress is killer."

The driver's door opened and the van rocked as a burly man they hadn't seen settled behind the steering wheel. The engine started and they were backing out of the warehouse.

Mark heard her sniffle and wished there was something more he could do. "Lottie."

"Don't worry about me, I'm fine."

He sputtered, barely containing an outright laugh over the obvious lie. "I *will* get us out of here."

"I know." She pulled again at the neckline of her dress. "You'll squash that creep like a bug and I'll give you a big round of applause."

"That doesn't sound like something a frilly girl would say."

"I wish I could do the squashing," she said. "Your sisters could squash him."

Mark didn't want to mention how Eaton had nearly destroyed Grace Ann. "In a fair fight, my money's on you, honey." He'd rip out the man's eyes for making Charlotte feel like a helpless object rather than a capable woman. And what would he do to himself for making her feel less important to him and the family? Once they were safe, he could work on making amends for that. "Try to relax," he murmured. "He has the advantage now, but everyone makes mistakes eventually. You know I didn't mean all that about—"

"Forget it," she said, her voice small. "It's okay."

He'd hurt her feelings when he should be a source of strength and hope for her. He wanted to be comforting, but he didn't have the luxury right now. Hope was fragile and wouldn't hold up long against whatever Eaton had planned for him.

Charlotte needed more than comfort. She needed the jaded, cold warrior the navy had carved out of him through the rigors of training and operations. Only his well-honed, lethal skills would get them out of this alive.

Charlotte was *not* okay.

In fact, this entire night was the polar opposite of

okay. From the moment they'd been attacked in the alley until now, she felt she was living a nightmare. Her fears for her own life were pushed behind ones for Mark's. Even if she were let go, what would happen to him? Her breath came fast, and she felt her pulse race, as anxiety flooded her.

And yet all she could think about was how much her heart ached. She supposed she should thank Mark for momentarily distracting her from the paralyzing fear of being kidnapped by a madman who had some perverse idea of revenge.

Her plans for a kiss were trashed, but worse, her fantasy of being his had popped like a bubble. A sphere of gleaming rainbows in the sunlight impaled on a blade of grass. That's what happened to lifelong crushes when exposed to the harsh light of reality.

She would never be a Riley. It was completely irrational to hurt this much over a few words tossed out in an attempt to protect her. Mark had no idea she'd imagined their wedding day in her head a thousand times. A silly figment of her imagination. Thank goodness she'd never shared that nonsense with anyone. She fought against another wave of tears, thoroughly annoyed with herself.

A kiss wouldn't have changed anything, even if she had pulled it off. He had five years on her and a career that included pressures and dangers she couldn't even fathom. In contrast, her life had been a cakewalk. Her biggest career challenges were snobby critics, obstinate patients and the occasional travel delay.

If they'd met as strangers, would they have any common ground? Would he have given her a second look?

She had to get control of her reactions and regain her perspective. Had to find a way to help him.

"I'm sorry this man hates your family." All her life, General Riley, his wife and their five children were a natural extension of her family. Her memories of all of them together created a vibrant canvas, infused with bold color and light and love.

"Not as sorry as I am that his hatred spilled onto you." He dropped his head back and stared up at the ceiling of the van. "He didn't bother concealing his face."

"That's a problem?" she asked when he didn't elaborate.

"It shows a troubling degree of arrogance." Mark muttered an oath. "You shouldn't be here. He knows that. What is he thinking?"

"You shouldn't be here either," she pointed out. He seemed to be forgetting they'd both been kidnapped, only one of them on purpose.

"If I hadn't been out there flirting with you, we wouldn't be in this predicament." He glanced toward her bare feet. "And you'd still have those sexy heels you were wearing."

Had they been flirting? He'd recognized the connection between several paintings, but the rest was a blur, thanks to Eaton. Her hopelessly romantic heart fluttered in her chest knowing that Mark found her heels sexy. She preferred to think of that rather than the situation they were now in. The idea of flirting with him, on purpose, was enticing. Tempting. She'd wanted him to look at her like a woman—an interested, available woman—for so long, it seemed too good to be true.

She wondered what Mark would say if he knew that's where her mind had wandered. She suddenly despised Eaton for intruding on her first real chance to connect with Mark as a consenting adult. Mark had noticed her heels. He liked the dress. Those were moments she'd thought beyond her reach. "Can I put in a request for when we get out of here?" she asked.

"Absolutely." He slid closer, a sexy tilt to his lips. "It's smart to have something to look forward to."

She cleared her throat and went for broke. "When we get out of this, I'd like to have dinner with you. Just you, not the family. It doesn't have to be fancy—"

"Why not? You deserve fancy."

The statement made her smile, something she'd thought beyond her a few minutes ago. "Thanks. In that case, bring on the candles and good wine."

He chuckled. "Count on it." He shifted on the bench. "Want in on a secret?"

"Absolutely," she replied, echoing him.

"I walked into the gallery tonight expecting to be bored. Then I saw you. All the color and movement of your art faded into the background. I suddenly wanted to steal Dad's new boat and take you out for champagne on a sunset sail."

"You thought all that?" Was this a new tactic to keep her calm? "About me?"

He nodded and she felt his gaze drifting over her as distinctly as if he'd touched her with those strong, long-fingered hands that mesmerized her almost as often as his face.

"It was the dress." His voice was quiet and warm and completely at odds with their surroundings. "Those blues and greens remind me of a Caribbean beach. You looked so…you. Grown up, confident, amazing. And your hair. If that isn't champagne-worthy hair, I don't know what is."

No one had ever said anything so romantic to her. Not even the fascinating guitarist she'd dated for a few months in Paris. Even better, she believed Mark. Those words resonated as true. The awareness was liberating, empowering and a bit unnerving. She could practically hear the water against the boat's hull, feel the wind teasing her hair while the sun sank slowly into the horizon. See the glint in his eyes just before he kissed her.

She was probably reading way too much into the moment. Flirting was one thing. Mark, older and more experienced, with his intense career, couldn't possibly be satisfied with her, a woman frequently lost to an image no one else could see. Not in the long term. Although, considering their situation, long term was relative.

If she asked, would he kiss her now? Pondering those odds and possibilities, she nearly slipped off the bench when the van driver took a corner too fast. Mark caught her before the cuffs could jerk her arms and chafe her wrists again.

"You're quiet. What are you thinking?" he asked, still holding her steady.

It wasn't easy to speak with his warm hands on her skin. Even in this dangerous situation, his nearness both roused and soothed her.

The van took another turn and she grabbed his strong forearm, feeling the strength under the fabric of his suit coat. "Someone up there could use a safe driver refresher course," she said, loud enough to carry to the driver.

Mark grunted in amused agreement. "Seriously," he said at her ear, as the ride smoothed out. "Before that."

She could hardly admit she'd been thinking of them together in the setting he'd described. "Dinner on the water would make a beautiful painting," she said. "Planning a canvas sometimes helps when I'm stressed or uncomfortable."

Once Mark got them out of this, she would go back to her studio and paint. For days. Only breaking for dinner with him. She would paint a sun-soaked ocean and layer in all of her longing for Mark. All of her romantic wishes could float safely there, just under the surface of the water and she'd never have to face the likelihood of his rejection. He'd be kind and let her down easy, but that wouldn't change the result.

Obviously it would take a series of paintings to address the wealth of emotion she carried for him. On the canvas, only the sunset, the water and the effervescent champagne she dreamed of sipping while stretched out under the muted light of an endless sky would show. Endless. Yeah, that about summed it up. Endless fantasies, endless hope, endless what-ifs. She wasn't so sure that dinner after this crisis was a good idea after all.

"Must be some painting."

She was glad the light was dim and irregular back here, so the blush heating her cheeks wouldn't be as easy to spot. "I guess we'll see if I can pull it off when I get back to my studio." Maybe then she would work up the courage to grab a little piece of her dream of Mark.

"I'd like to see that." He shifted a bit, his hands still

on her, lighter now. "Do you ever invite people to watch you work?"

"No. The idea of painting in front of an audience makes me queasy." Her hands cramped and her muse skittered out of reach, hiding until it was safe to come out. "Every artist has a process that works for them."

"That makes sense." He sighed and moved away from her. "I'm so sorry, Lottie. I can't tell you how badly I want you out of here." His voice was so low she barely heard him over the engine and tires. "No stops lately. We've been on a highway for a while. I don't like it."

Remarkable she hadn't even noticed. Apparently he could effectively distract her without losing his focus. His features were hard to pick out in the near darkness. "How can I help?"

"It would be great if you had a magic wand handy. Barring that, I'm open to ideas," he said.

He slid farther away from her until he was at the end of the bench behind the front seats. Slowly, he stretched his arms, then his legs, but the restraints kept him far from the metal screen between them and the cab of the van. He couldn't interfere with the driver at all. "Eaton is a stickler for detail," he grumbled.

Following his example, she slid to the other end of the bench, straining for the rear door. They couldn't get out because the door handle had been removed, but she just realized that what she'd been hearing sliding around in the back were her shoes. Maybe if she could reclaim one or both shoes they could use the high heels as weapons.

It was a balancing act and far from graceful, but she

stretched full-length, trying to catch her toe in one of the straps.

Obviously they weren't alone out here on the road. If they could find a way to make a scene, surely another driver would notice and possibly call for help. When their driver pulled over to deal with whatever scene they made, they could attack him with her shoes.

"Charlotte?" Mark said softly. "I can use the point of the buckle on your shoe on these cuffs."

"Almost there." She was sure she could stretch another inch or two. She was wrong. The stupid sparkly heels remained just out of reach. She slumped onto her back on the bench, willing herself to stay positive. That's when she saw the hatch overhead.

If they could get that open it might garner attention from other drivers, as well. Getting her feet under her, she stood on the bench.

"What are you doing?"

"Creating a diversion," she said. "Or trying anyway." She was disgusted, but not surprised, that the cuffs didn't give her enough slack to stand upright on the bench. Frustrated beyond bearing, she screamed and stomped her feet.

She startled the driver and he twisted in his seat, shouting about the commotion, and jerked on the steering wheel in the process. His curses blended with Mark's and hers too as she lost her balance, tumbling to the bench. Horns blasted from either side of them as the van swerved all over his lane.

Unfortunately, there were only near misses, no collisions that might have helped them escape.

Mark helped her get situated again on the bench beside him. "I'd rather you didn't break your neck before I have a chance to get you out of here. What was that?"

"Dashed hope, obviously," she replied. Pain sang up her arms from her wrists to her shoulders. "I thought opening that hatch might get some attention from another driver."

"Not a bad plan," he said.

"Really?"

"Really." He looked toward the hatch. "I should've thought of it."

Was that admiration in his voice? She gathered herself and rolled her shoulders. "The swerving probably wasn't enough."

"Probably not," he agreed. "Can you get your shoe back on and hook the heel into the handle of the storage bin?"

With all the swerving, one of her shoes had come within reach. She got it on her foot and then followed his gaze to the bin under the bench seat they shared. "I can," she said, determined to be useful.

She had to fidget and twist a little and ignore all the places that ached from her last attempt to raise havoc, but at last she hooked the heel of her shoe through the handle. A few seconds later, she had the right angle and the door popped open.

"Nicely done."

She felt a flush of pride. "What's there?" She couldn't see into it as well as he could. "Anything we can use as a weapon?"

"Looks empty."

She shook her head. Not even a scream would help this time. "What now?"

"Now you start banging that door back and forth."

She scowled at him, though he probably couldn't see her expression. She didn't think making noise would do them any good, but trusting him, she did as he asked. "We could've just stomped," she said.

Under the flash of a streetlight, she saw him shake his head. "This is better. Keep going."

Time and again, she did as he asked. The driver took his sweet time reacting, but finally he slowed down and pulled over to the shoulder.

The van rocked as he came to a hard stop. He was muttering to himself as he put the gearshift in Park. An overhead light came on and he turned in his seat to yell through the screen. "What's that noise?"

Charlotte held out her cuffed hands and Mark did the same. "It's not us," she said. She kept the bin closed with her foot so he wouldn't see the trouble immediately.

He glared at Mark. "What did you do?"

"Not a thing," Mark said. "Maybe you ran over something in the road."

"No. You're the trouble. Kidnapping is always a bad plan," he muttered to himself. "Unpredictable." He shoved out of the car and a blast of air rushed in as a big truck sped by.

He'd resorted to colorful swearing by the time he yanked open the back doors. Charlotte was prepared to jump him, distract him or otherwise assist Mark until she saw the gun.

"Stay back," the driver ordered. "One move and you're dead."

When she met his gaze, she believed he would happily follow through on the threat.

"He's bluffing," Mark said. "Eaton would kill him if he hurt either of us and wrecked the grand plan."

She noticed he'd angled himself to be more visible in the glare of headlights from passing cars. While the driver looked for the source of the noise, Mark's gaze went to the shoe, and he nodded, motioning for her to give it to him.

She raised her knee and the guard's attention snapped to her. "Don't you move."

She froze, once more finding herself on the business end of a gun. "I had an itch," she claimed. Catching Mark's movement from the corner of her eye, she chattered in an effort to hold the driver's attention. "What can I do anyway? You're holding the gun. Do you have any water?" she asked. "I'm so thirsty."

An object flew at the driver's head. The shoe, she realized as it connected with the man's head and he stumbled backward. She'd never wished so hard that a person would fall in front of a truck.

No such luck. On a tempestuous roar, the driver launched himself into the van with them. Grabbing Mark by his lapels, he hauled him forward, to the limit of the cuffs. He raised a big hand and brought it down hard across Mark's ear.

"You will sit still until you are told to move."

"Pardon?" Mark tilted his head. "Can't hear you. My ear's buzzing."

His face mottled with rage, the driver shoved Mark back to the end of the bench and rounded on her.

His hand came up, palm open. She braced for the impact.

"Don't touch her," Mark said.

"I'll do what I please." He reached out, his hand clammy and rough as he dragged his palm down the length of her throat. His thumb and fingers circled the base of her neck, squeezing just enough to let her know he was in complete control.

A blast of icy fear coursed through her. He could snap her neck at will.

"Cooperate," he said, applying more pressure. "Behave."

"Hey!" Mark stomped his foot against the floorboard. "Were you expecting friends?"

The driver spun as a car coasted up behind them on the shoulder. He hurried out of the van and slammed the doors closed again.

Charlotte coughed and tried to rub away the feel of the driver's hand. "I should've hit him when he was distracted," she said. "We're right back where we started."

"Hardly."

She lifted her gaze and caught Mark grinning at her. "Why are you smiling?" There was an imprint of the driver's fist on his cheek and a trickle of blood seeped from his ear. She'd expected to see something closer to anger on his face.

"You're fierce, Lottie," he said. "Looks good on you."

Fierce. The surprising compliment sent a ripple of warmth through her bloodstream, melting away the dreadful chill from the driver's touch. "I can think of better ways to spend an evening," she admitted.

"Sure. But misery is always more fun with good company," he joked. "More importantly you aren't huddled up crying in the corner. You're a variable they don't know how to solve. I think they'll figure out they should let you go, and you should grab the chance when it comes."

Despite everything, there was a glimmer of happiness in her heart. He'd called her fierce. "I've cried plenty tonight," she pointed out. She felt so much weaker than him. Fragile. None of her yoga or hiking or other fitness endeavors had prepared her for this. "He could've snapped my neck."

"Could have. Didn't." Mark worked his jaw side to side. "He has weight to his punches, I'll give him that."

The dome light in the cab came on as the driver resumed his position. A moment later, the light over their heads winked out. It seemed the Good Samaritan who'd stopped had been sent away. So much for the miracle she'd been hoping for.

Resigned, she curled up on the bench seat and Mark invited her to lean on him. It wasn't ideal, but it was a wonderful comfort to rest her head on his shoulder.

"Do you remember that summer we turned Mom's minivan into a fort?" Mark asked.

"We? That was all you and Luke." She closed her eyes, recalling those sweet days.

"You were there," Mark said. "Guilt by association."

"Maybe so." She opened her eyes. "This place could do with some pilfered couch cushions and a hanging sheet or two."

Mark chuckled. "And gummy bears."

"Yes." She rolled her wrists, trying to get some relief from the handcuffs. "What made you think of Fort Van…whatever it was?"

"Fort Van Dodge," he supplied. "You slept in there. I remember your eyelashes."

She sat up and blinked said lashes, wishing for better light to read his expression. "What are you talking about?"

He rested his head against the panel. "Your eyelashes turned into little gold fans on your cheeks when you slept. Still happens, I bet."

Weary and uncertain, she drew his words straight into her heart. She should probably find something witty to say or a memory to share, but her adrenaline spikes were giving way to pure exhaustion. Better to stay quiet than say something that made him feel obligated to take on more of her stress.

"Sleep if you can," Mark said, as if he'd read her mind. "I won't let anything happen."

He clearly wanted to spare her, and she appreciated his efforts, but she had a feeling it would take both of them, working together, to escape this mess.

Chapter 4

With Charlotte leaning into him, her head resting awkwardly on his shoulder thanks to the cumbersome handcuffs, Mark kept watch. Not that he actually saw much, but he took in all the information available from the sound of the pavement to the brief glimpses he caught through the windshield.

He had to get her out of this mess. It was his fault she was stuck in this dangerous situation with him, and he wouldn't let an innocent suffer on his watch. Especially when that innocent was Charlotte.

A shame they hadn't been kidnapped in the daylight. That would've made things much easier. Of course, in the daylight, he'd have been behind the gates of a military installation, putting him out of Eaton's reach.

The effort to pick up on any location clues helped divert him from the enticing woman leaning against him.

Whatever she'd used in her hair smelled amazing and her skin felt as silky as her dress. At first glance, she might be mistaken for soft or fragile. She wasn't. Charlotte had shown tremendous fortitude under pressure. He wondered how long she would hold up, wishing it didn't have to be a concern for either of them.

He could smell the ocean nearby, though that didn't necessarily mean anything since they'd started the evening in Virginia Beach, just a few blocks in from the coastline. When the rear doors had been opened earlier, he hadn't seen much of their surroundings, but he guessed they were headed south and though traffic had been steady, it seemed the driver had been routed away from the major thoroughfares.

Having been read into the ongoing investigation and search for the man harassing his family, Mark decided Eaton enjoyed putting Rileys into ridiculous situations. The man had mastered how to provoke and divert and he went out of his way to fabricate high-visibility moments that would create havoc and blow back on General Riley.

Mark's dad had been candid about why Eaton had been removed from the unit during a deployment. Several evaluations had been conducted at the time and all of those professionals concurred that Eaton had snapped. Every step had been taken to ensure Eaton got the care he needed, that his family was provided for, but somewhere along the line his wife had walked out, taking their daughter.

Consequences happened. It was a standard by-product of living. Rather than take responsibility for his actions and the fallout, Eaton pinned all the blame on the general and set in motion an elaborate plan of revenge.

The file on Eaton was frightening. Led by army investigator Hank Lawson, the team was uncovering a history of odd jobs that led Eaton to work with mercenary teams abroad. It seemed a superior sniper without a conscience was always in demand. Through the years, he'd found and cultivated a network of people willing to carry out his orders. He used that time for planning and fine-tuning his revenge against Mark's dad. As of the last update, no one had an accurate location for Eaton's home base. Somehow the man had effectively fallen off-grid.

Mark couldn't help but wonder if Eaton had managed to compromise someone inside the investigation, someone who'd taken out the eyes and ears of the team running security at the gallery. What else explained the lack of response?

He was debating the wisdom of faking another crisis to further interfere with whatever timeline Eaton had in place when the sound of the engine changed and roused Charlotte.

"Mark?" She pushed her hair out of her eyes. "Did I sleep?"

"Not well," he replied. "It's just an exit ramp. No worries."

"If you say so."

The doubt in her voice made him want to crush Eaton. She shouldn't even be here. He tried to tamp down his rage at the man who'd taken them prisoner, or at least channel it into how he'd use it to crush Eaton. Going after the Rileys was bad enough. Snagging Charlotte in his snare was stupid and cruel. He thought of the sunset cruise he'd described in an effort to give them both a diversion from the crisis. A flash of curiosity left him wondering how her voice—all grown up now—might change with a bit of healthy flirting. Jaded or not, he couldn't deny his attraction.

Assuming she harbored a similar interest in him, maybe they could spend some time together. Picturing his mother's concern for Charlotte, he would be crystal clear with her about his limits and expectations. He didn't want anything fun to hurt either of them. Charlotte was the kind of woman who would eventually find someone, a lover and partner to share forever. Not him. Life, in the form of Maria, his near-miss fiancée, had taught him he wasn't the kind of man who stirred that kind of lasting devotion.

Of course, that was assuming a great deal. He had no illusions about the severity of the situation. Surviving Eaton's plan was likely to require hard decisions and ruthless action Charlotte might not appreciate. Though he admired her determination to help them escape, she wasn't equipped. He didn't doubt her loyalty, but she didn't have the training necessary to go toe-to-toe with their notoriously vicious captor.

His first priority was to get her safely out of this mess, and to protect her every step of the way. Not a hair on her head would be harmed if he could help it. She'd already suffered too much.

When she'd dozed off, he remembered her the way she'd been as a kid in Fort Van Dodge. Even back then, he'd found her determination more adorable than annoying as she and his younger sister, Jolene, tried to keep up with the older kids. That willpower and cleverness were still evident in her sky blue eyes, despite the fear. Those intangibles, wrapped up in the beauty she'd grown into, left him wishing he were a different man.

A man who could inspire a woman to wait for his return, to put up with an unpredictable schedule for just a few more years. A man confident in his ability to be a content civilian after a high-action career.

"We've reached a town," he said, as the red haze of a street light glowed through the windshield.

"Near a wharf or dock." Charlotte wrinkled her nose. "There's a smell you never forget."

"You don't like the scent of the ocean?" That could be a deal-breaker for a long-term involvement. Good thing he wasn't looking for one of those.

"Of course I do," she said, clearly exasperated. "We must be close to another industrial area. Instead of salt water, sunscreen and candy, I smell stale oil and grease."

"That's a good nose on your face," he teased. "No tires this time," he said.

"Painting isn't just about what I see. The real trick to making it come alive is layering in all the cues about other senses in that moment."

He could imagine the passion shining in her eyes. Her enthusiasm for her work wouldn't be muted, not even in this grim van on their way to who-knew-where. He wanted to kiss her, to taste the excitement evident in her voice. Suddenly, in the moment, she was everything. Air, light, movement. *Everything.*

Blaming the reaction on a wayward surge of adrenaline, he shifted as far from her as he could get and rubbed at his chest. The combination of new attraction, danger and old memories had inexplicably ripped the cover off a void near his heart and Charlotte poured in something he didn't know he needed. Maria's betrayal had left him feeling unbearably weak and full of self-doubt. To get through, he'd deliberately closed himself off from intense emotions. On a mission with his team, second guesses were a land mine waiting to blow the operation apart. He hadn't let them down. He wouldn't let down Charlotte.

"Are you hurt?"

Not in a way he could explain. "It's nothing."

Thankfully the van came to a stop before he had to drum up a better explanation. He prepared himself for another confrontation with Eaton, but there was no sign of him when the doors opened. Four men faced him, not one of them familiar. How many men did Eaton trust? This team was dressed head to toe in muted black from their knit sweaters to their thick-soled black boots that didn't make a sound as they approached.

"Take me to Eaton," he demanded.

The burly bald guard at the door shifted, making way for another man who carried a ring of keys. "You'll see him soon enough."

The second man had pale blond hair, fair skin and a wiry build. He withdrew standard handcuffs from his back pocket and slapped them on to Charlotte before freeing her from the cuffs chaining her to the van. He picked up her shoes and, with almost reverent care, he handed her out of the van.

Mark clamped his mouth shut against the urge to demand where they were taking her. Divide and conquer was a classic tactic for a reason. He had to stay focused on the big picture and the primary goal of escape. *Patience is key*, he coached himself. He'd find an opening, make it wider and get her free and clear of this nonsense.

The wiry guard returned, the cuffs in his hands clinking lightly. The driver must have tattled on their antics during the drive because he removed Mark's shoes and put on leg shackles before tightly cuffing his wrists and then freeing him from the bar set into the van wall.

"Where did you take the girl?"

The man shoved him out of the van without any of the care he'd shown Charlotte. "You know who she is, don't you?" Mark asked under his breath. "The star of that party you dragged us away from. People are searching for her. Your boss won't care if you're a casualty in that fight. Maybe think of that and let her go."

The guard halted, his strong fingers digging into the tendons and muscles of Mark's arm just above the elbow. It was an effective pressure point and the nerves in Mark's hand tingled. Someone had trained this man well.

Mark looked around. They appeared to be in an oversized garage. They'd pulled the van in and put the door down. Nearby he heard the unmistakable creak of boats and bumpers against docks.

"You're now the property of John Eaton," the bigger, bald guard said. It seemed he was the one in charge at this site. "From this point forward, you won't take so much as a breath without his permission."

Mark slowly filled his lungs, proving the ridiculous nature of the statement. He got a big fist to the rib cage for his trouble. "The girl?" he asked, grinning. If they were hitting him, they weren't bothering her.

"Not your concern."

"You should let her go. Keeping her will backfire," Mark said. "Ask the skinny guy here." He tilted his head toward the blond man. "She's adored by tons of fans. Taking her from her own showing will bring the police down on you with more force and sooner than you expected. There's a good chance most of you won't make it out alive in that fight."

"You Rileys should start minding your own business." Eaton emerged from the shadows. "We've planned for every contingency and we are experts at tactical adjustments. We've anticipated every outcome, run all the scenarios. *You* will not win," he finished.

Mark shook his head. "I didn't get goose bumps. You can try the speech again if you want."

Eaton didn't reveal any reaction, merely glanced down at Mark's feet. "I see you've lost your shoes."

"Art showings get wild," Mark said. The floor was cool under his socks. "You talk a big game, but we both know you weren't expecting two hostages."

"Your reputation as a ladies' man precedes you, so we created a contingency for two prisoners." Eaton smiled. "My team is the best."

Mark didn't care for the man's confidence and matched it with bravado of his own. "You're a fool to keep her," Mark said. "Do what you want with me, but you'd be smart to let her go before your game gets cut short. If something happens to her, nowhere on earth will be safe for you or your hired hands."

Eaton chuckled. "After the drive, I thought you'd

have a better argument prepared. I guess what they say about SEALs is true. You're only the tip of the spear, not the brains behind it. Rest easy, you'll have a chance to show me your skills."

Mark was increasingly unsettled, though he'd never let it show. "Tip of the spear, huh? That's unfortunate," he mused. "I didn't expect to have anything in common with you, *sniper*."

Eaton slapped him. Mark didn't care. It was satisfying that he'd hit a nerve. At some point, one or more of the team would figure out this wasn't worth it. He would turn that into an advantage as Eaton's plans played out.

"Tell me you've sent Charlotte home," he said, glancing at the closest guards. "Letting her go doesn't spoil his plans for me. My family and team already know I've been taken. Letting her go will be save your sorry asses though, because you won't be responsible for anything that happens to her. A smart boss would operate from wisdom rather than pride and spare his team the risk and embarrassment."

Eaton's confident grin would only have been more terrifying if he'd added clown face paint and a red wig. What was the man up to?

"Didn't you get the memo, Riley? *I'm* in control. This is my world. Neither you nor your pretty friend have a say in how things will go here." He cocked his head. "However, I do believe in fair play."

"Fair play?" Mark echoed. Mentally he took a step back. This guy wasn't teetering on the edge of insanity— he'd embraced the free fall. "Then why am I restrained?"

"Because our game is just getting started."

Eaton stared at Mark for a long bone-chilling moment. Turning on his heel, he began barking orders to his men. Pausing, he cast a look over his shoulder. "Do cooperate for my team, Riley. An injury will only delay the inevitable."

Mark had a few inevitable ideas of his own. "Where is Charlotte?" he shouted.

Eaton raised a hand and Mark sensed movement behind him. He didn't have time to turn or dodge before a heavy blow struck the back of his head. He staggered under it, seeing stars, but he wasn't completely out as two men hooked him under the arms and dragged him away.

He fought to stay conscious, seeking out any pertinent details as they hauled him out of the garage, over a gangway and down to a waiting boat.

"Charlotte!" In his mind and heart, he'd shouted it. Based on the guffaws around him, it had been more of a whimper.

That was fine. Let them laugh. If they were convinced he was too weak to fight, he'd have his opening sooner than expected. And he'd seize that opening just as soon as he found Charlotte.

He heard the rasp and rattle of a lock on a door and felt the sharp nip of a needle at his neck before everything went dark.

His son was missing.

The thought lodged in Ben Riley's mind, making it impossible to think of anything else.

He stared out the window of the hotel room. His wife was behind him on the phone, quietly speaking to Charlotte's mother, Sue Ellen. When it had become

clear Charlotte had ducked out of her first solo showing, they'd all covered for her. No one was surprised.
The girl was immensely talented, but she was shy, had
always struggled with being the center of attention.

Then another scenario circulated. The consensus
was that Charlotte had left with Mark. Ben didn't find
that cause for much concern; the kids had been friends
all their lives, though Patricia had been inexplicably
disappointed.

No, the real worry hadn't set in until another hour
had passed, another hour for the kidnappers to take
Mark and Charlotte farther out of reach.

Ben scrubbed at his hair, freshly trimmed for Charlotte's big night. He'd long since shed his suit coat and
tie and rolled his shirtsleeves back to his elbows. He
was ready to do something, to take action, but the authorities had told him to stand down.

Ben had been assured retirement would be relaxing.
His wife and friends who had retired ahead of him told
him it would be great, that they enjoyed themselves immensely. It all rang hollow now.

He'd barely had time to acclimate to their new beach
house when John Eaton came out of his past, targeting
the Riley children as revenge for Ben putting an end to
the sniper's army career.

Why couldn't they drop a net over the bastard?

A hitch in Patricia's voice drew his attention. He
turned, ready to comfort, but she waved him off with
a brave smile and continued her conversation with her
best friend. His wife had always been a rock in a crisis and he'd always been honored and grateful for her
partnership, loyalty and love.

What Ben wouldn't give to have a unit at his back. He was ready to lead an all-out assault to track down Mark and Charlotte and put an end to Eaton. Being sidelined was hell.

On the verge of losing his temper, Ben walked into the bedroom and closed the door. The view through this window wasn't any different. A dark Atlantic Ocean stretched out under a deep sky and foam-tipped waves gleamed under the pale moonlight. He'd planned a romantic evening with his wife after they'd showed Charlotte their support. Instead the evening was a disaster.

Once the team running security at the gallery had recovered from Eaton's coordinated attack, they'd done their best to pick up a trail. So far no one could say for sure that Mark and Charlotte were still in the city. He and Patricia had left the gallery in a daze, returning to the hotel room to wait for information.

Ben had never felt more defeated than he did right now. Considering some of the places he'd served, that was quite a statement. He'd let down his family, exposing them to a threat he wished he could have anticipated.

His hands curled into fists as he ran through his memories of Eaton, a skilled sniper who had snapped in a startling display of cold-blooded violence. There had only been one way to deal with a scenario most commanders never faced. Get him out of the service. Somehow, despite the army's disciplinary actions, Eaton had recovered and spent years recruiting aggressive mercenaries to harass and endanger his family.

Not for the first time, he wished the man would come straight at him, instead of taking aim at the kids.

All five of his children were capable adults. He and

Patricia had seen to that by setting high expectations and giving them the best foundation they could provide. And Hank, the soldier he'd taken under his wing early in his career, was considered family now, and fully capable of leading this investigation to a just conclusion.

But would they lose Mark and Charlotte in the process?

Pulling his cell phone from his pocket, he started to text Hank and caught himself. Pestering would be more of a hindrance than a help. Hank would update him when there was news to share. He took a deep breath. That was the crux of it; there was *nothing* for him to do but wait. He'd given Hank all the details he could recall about Eaton's habits as a soldier and his basic demeanor and attitude as a man.

Ben never anticipated the man could organize and pull off the stunts he'd accomplished against the family so far. His vengeance had almost been the end of both Matt and Grace Ann. He'd set traps for both of them, and used those stunts to torture Ben.

The bedroom door opened quietly and Patricia joined him at the window, sliding her arms around his waist and leaning her cheek to his back. "Everyone is doing all they can to find the kids. We'll have them home again soon."

"And here I stand, useless." Hank and the local authorities had expressly prohibited him from joining the search. "We can't even give a statement to the press."

"Can you imagine how Eaton would gloat if we did? His team managed to snag a navy SEAL."

He turned his back on the view to study his wife. Stronger now, lovelier than she'd been the day they'd met. Her unruffled calm shouldn't be a surprise. "He took your child."

"Two, really." She pressed a hand over her heart. "I'm as furious as you are. The man is a monster and, given a choice, I'd have him drawn and quartered for coming after our family."

Ben traced her cheek and brow, smoothed a strand of hair behind her ear. "I don't do helpless."

"I never would've stuck around this long if you did." Her lips tilted into a small smile.

"There must be *something* we can do." He caught her hands in his. "Waiting with no information is worse than all the pictures he's sent before."

"Knowing Eaton, he'll send us something soon," she noted.

"Charlotte's parents will never forgive us," he said.

"Mark won't let anything happen to her." Patricia stepped into his embrace and he hugged her close. "Our boy will bring her back."

Neither one of them could voice the thought that Mark wasn't alive, alert and able to protect Charlotte. "Are you concerned they're more than family friends?" he asked.

"No," Patricia said with a soft laugh. "Although I caught him looking at her with something more than friendship in his eyes. If I hadn't assumed he'd swept her away from her own party, we might've recognized the trouble sooner."

"Mark's an incorrigible flirt," Ben said. "He gets that from you."

She swatted his chest lightly and wriggled out of his embrace. "I can't help thinking Charlotte could be just what Mark needs," she said. "I'm not sure the reverse is true after what Maria did."

She never failed to surprise him. "So you finally admit you have a favorite child and it's Charlotte."

"I should've thought of that answer ages ago." Her eyes crinkled at the corners. "There's no secret relationship between them, Ben. I learned that much. She was simply in the wrong place at the wrong time. And she probably tried to help him."

"True." He hadn't considered that angle. "She has spunk."

"She's so quiet it's easy to overlook."

Ben sat down hard on the end of the bed. He gazed out at the night, racking his mind for any stray thought that could prove helpful. "Tell me what to do."

"We do as Hank asked," Patricia replied. "We wait."

He swore.

She shook her head. "If we jump the gun, we only cause more problems. We'll wait, together, and think positively until it's time for us to do more."

"You amaze me."

"Up close or from a distance?" she teased.

"I'm serious," he said.

"Oh, honey, I know you are." She sat beside him and rubbed his shoulder. "Whenever you were overseas, there were times I thought the waiting would do me in."

He laced his fingers with hers. "I took you for granted."

"Of course you did. That's part of the deal. My job was keeping the house and family going while you did your job. Now, at least, I can wait *with* my best friend rather than *for* my best friend."

"That's not as comforting as you might believe."

"Maybe not for you."

She rested her cheek on his shoulder, his wife of more than three decades. In Love and Life Together had been their motto from the beginning, whether they'd been in the same room or thousands of miles apart.

"I'm sorry," he whispered.

She turned, taking his face between her hands, hands that had raised five children, too often alone. "Don't be. Eaton's quest for revenge is *not* your fault. He's a criminal and you did what was necessary. These attacks are on his head, not yours."

He closed his eyes so she wouldn't see the guilt churning inside.

Her hands gripped his shoulders and she gave him a little shake. "Benjamin Riley, you know I'm right."

She was. Still. He pressed a hand to his gut. "I can't shake this sense of dread over what Eaton has in mind this time. I want to get out there."

"Then we will. As soon as Hank has a solid direction, we'll find a way to help the search."

"Together," he said emphatically. He didn't trust himself to get out there and look without her at his side.

"Always." She touched her nose to his. "There's no other way for us, my love."

Charlotte sat on the end of the narrow bunk in a tiny cabin. She'd been led onto the boat and down to this room by a guard who'd shown surprising courtesy and compassion. He'd removed her handcuffs, thankfully, but she was still barefoot in a dress she was ready to be done with, despite Mark's compliments.

What had they done to him?

The courteous guard had locked her in and she'd heard him order someone else to stand watch outside the door. She was still a prisoner with no idea what might be coming next. Her fear was on the rise again, tightening her chest and making her palms damp.

Breathing deeply, she closed her eyes. *Inhale calm, exhale panic.* She heard a noise in the corridor and her eyes popped open. Mark had been emphatic the search for them was already underway. He'd told her to grab a chance if she could to get away. But how could she leave him, knowing he was in danger?

When he didn't charge through the door, she tried the calming breath again. Inhale, exhale. It wasn't working. She jumped up from the bunk and shook out her hands, trying to imagine herself at her studio or at the campsite by the lake.

Nothing worked. Panic had been perched on her shoulder, ready to pounce long before they'd separated her from Mark. Now, calm was a vague concept she couldn't grasp. Like algebra. Or cubism. Well, she understood cubism—she just didn't like it much.

She tapped her hand against her forehead. That was a perfect example of freaked-out, useless thinking. Mark would be searching for a way out, and she could do the same. Giving up on the breathing exercise, she kneaded the muscles in her hands and forearms, avoiding the abrasions on her wrists from the handcuffs. Something in the room might be useful. Had to be if she was going to escape and find Mark.

They were on a boat, still at the dock. No sounds of an engine or the noises or motions that indicated they would soon be underway. If she set the bunk mattress on fire, someone would have to come in to put it out. A quick search of the room proved futile. Anything that might help her start a fire had been removed. She looked at the light switch, wondering if she could get that to spark and flame. Knowing her lousy track record with most things mechanical, she'd electrocute herself before she worked the switch plate off the wall. Besides, how would she control the blaze before help came?

The space had a functional, if miniscule, bathroom. She supposed she could flood the space. She opened the faucet and stifled a groan at the tiny trickle. No water pressure and no stopper for the sink. She could tear apart her dress to clog the sink drain, but even then, flooding the room would take days. Did she have days?

Shying away from that slippery slope of despair, she continued her search for anything that could become a weapon. Lifting the mattress from the bunk and removing all three drawers from the dresser one by one, she came up empty again. "Come on, Charlotte. Think."

The closest thing to a weapon was a drawer. Not an item easily hidden if, say, she coaxed the guard into opening the door. "I could ask nicely," she muttered to the empty room. "Please lie down and be nice enough to pass out the first time I strike you."

Even if that absurd scenario worked, there were at least four other guards she'd seen around the boat and dock. Odds were good they wouldn't all be as accommodating as the guard in her imagination.

Frustrated, she flopped back onto the bed.

What would Mark expect of her? He'd asked her to trust him. To hang in there. Both trust and the hanging-in were easier when he was in sight and within reach. She didn't even have a good idea of how much time had passed while they were locked in the van.

Mark had called her fierce and she did her best to cling to his view of her. Just because she couldn't see any action to take right now didn't mean there wouldn't be an opportunity. A fierce artist. She liked the sense of empowerment that surged through her along with the images dancing through her mind. Closing her eyes again, she imagined herself strong and determined, standing against the bullies holding her and the man she loved.

The man who had no idea she loved him.

Well, he knew she loved him like family. He just had no idea she'd been *in* love with him for as long as she could remember. The idea of him anyway. She wondered what he'd say if he knew he was the star of her fantasies that had grown from a crush to infatuation to something no other guy could possibly live up to.

Knowing Mark, he'd be flattered. His ornery grin would flash before it melted into a warm and sincere smile. And then he'd dash off to do something athletic or heroic or date someone more beautiful and confident, and she wouldn't see him until the next holiday or family event.

Life was precious; the past few hours proved how quickly things could change. It shouldn't matter if he left her for a new assignment or because he didn't return her feelings. She wanted to be fierce, to seize the moment, but she couldn't shake the potential fallout. It was probably a good thing she hadn't managed that kiss. That would've changed things between them too much and he needed to focus. She'd do everything in her power to help them escape and then channel all her love for him into her art.

Though she longed for that fancy dinner, it wasn't the smart move. As well as she knew Mark, she knew herself better. A fancy night out would turn romantic in her mind and another decade of her dating life would slip by in a blur of men who weren't Mark.

Even if he did look at her in the romantic way she longed for, he wasn't ready to leave his career and his SEAL brothers. She certainly wasn't ready to do the military-wife-and-family thing, despite the example set by her mother and his. Throwing away a good, solid friendship on a dream that couldn't come true made no sense.

Her heart could go back to all that wishing and yearning later. Right now, survival was paramount. If they didn't escape this situation—*together*—Eaton would make sure neither of them would be yearning for anything ever again.

She stood at the narrow bathroom door, wondering if she could dismantle a pipe or the towel bar. Her hands slipped and slid for purchase as she tugged at the towel bar. She was reconsidering the drawer as a weapon when she heard the slide of the lock and the door opened. She froze and then her knees started to quake. So much for Mark's fierce artist.

"Hello? Is this a bad time?"

Eaton. She stepped out of the bathroom and glared at him. "Is there really a *good* time for kidnapping?"

He spread his hands wide and smiled. "Welcome

aboard, Miss Hanover. You're satisfied with the accommodations?"

"Where is Mark?"

"He's close."

She didn't care for the sly glint in the man's eye. "You killed him."

"No." Eaton's brow flexed into a frown. "He isn't my true target."

"He told me you're pursuing some revenge thing against General Riley."

"That would be more accurate."

She folded her arms over her chest, trying to hide her nerves. If she could get some information, maybe she could also leave a clue for anyone who found their trail. "Is it accurate to say you've caused harm to innocent Riley children?"

"No." He was emphatic. "General Riley is *not* innocent. His children, adults in the military, are not innocent. My wife and daughter were *absolutely* innocent. Whatever pain I manage to inflict on the general, it will never be enough and never be equal to the pain he caused them and me by hurting them."

His rage filled the room. She wasn't sure *madman* was the right term for Eaton. He was calculating. Remorseless. And he knew exactly what he was doing.

"Out of words, pretty painter?"

"Not yet."

His sneer brought to mind crocodiles rising from the murky water to assess their prey.

"I'm listening," he said.

She'd planned to make another plea for their lives, but she could see there was no point in wasting her breath. "I'm sorry you were hurt." She could give him compassion without throwing General Riley under the bus. He would never do anything to intentionally harm anyone under his command or that person's family. Whatever Eaton had done, she was sure the general had responded appropriately. "I'm sorry your family was affected."

"Affected?" Eaton cocked his head. "Their lives were ruined."

He didn't shout. It would have been easier to deal with him if he had. Instead it was as if the bitterness had settled into his skin and lodged itself even deeper into his bones, altering his entire framework.

"That's horrible." She clung to compassion when she wanted to shout and rail at him. He probably expected her to fly into hysterics. Lulling him into complacency might be what she needed to escape.

His gaze narrowed and he stared at her as if he could see under her skin. At least he wasn't leering down the front of her dress this time. Maybe he'd done that to draw a reaction from Mark.

"Please reconsider and let Mark and me go."

He acted as if she hadn't spoken. Checking his watch, he planted his legs wide and folded his arms over his chest. He presented himself to the world as an average man, easily overlooked or forgotten. She was sure he'd cultivated that effect during his service as a sniper. When she looked, the man she saw wasn't average or forgettable. His righteous self-assurance was terrifying.

"I was furious when I saw you in the van," he said conversationally. "It took some time to warm up to the unique opportunity you present."

Opportunity had never sounded so frightening. The motors rumbled and the boat lurched under her feet. She lost her balance for a moment and caught herself on the bunk before she pitched forward into Eaton. He didn't strike her as the chivalrous type.

"Won't you please let us off this boat?" she asked.

"Eventually, yes. In the meantime, rest and enjoy the ride." He gestured to the bed. "You'll be provided with all the necessities in due time."

He walked out and she heard the lock slide back in place. The small window high in the wall of the cabin had been covered, but she didn't need the visual. They were leaving the dock and he could take them wherever he pleased.

Her only consolation was that Eaton's presence meant Mark was on this boat too. He might have let someone else drive the van that brought them here, but he wouldn't relinquish control over the current prize in his revenge game.

She considered pounding on the door or tearing apart the cabin. None of it would change the reality. For the immediate future, she was stuck. A captive in a war she didn't understand.

Chapter 5

Mark came awake with a bad case of cottonmouth and a terrible whining in his ears. Mosquitoes? Bees? A flock of drones? He blinked away the fog muddling his brain and found himself handcuffed and chained like a dog to a loop of rebar bolted into a cement pad. He'd been stripped to his slacks and dress shirt. They'd even taken his socks. He tugged on the restraints, tested the grip of cement on the rebar as he worked himself into an upright position so he could get his bearings.

An industrial fan mounted in the ceiling was the source of the sound. Naturally, it wasn't blowing at him, but rather toward an old metal desk, currently unoccupied, at the opposite end of a long, narrow room. A modified shipping container, he realized after further study. The air was hot and the humidity high. How far south had Eaton taken him? And how?

He recalled the drive and the marina. After Charlotte had been escorted away, Eaton and his men had harassed him. Drugged him. He didn't need to touch the back of his head to feel the knot there. His scalp was tight from swelling and probably more than a little dried blood.

"Charlotte?" His rusty voice sounded pitiful in his ears. Clearing his throat, he shouted her name.

The only response was his rumbling stomach.

Mark twisted as far as the restraints allowed, trying to get his bearings. There was remarkably little to go on. Rusting corrugated walls and one door. When his eyes landed on a bottle of water near the wall, he didn't even try to stretch for it. It was either out of reach or laced with drugs. Let the games begin. Mark scanned the windowless room again and spotted two cameras. Was Eaton already sending out the feed meant to torture his father?

"Charlotte!" he called again. What had Eaton done with her? Mark forced back the swell of panic. He had to stay calm. One step at a time, just like he'd told Charlotte.

Eaton had to know the army investigators were closing in on him. Why else would he go to such extremes with this elaborate kidnapping?

The man wanted to get caught, everyone agreed on that. More specifically, he wanted to get caught on *his* terms, after he'd accomplished his goal of ruining the general. Hank's team had managed only a few successful interrogations of people they'd connected to Eaton. Still, Hank and his team were piecing together a picture.

Power was Eaton's drug as much as control and

impact. Whatever misfortunes he blamed on General Riley, Eaton intended for the general to suffer and keep on suffering as everything he valued dissolved into a wasteland. He blamed the general for the destruction of his family and seemed intent on dealing the same crushing blow to the Rileys.

"Charlotte!" Mark shouted her name again.

"Mark!" The faint response motivated him. If she was within earshot, they still had a chance. He hauled himself to his feet and tried to budge the cement pad. The door opened and Eaton walked in, followed by a man tall enough that he had to duck to get through the doorway. The man was bald and a wall of muscle. His uniform, likely in deference to the humid climate, was a black tank top with black cargo pants and black jungle boots.

If he was part of Eaton's plan, Mark anticipated a great deal of pain in his own future.

"We're glad to hear you're back in fighting form," Eaton said. He propped a hip against the desk, staying well clear of Mark, and folded his arms over his chest.

Mark stilled, refusing to give any hints about his condition. "Where's Charlotte?"

Eaton looked at the muscle man. "So predictable."

"Just as you said," Muscle replied.

"What did you do to her?" Mark demanded.

"We've shown her every courtesy," Eaton said. "Haven't touched a hair on her head." He took two strides forward, tucking his hands into his pockets. "Yet."

Mark strained toward him, wanting a piece of Eaton

more than a gallon of water. "I'll get free," he vowed. "You'll pay."

"You will get free," Eaton agreed. Then his eyes narrowed to slits and his nostrils flared. "When I'm ready for you to be free." To Muscle, he said, "Go on and introduce yourself."

Mark watched the big man advance, learning what he could in the few brief strides it took the thug to reach him. He dodged the first ham-sized hook aimed at his jaw and, thanks to the restraints, got caught with an upper cut. Wheezing, cuffed, he couldn't do more than offer a few weak blocks against the rest of the beating.

"That's enough for today." Eaton gave the order just before Muscle's boot connected with Mark's rib cage.

The big man pulled the kick, sparing his ribs, and Mark smiled. His teammates always claimed he lived a charmed life. He was starting to believe it.

Eaton walked over and unlocked the cuffs linking Mark's hands to the rebar and Muscle shuffled him out of the room.

Definitely a modified shipping container and not pinned down well, Mark noted as the floor gave a bit under their feet. He hoped it wasn't just his imagination that beyond Muscle's body odor and the smell of rust he caught a whiff of clean salt air nearby.

"Tack up some plywood, add a window or two and the place won't be half-bad, Eaton," Mark mumbled through a swollen lip.

"Something to think about," his captor replied. He stepped in front of Muscle and led the way to a second heavily reinforced door. "Why don't you consider the color palette for me and we'll discuss it at our next meeting."

"Sure. I'll bring color swatches."

Muscle walked through the opening first, dragging Mark through the doorway and tossing him into a cell that resembled a dog kennel with plywood on one side. The cell door clanked shut and Muscle locked it with a standard sliding bolt before walking out of the room and slamming the reinforced door closed with a loud bang. Eaton and Muscle had to know his ears were ringing.

Swiping away the blood trickling from his eyebrow, Mark took stock of the surroundings. He looked around for a camera and didn't see one. That didn't mean it wasn't here, he thought, leaning on the cage door. The bolt held firm and there wasn't enough space to get his hand through to manipulate it. He gave his captors points for confidence.

Wire fencing made up the walls and a ceiling of the cell that was a few inches too short for Mark to stand up straight. The jerk knew how to make a prisoner miserable.

He kicked at the gap at the bottom of his cage door. A convenient food slot, though Eaton probably wouldn't bother feeding him. Next, he poked through the chain links at the plywood pressed against the outside of one of the cage walls. When it didn't fall, he assumed it was there to block his view of anyone in the next cage.

"Mark? Is that you?"

Charlotte's voice, stoic and clear, erased every pain as relief surged through his system. "Charlotte, are you okay?"

"I'm fine. Well, I'm terrified, but they haven't hurt me."

Mark sat down hard, as close to the plywood as possible with his back to the cage door. She sounded all right. He just had to keep her that way. He rapped a fist against an upright support post and the sound reverberated all around. "Good acoustics in here," Mark muttered. Eaton or the guards would hear every movement.

"If you say so. What did they do to you?"

"Nothing serious," he replied. He didn't expect the reprieve to last, but no point in talking about something neither of them could control.

"I don't believe you."

"That's rude." He tried to laugh, but it turned into a wheeze. "Where's the trust? I've never lied to you."

"Mark, I'm serious," she pleaded. "Have they hurt you?"

He couldn't ignore her plaintive tone. Maybe knowing the facts would keep her vivid imagination in check. "They drugged me at the dock. Typical tactic, but it's out of my system now. A big bald guard roughed me up a bit. I've had tougher training sessions." He knew he was in for it later if Eaton had devices in here to pick up this conversation, but Charlotte's peace of mind was more important. "Now it's your turn to be honest with me." He remembered the way the older man had ogled her in the van. "Has he hurt you?" He held his breath.

"No."

Her voice was firm. She wasn't lying to him. Thank God. He exhaled slowly. He heard her shifting closer and envisioned the flow of that dress over her body.

"He locked me in a tiny furnished cabin on the boat for the duration of the trip here."

"How long were you on the boat? Did you stop anywhere?" How many days had he been unconscious? "Did you recognize anything on the way here?" He paused, listening. She didn't respond. "Charlotte?"

"Oh, I'm here, just making a list. Did you want those answers in order?"

"Ha ha." He was glad to hear her spirits were still good. But he needed information to make a solid plan.

"We left the same night we were kidnapped. We were on the water all through the next day and night. Then we arrived here in the afternoon. There's a dock and this building we're in. I saw a generator, but not much else."

"Okay, good." Her voice grew stronger with every bit of information shared. He used his shirtsleeve to blot the sweat from his face, ignoring the smear of blood. One more stain on a shirt that wouldn't last much longer. "It's hot in here. Has he fed you anything?"

"They've given me bottles of water and meal bars. It's better than starving."

She wasn't wrong. "Unless you have a fake-food allergy," he quipped.

"You know that's not a thing."

"Maybe not." He did know she'd rolled her eyes and that made him smile. The smile tugged his busted lip and made him wince. It was worth it.

"Have you seen any cameras in here?" he asked.

"Not in here. There might have been a camera near the dock."

That made sense. "What else can you tell me?"

"There's a narrow beach near the dock and we walked through a wide path. Sea grasses and palms, and thicker trees farther inland. You and I are the only two people in this room."

"Good job." He'd had less intel on combat operations and the team had still succeeded. He had to assume Eaton knew his service record, so why allow her to tell him any of this?

It could be a test, but more likely it was one of the mind games Eaton liked. On his quest to destroy the general, he demonstrated a pitiless determination in setting up ordeals designed to create as much pain as possible for General Riley's children. And their father had been kept apprised of every grim moment via text messages, photos and live videos.

"Charlotte, you're amazing." She'd wanted to help and she had. "They'll find us soon. Whatever he does or says, remember good people are out there looking for us."

"I'm uncomfortable but I think you're in more danger," she said. "He talked to me that night on the boat, Mark. He's organized and deliberate. He has something very specific in mind."

"We'll get our chance," Mark promised. He was more concerned with the improvising Eaton had in the works now that Charlotte was here. Mark couldn't deny she was a weakness Eaton could use against him. He didn't care. He'd do anything to spare her pain or humiliation.

"Charlotte—" He snapped his mouth closed, feeling the footfalls through the metal floor a moment before they were audible. The door opened and Muscle appeared again.

He sneered at Mark and walked right past him to Charlotte's cage. Mark wanted to coach her, to encourage her and reassure her he'd find a way to get her out. Muscle's body blocked most of his view of her as she crossed in front of his cage, but he could see she'd been forced to change out of her dress and into hospital-like scrubs in a drab olive green color. Her high heels were gone and in their place she wore slip-on prison-issue shoes that were a little too big for her feet. Mark clutched the front of his cage. Willing her to hear all the things he didn't dare say.

Muscle hurried her along. Her hands were cuffed in front of her and she craned her neck to look at him as she walked by.

Her eyes went wide and she dug in her heels. "You *are* hurt."

"I'm *not*," he insisted. No matter how bad he looked, he was strong enough, smart enough to get them out of this.

He had to be.

Charlotte's heart hammered and pulses of terror zipped through her system. She paced the length of her cage, tripping over the floppy shoes. Taking them off, she shoved them into the back corner. What were they doing to Mark?

She'd known he was worried for her, but the big guard had escorted her to the other room and parked her in a chair in front of the desk, not before she noticed the drops of blood on the floor near where they must have secured Mark. Eaton had asked her several vague background questions about her association with the Riley family. She couldn't figure out what he expected to accomplish with her. He'd seemed to be killing time, and she hadn't had the courage to ask him why. Eventually he'd sent her back here.

Her cage door had barely locked before they were dragging Mark away. In the hours since, she'd heard only angry shouts and the occasional pain-filled cry. From the vent cut into the top of the wall, their only source of fresh air in here, she watched the light fade as night fell.

Feeling helpless, she piled her hair on the top of her head and scraped her knuckles on the wire fencing that created a ceiling. It dawned on her then that Mark wouldn't be able to stand up straight unless his cage was taller. Eaton wouldn't bother to do anything to make a Riley more comfortable. She pressed her cheek to the cage door, but she couldn't get the right angle to see anything helpful about the height of his cell on the other side of the plywood barrier.

For reasons she couldn't articulate, learning the answer became imperative. At the plywood side of the cell, she gave the fence wall a hard shake and then climbed it, shoving her fingers through in an effort to reach over the barrier.

No luck. Hopping back to the floor, she stifled a curse. She would just ask Mark when Eaton brought him back. Because Mark *would* come back. She had to believe it. She rubbed her arms against the chill of doubt that chased that thought. Negative thinking wouldn't help either of them.

Frustrated and desperate, she rattled her cage door again. Outside, a light winked on and gave her enough brightness to search again for any structural weakness in the cage. The wire fencing wasn't exactly top-of-the-line security, but she couldn't make any useful progress where it was strapped to the floor and walls of the container.

At the sound of the door unlocking, she hurried to the front of her cage, hoping for a glimpse of Mark. The door opened and the bare bulb overhead flashed on. She squinted at the flare of light. Despite pressing her cheek close to the cold fencing, all she saw was the smaller of the two men who had alternated guard duty. "Hey!" she called out. "What's going on?"

He didn't acknowledge her. She listened to the footsteps. Someone was dragging something. *Please, please, please don't let that be Mark.* With a grunt and a curse, the big guard shoved the heavy object or person into Mark's cell. Her heart sank.

"Is that Mark?" she asked, demanded. "Mark, talk to me."

The only response was a pained groan.

"What did you do to him?" She shook the door of her cage, slammed her body against it.

The big bald guard suddenly stepped in front of her. "Back up, missy."

She didn't have to be told twice. The smell alone had her wishing for a fan. A stench of blood and something hot, like melting wires, hovered around him like a thick fog. "What did you do to him?"

The guard's hard eyes glittered and he traced the hasp of the lock on the door. He had the key and they both knew it. "Be glad the boss put you off-limits."

"L-leave 'er…'lone."

Mark's words were slurred, but he was alive. The guard's attention shifted and she watched, horrified, as he hauled Mark out of the cell and pinned him to the wall in front of her.

"You don't give the orders," the guard said.

"You either," Mark retorted.

Charlotte's breath caught in her chest. He looked dreadful. One side of his face was swollen from jaw to brow bone and blood trailed over the terrain into his beard. They'd replaced his suit with a pair of thin pants like the scrubs she wore. His feet and chest were bare.

"Mark," she whispered, afraid for him. His appearance didn't put her off; it made her want to help, to comfort, to soothe. "Oh, Mark."

His gaze flitted to her and his lips curved into what was probably intended to be a grin. "Hi, Lottie."

She shook her head. With the damage to his face, he was a caricature of himself. What was she supposed to do now? Priority one was *not* to blurt out she loved him. That was a declaration and a moment best not shared here.

Better to focus on solutions to the immediate trouble. It looked as if the only thing keeping Mark upright was the guard's meaty hand. She was livid with Eaton. At the first opportunity, she'd attack the jerk, to hell with the consequences.

Furious and afraid for Mark, she shook the cage door. "You've made a huge mistake. Open this door and I'll kill you myself." Senseless, likely impossible, but she wanted the chance.

"She'll do it too," Mark said. "Fierce."

The guard muttered something unintelligible and shoved Mark back in his cell. He locked them into the room and the light overhead went dark again. Charlotte pressed her forehead against the side of the cage that bordered his.

"Do you have any water or food?"

"Both," he grunted, sounding surprised.

"Good." She'd been trying to figure out how to help him. "Don't talk, just take care of yourself."

"Mmm-hmm."

She heard the wrapper tear as he opened a meal bar, then a short bark of laughter. "What's so funny?"

"Hard granola bar. Sore teeth."

His words were still a bit slurred, but she understood. "That's mean."

"Uh-huh."

A moment later, she heard the crinkle of plastic as Mark drank the bottled water. "You should drink more," she said when he was quiet.

"All gone."

She felt so bad for him. Worse when she realized he would've been dealing with this by himself. She had four more bottles in the corner of her cage, along with three soft oatmeal breakfast bars. "I hate John Eaton."

A snort came from Mark's cell.

Now that she was looking for them, she'd noticed the cameras in the office where Mark had been beaten. Clearly they were doing a number on him to make the general miserable. Mark had told her that was Eaton's strategy, but seeing it play out was dreadful. "We have to do something."

"In time," Mark said.

"Tell me how to help." There had to be something more she could do here.

"Can't."

Not what she wanted to hear. Beating up Mark seemed to be Eaton's only goal, anything to make General Riley suffer while he watched. A man like that would want verification that his tactics were effective. "How does Eaton know your dad's watching?"

"Dunno," Mark replied. He sounded half-asleep.

Maybe he was conserving his energy to heal while he could. His training would've prepared him for this kind of situation. Charlotte knew he wouldn't cave to the torture anytime soon. Her heart broke for Mark, his father and the whole family. The next time Eaton hauled her in for a face-to-face, he wouldn't find her so cooperative.

"This is intolerable." She slumped to the floor and leaned against the barrier between them, wishing her presence offered him the same reassurance that being near him gave her.

"Life sucks sometimes." Mark's voice was a bit clearer now. "We'll get through it."

Would they? She tugged at the fencing, stretching her fingers through to touch the plywood. The fence panel was looser at the middle and the barrier between their cages didn't reach the ceiling. Maybe she couldn't fight back directly, but she could help him recover.

"I have an idea." She grabbed a bottle of water and one of the soft meal bars. She tried to lift the plywood and slide the water through, but she couldn't get the barrier quite high enough.

"Not up. Forward," Mark said.

She heard him move toward the back wall and hurried to follow. Together, using their fingertips through the chain links, they pushed the plywood far enough out of the way for her to pass him an oatmeal bar and another bottle of water.

Her fingers brushed against his and, despite the crisis and his injuries, that familiar combination of awareness and longing zinged up her arm and straight into her heart. She couldn't suppress the gasp.

"Don't worry about me, Lottie," he said, misunderstanding her reaction. He opened the meal bar. The homey scent of oatmeal was a strange counterpoint in their makeshift prison.

"Of course not," she said, trying to follow his habit of keeping things light. "You're obviously doing fine."

"I am," he whispered, his voice low. "This helps."

Through the narrow gap, she watched him wolf down the food and guzzle another bottle of water. She took both the wrapper and the empty bottle into her cell to hide that they'd shared resources. "Do you want more to eat?"

"Better not," he replied.

"What can I do?" she asked again. "There has to be something."

He reached through the gap and touched her fingers, the closest they could come to holding hands with his still handcuffed. "This." He sighed. "This helps. Knowing I'm not alone."

She wished she could see his face, but it was too dark again. She almost lifted his hand to her lips, as she had so many times in her imagination. Her mind would always go there with him, whether they were in a dark cell or surrounded by his family at one event or another. "You're not alone," she whispered.

"That's the best part of a SEAL team," Mark said after a few minutes. "Someone has your back."

Oh, how she wished she could have his back here. "I'll help you any way I can," she said.

"You've made that clear." He turned his head and even in the low light, she caught a bit of that familiar grin. "At this point, I think it's best if we let things play out."

"How much can you take?"

"The SEAL training drummed all the quit out of me years ago."

Not exactly quantifiable. "I'm serious." She wanted a timeline, something to track or prepare for.

"So am I." He turned his whole body toward her. "I know you're scared. I'm sorry."

For you. For herself too, but seeing him bloodied and exhausted, she was terrified Eaton would kill him. She kept the revelation locked up tight behind her closed lips. How could she convince Eaton to let them go?

"They're looking for us," Mark said. "We just have to stay tough. This is a performance," he said. "An attempt to prove he can best a navy SEAL, that's all."

"Well, it's not even B movie material."

He sputtered a small laugh. "Let him have his fifteen minutes of fame." He raised his hands and bumped into the fencing, as if he'd meant to touch her cheek and forgotten the barrier and restraints. "I can take whatever he dishes out."

"How?" she blurted the question aloud.

"Training," he said. "Belief."

"Hope," she summarized.

"In a word." He squeezed her fingers. "Mind over

matter. When I get an opening, I'll jump on it no matter how bad I look right now."

"*We'll* jump on it," she said.

She heard the brief hesitation before he agreed. No matter the compliments about her being fierce, he must see her, an artist without any survival skills to speak of, like a millstone around his neck.

If she proved herself valuable here, in this pressure cooker, would he look at her differently once they were rescued? See her as an equal rather than someone he needed to shield, even from his own life choices? It was a ridiculous twist of logic to think if he could believe them out of this ordeal, she might employ the same tactic and believe him into an integral part of her personal life when they were free.

And still her hopelessly romantic heart insisted that anything was possible.

Chapter 6

Mark's head weighed a ton as he came around. Resting his cheek on his raised arm, he instantly regretted this latest return to consciousness. It wasn't a nightmare; he was still in Eaton's office, his body serving as a heavy bag for Muscle and the guard Mark had labeled Quick-Punch Kid. The two had strung him up by his wrists to a loop mounted to the ceiling and had worked him over until he'd passed out.

For hours on end.

For the first time in his life, Mark wished for painkillers. A lowering admission, but there it was. Thankfully Eaton's cameras couldn't expose his weak thoughts.

Two things kept him going: Charlotte needed him to keep breathing; he was going to have fun retaliating when the opportunity came; and his dad was surely watching.

Whoops. That was three things.

The more motivation, the better. Eaton didn't want him dead, which he found interesting. He wanted him weak. Mark supposed it was okay to lose these skirmishes as long as he eventually won the war. And he would. Strange thoughts flitted through his head as he hung there waiting for the next round. *Eaton must be afraid of the reputation and strength of navy SEALs.* Mark smiled, making a mental note to keep that fear fresh in Eaton's mind.

All the way up to the moment when he killed the man.

"Is that a grin of the damned?" Eaton asked.

Mark hadn't heard the door open. Oh, right. One of his ears was full of blood from a punch or a cut. He shook his head, trying to clear it. "No," Mark managed. He focused on the smell of the ocean somewhere outside this pocket of hell.

Eaton carried a white paper bag to his desk and sat down. He opened a rugged laptop computer and then the bag. The savory aroma of a Philly cheesesteak sandwich filled the room. That scent would linger in the humid air. Mark's stomach growled. Eaton's bark of laughter was low and mean.

"Tell me about Miss Hanover," he said.

"No." It had been the first question every time for the last two days. Eaton wanted to know what Charlotte meant to Mark and the Rileys. He asked about her family, her career, her artwork and where she'd studied.

Mark had been grateful he didn't have too many details about Charlotte's recent choices to blot from his mind when Muscle and Quick-Punch Kid pummeled him during the interrogations. On the flip side, a piece of Mark that resided dangerously close to his heart had other questions about Charlotte.

Would she have let him kiss her behind the gallery? Was every kindness she'd shown him since the kidnapping rooted in concern as a family friend? Would she ever forgive him for this fiasco? Would they ever enjoy champagne on a sunset sail?

Mark struggled to catch his breath, a significant challenge when hanging like a side of beef on a hook. Eaton asked another question about Charlotte.

"I will kill you," Mark replied, the words lacking in volume, but full of conviction.

Eaton approached, carrying a chunk of his sandwich. The savory aroma taunted Mark. It took all his willpower not to beg for a bite. "Tell me about Charlotte and I'll give you my sandwich."

Mark didn't want to think about the condition of the sandwich he'd receive if he played along. "Not hungry."

"You would be if she stopped feeding you from her stash."

Mark wasn't surprised Eaton had cameras in the cage room. The man enjoyed his live surveillance feeds the way most people enjoyed chocolate. Mark was more curious about why Eaton allowed Charlotte to help him. The man had a reason for everything he did.

"I don't condone torture," Eaton said, gesturing with the sandwich, sending that aroma floating around Mark's face. "Always my preference to strike first and let the vultures clean up the mess."

The beef and peppers and mushrooms made his mouth water. Proper nourishment would go a long way about now. Where had he even come up with fresh hot takeout? From what Charlotte had said, based on the little she'd seen and heard, Mark was sure they were on an undeveloped island. Maybe he kept a chef chained to the stove on that boat.

"Tell me about Charlotte," Eaton ordered.

"No."

Eaton threw the sandwich to the floor and stomped on it.

"I knew it," Mark mumbled.

"Knew what?"

"Knew you were crazy," he said. "That smelled like a great sandwich."

"You…" Eaton threw several punches into Mark's gut, but after Muscle and Quick-Punch Kid, the strikes felt more like a deep tissue massage than a beating. Mark's laughter enraged Eaton.

"Not personal," Mark said, gasping. "Pain response."

Eaton lit into him again.

A phone rang and, with an annoyed curse, Eaton stalked back to his desk.

An island with cell service? Charlotte described it as little more than a forested sandbar, yet with the generator and phone, Mark wondered if it was a time-share for criminals. He wheezed out a laugh. His pain-addled brain came up with an infomercial script and sales pitch. His body creaked with the ensuing giggles and the chain holding him jerked and clanged.

"Shut up!" Eaton hissed.

For a man in charge, Eaton behaved as if he was re-porting to a boss. Weird. Mark watched the body language and regretted it when a reptilian smile creased the other man's face.

"We'll have two ready for you," Eaton was saying. "One in prime condition and the other less so." He paused, eyeing Mark. "Yes, wounded animals do make for delightful unpredictability."

Eaton swiveled in his chair, listening again. "The island is low on creature comforts, but we have the basics in place." He smiled. "Yes, more motivation to complete the hunt quickly, I agree."

Mark's blood chilled as the situation crystalized. Eaton was inviting a hunter to the island and he and Charlotte were the trophies. Had this been his plan for Mark all along?

Eaton finished the call and polished off the rest of his sandwich, treating Mark like a sculpture in the corner.

"Charlotte is talented and young," Mark blurted. "She's not a survivalist. Let her go."

"I most certainly will, in due time."

"Don't do this, Eaton. Take her out of the equation. Please," he added, though it cost him. "You can't let some jackass with too much money and no soul snuff her out."

"How much is her freedom worth?"

"Anything," he said. "I'll give your hunter a good chase. She won't. It'll be shooting fish in a barrel."

"Maybe that's what my client wants."

"No hunter worth his ammo wants that. It's the thrill of the chase."

"Not for everyone," Eaton countered. "For some, a live capture is the thing."

Mark strained against the chain holding him. Did he

mean the hunter wanted to take Charlotte alive? "What do you want? Let Charlotte go and you'll get anything," Mark pleaded. He had to spare Charlotte. He knew he was being manipulated by a master and didn't care. He didn't know if the room was wired for sound, or if his father could only see his struggle, but that wasn't important now.

During his military service, it was rare for Mark to meet the people their operations saved. As a kid, it had been difficult for him to understand why his dad left home to help strangers. Sure, he'd connected with others through various service projects and as an adult he'd worked in tandem with military personnel from other countries. When he and his team made rescues, they chatted briefly with survivors.

None of that was the same as *knowing* Charlotte would be the victim if Eaton had his way. She was too close, too precious. His stomach twisted at the thought of any harm coming to her.

"*Anything* sounds good, but I want more than you can give." Eaton advanced on Mark once more. "I want your father on his knees, begging me to spare your life. I want to stand over the precious, decorated, idolized General Benjamin Riley and see that he's broken. The way I was broken when he ended my career, destroyed my family."

Eaton had lost his career and family because he'd gone off the rails and slaughtered innocents. He'd brought every rotten consequence down on himself. "Never happen. He won't give you the satisfaction."

Eaton knocked Mark off balance and for a moment all his bodyweight was suspended from his wrists. The cuffs bit into his skin and his shoulders burned. "Look at you," Eaton taunted. "You're in no condition to stop me." He rested his palm on his gun and his trigger finger drummed against the holster.

Mark clung to the last shred of dignity, refusing to be cowed. He'd beg for Charlotte's life, no problem, but he wouldn't show any fear for himself.

Eaton took a step back, reaching for the radio on his opposite hip. "Take him back to his cell."

Quick-Punch Kid walked in alone and Mark had a flash of hope. Even cuffed and exhausted, he had enough to take this guy. Muscle was looming just outside the door and Mark had to bide his time. Again. At least he'd learned that Eaton didn't intend to toy with them indefinitely, in or out of the cages.

He glanced down, eyeing the contrast between Quick-Punch Kid's forearm and his own. They'd only been here a few days, but the man's skin showed a deeper tan every day. "Good genes, man," he said.

"Huh?"

Mark repeated himself, with excruciating slowness. "You're tanned," he added. "Weather's been clear?"

"Gorgeous," Quick-Punch Kid replied. "Last night I slept out under the stars in the hammock. The breeze off—ow!" Muscle cut him off with a hard pop to the back of his head.

"He's fishing for intel, you idiot."

"That's harsh," Quick-Punch Kid complained while Muscle unlocked the cage room.

Seeing a chance to get in a few licks, Mark head-butted Quick-Punch Kid, hearing the man's nose crunch as Muscle pulled the key from the lock.

The door swung open and Quick-Punch Kid, reeling from the pain, stumbled through first, tripping over his feet and landing hard on his backside. Mark drove a shoulder into Muscle's midsection, sandwiching him in the door frame. The man doubled over, gasping like a fish out of water and Mark went for the keys.

Charlotte shouted a warning a beat too late. Mark dodged the kick to the head, but Quick-Punch Kid advanced with a series of punches and another kick, this one aimed at Mark's knee.

Mark tucked and spun, and took the blow in the back of his leg. It didn't feel great, but it beat the alternative of not being able to walk. Just as he twisted back to make another dive for the keys, Muscle caught him by the throat and squeezed until Mark's vision hazed.

He heard Charlotte and Eaton yelling. Mark coughed and sputtered as the big man dumped him back into the cage. Another win for Eaton. Mark didn't mind letting them think they had the upper hand. He couldn't show it, but he was just as satisfied with that exchange as they were.

"Are you okay?" Charlotte asked when they were alone.

"Okay enough," he replied. "Looked worse than it was." Except now that he was in this cramped cell, he could feel the price he'd paid in every tight muscle and aggravated nerve ending.

She scooted the plywood back. "Here."

He looked over and smiled at the sight of her fingers reaching through the fencing. "I'll be fine." In an hour or two. Maybe a week.

"Maybe I'm not," she admitted.

He caught her fingertips and held on. "I just made my move too soon. Do you have an oatmeal bar?"

"Of course." She released his hand.

For a moment, he felt entirely alone, though he knew it was a silly reaction. Remembering that Eaton knew about her sharing her stash, he took a closer look at the ceiling and still couldn't spot the camera. Not much point in worrying about it now. He dragged himself back to lean on the wall where he could see her better.

He rolled his shoulders. Slamming into the wall of muscle that was the big guard after a daylong beating might not have been the brightest move.

"Here." The oatmeal bar came through the space they'd made, followed by a bottle of water. He downed the bar in greedy bites, his mouth too full to talk.

He was torn between telling her about Eaton's likely plan and just letting things play out. Knowing would only scare her more. If he had a chance, they'd get out of here before it became an issue.

If. Was he actually relying on something as flimsy as *if* now? "Since we've been here, have you seen anyone other than those two guards with Eaton?" he asked.

"No."

"And none of them have threatened you?"

"No." She urged him to drink the water. "He talks and postures. But I don't think he knows what to do with me."

He wasn't about to correct that assumption. "What do you know about survival in the wilderness?" he asked.

"Obviously I'm not a SEAL," she said. "But I'm not useless. If we escape—"

"When," he corrected.

"Yes," she said enthusiastically. "*When* we escape, I'll be an asset."

"Of course, you're an asset." There would be challenges, and more of them, if he didn't give her a few tips. "Are you up for a crash course?"

"Absolutely," she said, scooting as close as she could get. She listened attentively, urging more water on him as he relayed the basics of surviving in an environment she didn't know.

"You're talking like you won't be with me," she said quietly, as he drained another bottle of water.

"I'll be with you," he promised. "I feel better knowing you're as prepared as possible in case Eaton does something to separate us." Something like kill him outright, maim him or sell her off.

Once the trials of the day caught up to him, the aching started in earnest. Every time he dozed off, he slid closer to the nightmare of the plans Eaton had for Charlotte.

"Mark? Can you hear me?"

He jerked, his hand seeking hers and coming up against the plywood. She must have moved the barrier back into position at some point.

The room was completely dark now. He focused on the soft sound of her breath, matched his to hers. He couldn't help her plan paintings, but maybe there was another way to carry her away from this place, temporarily. "When we get out of here, I'm taking you to the nearest five-star hotel."

She moaned. "Clean linens," she said. "I can almost smell them."

"Soft mattresses. Room service," he said, continuing the list.

"Roomy hot showers," she said. "And a massage."

"Fluffy towels and robes. A swanky bar and good whiskey." He started laughing and ignored the pain that followed. "Did we say room service?"

"You did, but it deserves to be on our list twice." She giggled.

The sound rolled over him, warm as sunlight, simultaneously soothing and arousing. The game had helped him. Had it helped her?

"Do you remember that time we had to abandon our campsite after the hail storm?" she queried.

The sound of her shifting around filled him with a sudden urge to pull her into his lap. He wanted to discover how her curves felt under his hands. "That was the summer we were in Colorado," he recalled.

"Right. You tried to convince Grace Ann to imitate Aunt Patricia and order room service for us."

"Dinner had been washed out," he said defensively. "We were all hungry."

"Your dad tried to make the MREs sound like an adventure in fine dining," she reminded him.

"For the record, navy food is better."

She giggled again. Maybe hysteria was setting in, but he couldn't get enough of the sound. Or maybe laughter really was the best medicine. He certainly felt better when she did the laughing.

"I've loved your family forever," she said, her voice wistful. "You were all so bold and loud and a good influence on a shy kid like me. You remember how aggravated Adam would get when he couldn't pull me away from my sketchbook. Being with all of you was good for both of us."

"Don't forget ornery." They'd all taken turns involving her. "Why wasn't Adam at the gallery?" Her brother wouldn't have missed that kind of event without a good reason. Mark was sure Adam would be at the head of the long line of people ready to kill Mark if he didn't get Charlotte out of here safely.

"He's overseas, working with Doctors Without Borders. He called the day before and I gave him a private tour over the phone."

"That's good." He wished he could see her expressive face. "You were such a quiet kid. I admit it mystified me."

"You're kidding."

"Not a bit. At my house, the volume was cranked to ten from morning to night." It seemed she'd appreciated being around his rambunctious family as much as he'd appreciated being in her quieter orbit. "Did Adam ever tell you what happened the day you came home from the hospital?"

"The day I broke my arm?" she asked. "Were we still neighbors then?"

"No." He should stop talking before this turned too sappy. "I meant when you were born. Mom dragged us along to play with your brother. I wasn't impressed with baby you."

"Gee, thanks."

"You looked like a doll until you cried," he continued. "Then you were so loud the moms were distracted and we snuck outside to climb a tree. Luke got stuck and Adam and I got grounded for daring him to go too high."

"Hellions."

"Every chance we got," Mark agreed easily. "But not you."

"A natural-born observer," she said. "That's what my mom called it."

That wasn't how he remembered her as a kid. "Oh, you dive in. You just need the right motivation."

"Maybe," she allowed.

The wistfulness was back. He nudged the plywood so he could hold her fingers. "Your mind is wandering again."

"There are things I've left unsaid. When I'm in here alone I... I wonder if I'll ever get the chance. I know it sounds depressing or weak, but—"

"Lottie." Her words tore him up.

"I know. Ignore me." She cut him off before he could reassure her. "I get moody when I'm away from the creative process too long. Drawing in the dust isn't the same thing."

"Anyone in this situation would feel those things. It's normal. We'll get out of here. Trust me."

"I do." She coughed a little. "I've always trusted you...and your family."

And he'd sucked her into his family's trouble. Guilt was an unwelcome guest in the cage. "What was your favorite of the vacation trips we took as kids?"

"Monument summer in DC."

Her immediate answer startled him. "Why?" He'd been sure she would've mentioned a quieter place. "The museums," he said, answering his own question. "You would've spent days in the Smithsonian American Art Museum."

"Weeks, really," she admitted.

That was the summer after his high school graduation. He'd been eighteen and so sure of himself. That would've made her thirteen. Funny, when he thought of that day he didn't remember her that young.

Adam had been so exasperated with her for wandering off or falling behind that Mark volunteered to track her down. Like her brother, he'd been eager to move on to a museum with more action. In his opinion, the exhibits ranged from nice to interesting, but it was *art*. It didn't do or change anything, no matter how much their parents lectured them about culture and enrichment.

Then he'd turned the corner and found her on a bench in the center of a room, gazing intently at a painting of New York City at night. Light poured through a skylight overhead, turning her hair to spun rose gold. In that gallery, she'd looked nothing like the young cousin reluctant to join their more boisterous adventures. He didn't know how long he watched her, so still and intent, before he finally sat down beside her.

If he closed his eyes, he could see them there now, sitting together in a safe and tranquil quiet, far from this cage and the danger to come.

"You asked me why that painting," she said.

He nodded, the memory granting him exquisite comfort. "You said it was the light and shadow."

He heard her breath catch, a small sound that seemed much bigger in this terrible, uncomfortable room. "How do you remember that?"

He shrugged, belatedly recalling it was too dark for her to see his reaction. "Guess it stuck with me." *She'd* stuck with him.

"Me too." She sighed. "Mom lectured me about getting lost."

"You knew exactly where you were," he pointed out.

"Yes, I did."

Her breathing, the softness of her fingers in his, the pleasant recollections lulled him, easing the aches and pains. "I'll take you back," he promised. "Stay for days or weeks. I'll stand guard so no one bothers you."

He was floating at the edge of consciousness, savoring that sweet memory of Charlotte spotlighted by the sunbeam, dozing at last as the peacefulness carried him away from his throbbing bruises.

That's where she belonged, in the light. Then and now.

He'd get her back there just as soon as he caught his second wind.

Ben slouched in the desk chair in the hotel suite, staring at his phone. He gave Eaton credit for knowing how to wreak havoc in a man's soul. It was nothing short of agony watching Eaton's thugs beat and torture his son day in and day out, yet Ben felt an obligation to watch. To know.

Mark, the perpetual charmer, never talked about negative experiences. Somewhere along the line, Mark had decided that rehashing trouble didn't help unless it revealed a solution. Once they were rescued, Mark wouldn't bring it up again. Unless it was to testify against Eaton.

Ben didn't want to be surprised in a court of law. Bad enough that Eaton was only feeding them the pieces he wanted Ben to see. This time around, they weren't getting so many live feeds. As much as he wanted to believe the videos were edited for maximum effect, he knew better.

Time and again, he watched the replays, desperate to help, praying for Mark to stay strong. Hank and his investigators picked apart the same videos, searching for the smallest clue about where Eaton was holding Mark and Charlotte.

Eaton had shared footage of both kids through the past few days. When Charlotte was on screen, she was always seated in front of a desk and engaged in what appeared to be a conversation with Eaton. Oh, how Ben and Hank wished for audio. Other than looking a bit weary, with shadows under her eyes, it seemed she was in fair health.

Hearing Patricia's soft footfalls behind him, he lowered the phone. Her hands landed on his shoulders, rubbing at the knots of tension there. "You have to stop, sweetheart."

"I can't," he confessed. His fingers itched to pick up the phone and hit Replay again. "He's hurting."

"We all are," she said. "He's strong. All of us need to be," she reminded him. She leaned close and kissed his cheek. "Isn't he the one who pestered us day and night about how perfect the SEAL training is?"

Ben chuckled. His wife had a way of knowing just what to say. At sixteen, when Mark had decided to pursue the SEAL program, he'd been a nuisance, touting all the ways the navy's elite teams out-performed the army elite forces. Those years had been an exercise in parental patience and Ben couldn't deny he'd been happy to be overseas for part of that time.

"Did you ever get your medal for grace under the assault of youthful arrogance?" he asked.

"They call it motherhood." She smoothed her hands up to massage his neck. "And it keeps an entire cosmetic industry in business."

"We have another meeting with Hank in the morning," he said. "He'll update the Hanovers at their house afterward."

"Probably smart. Sue Ellen is a wreck and rightly so. Ron is desperate for a target." She sighed. "Staying up all hours and wishing you were taking those blows doesn't change a thing." She brushed her lips to the top of his head. "You're not doing him or me any favors, Ben."

She was right, though he was reluctant to voice the admission.

"We should go home and wait." Leaving the area was the last thing he wanted to do, but every inch of the waterfront had been searched along the trail they'd pieced together from traffic cameras. A kidnapped SEAL had brought out the best in community cooperation from civilians on up through the police departments and military to local stevedores working the docks that night.

No one believed Mark and Charlotte were still in Virginia and the trail had gone cold.

"Ben." Patricia nudged the chair, swiveling it so he faced her. "If this were happening in a container yard nearby, we'd know. You need real rest if you're going to be any use once we do have a search area."

"How is it you're so calm?"

"It's an illusion, love. One you need to embrace right

now. Plus, I've had practice saving my breakdowns for after the crisis."

"It's a nursing thing?"

"And a military wife thing," she confessed in a whisper.

He pulled her into his lap and held her close. She kissed his brow and relaxed into his embrace. "The enemy isn't supposed to be over here," he said.

"I know."

Too many emotions to name were winding around his heart, gripping tight. "The enemy isn't supposed to be one of our own."

"I know that too." Her fingers combed through his hair.

"When they find Eaton, I'll kill him for this."

"I know you'll want to." She sat back, holding his gaze. "But Mark's team will probably beat you to it. They're so big and strong and perfect, you know."

His heart eased with her humor, even if the laughter itself got bottled up in his throat and caused his eyes to sting. "What would I do without you?"

"You'll never have to find out." She kissed him again and slipped out of his arms. "Come to bed now."

Dawn arrived a few hours later and Ben felt marginally better, though hardly well rested, plagued by the lingering images of his son suffering. He and Patricia both picked at their breakfast before giving up on food. Her lack of appetite was the only obvious sign of her distress.

When they reached the temporary office Hank had established on the nearby naval base, the young man they considered a son was waiting outside the door, his expression grave. Ben caught Patricia's hand in his and held on tight. They'd get through this together.

Hank looked as if he'd been up all night and just changed into a clean uniform. He probably had. "Come on in."

Patricia paused to hug Hank before they walked into the room. Ben saw a series of still shots, apparently from the video, taped to a whiteboard and moved to shield his wife. With a tiny shake of her head, she stepped around him and studied the images.

"Why isolate these?" she asked, turning to Hank.

"The lip readers," Hank replied. A day or two ago, he'd told them he was bringing in specialists to pick apart every video for clues to Eaton's plan and location. "We still don't have enough to create a search grid, but we're getting closer."

None of the videos Eaton sent showed even a sliver of a window in view of either camera in the area where Mark was being tortured. "Did the lip readers pick up anything?"

"Pictures have been too fuzzy to get an accurate read," Hank said. "But we're working on it."

"The sandwich indicates lunch or dinnertime?" Patricia put her back to the pictures and took a seat at the long table in the center of the room.

"Or just what was available at the time," Hank replied. "There's been no rhyme or reason to the food in any of the shots with Mark."

"It's a tactic," Ben said.

"Yes, sir. I believe it is." Hank urged Ben to sit as he did the same. "We've gone over everything from the first live broadcast, moving forward. Eaton seems most consistent and conventional when he brings in Charlotte."

It had been a blessing that Eaton hadn't done anything physical to her so far. Ben knew all of them were holding their breath every time another video came through, waiting for Eaton to cross that line. They'd done all they could to keep her parents informed without worrying them unnecessarily.

"Using the best timeline we have," Hank was saying, "I'm thinking he's holding them somewhere south of here."

Ben lurched to his feet. "So let's go."

"Not so fast, sir. That's still too much coastline, private and commercial, to search."

"Why not north?" Patricia asked.

"There have been storms north of us that most likely would have knocked out the live feeds that have come through. At the least we would have seen signal interference and poor video quality." Hank stacked his fists on the tabletop. "Other than that, it's a guess."

"How far south?" Ben queried. He wouldn't put it past Eaton to stage this somewhere close to their beachside home in North Carolina.

"I sent a team to search the immediate area around your beach house," Hank said. Clearly his thoughts were similar to Ben's. "It's clear."

Catching Hank's gaze, Ben asked, "Is there something we can add to your investigation or search effort?"

"Not yet," Hank said. "He has help on the technology side. I have experts countering that. None of the mercenaries who've worked with him can shed any light on this site."

"He keeps them compartmentalized."

"Yes." Hank pressed his thumb to the furrow between his eyebrows. "The money has been almost untraceable."

"Almost?" Patricia sat forward.

"We've learned he didn't go straight into mercenary work. We have people dedicated exclusively to unraveling the money trail from the legitimate business he sold a few years ago to the present. I'm hoping that will give us more clues to his current location.

"One last thing," Hank continued. "Based on the bits of conversation we *think* we've interpreted correctly, Eaton is about to change up their routine. Hopefully that means we'll have some external clues that will allow us to search properly."

"And make a rescue," Patricia said.

"Yes," Hank confirmed.

The door burst open and they all turned. "The live feed is back and we have some audio," a young man in uniform announced. "Begging your pardon, sir," he added, his eyes wide when he recognized the retired general.

Ben waved off the interruption.

"Stay here," Hank said. "I'll forward what I can."

Less than a minute later, Ben's phone hummed as the live feed came through. Damn Eaton for being so persistent with this tactic.

"He knows it bothers you," Patricia said.

"It's hardly original. This would bother anyone," Ben grumbled. "You shouldn't watch."

"You shouldn't keep trying to protect me, Benjamin Riley. I'd rather deal with facts than speculation."

As the video began, Ben and Patricia both sucked in a breath at the sight of Charlotte chained to the rebar embedded in the pad of cement.

"Any last requests?" Eaton asked from off camera.

The audio quality was excellent. Patricia clutched Ben's free hand as they watched.

"Let us go," Charlotte said.

"You'll be free tomorrow."

Charlotte's eyebrows lifted in disbelief. "Free?"

"Yes."

"You're setting us free tomorrow?"

Patricia covered her mouth. They both knew it had to be a trap.

"That's the plan," Eaton confirmed. "No more cuffs or cages. You can walk right out the door."

"What's the catch?"

Eaton laughed and the vile sound struck hard against the corrugated metal walls and bounced back. "You are the clever one, aren't you?"

Charlotte only glared at him.

"I hear you miss your creative process." Her eyes went wide, but she kept quiet. "I have a proposition for you," Eaton was saying. "Before I let you go, I want a Charlotte Hanover original painting. It's an investment sure to increase in value."

Patricia gasped at the veiled threat that her art would be worth more when she died.

"You and Mark had such a nice conversation last night," Eaton continued. "Vacations, antics, family fun. It was very enlightening."

"Go to hell," Charlotte snapped. "That was private."

"Little girl, *nothing* is private in a prison. I'm surprised Mark didn't share that tip with you." Eaton circled behind her, motioned for something to move or adjust. "Your feelings and devotion to the Riley clan is nauseating. Still, it got me thinking."

A thin guard dressed in black from head to toe set up an easel within Charlotte's reach, adding a canvas and a small folding table of supplies. Through it all, Eaton droned on, talking about the vacation he'd taken with his family to Hawaii after a deployment.

"I want you to give me a painting of that time when I had a family," Eaton said. "Before General Riley destroyed us."

"It can take weeks or more to finish a painting," Charlotte said, clearly resistant to his demands.

"You have today if you want to walk free tomorrow." Eaton handed over what appeared to be an old photo. "Use this for reference. Better get busy. If you don't finish to my satisfaction, you both stay."

"I knew there was a catch."

"Oh, there is. If you stall, Mark will pay the price." Eaton walked out of the camera view and Charlotte took stock of the provided supplies.

Hank returned, putting the live feed up on a wall-mounted monitor. They all watched in silence as Charlotte began to work.

Occasionally they heard noises from Eaton, presumably at his desk, but it was too far from the microphone to be useful.

"That's not the right vegetation for Hawaii." Hank cocked his head. "She knows she's on camera and she has the picture for reference right there." He pointed to the corner of her canvas. "I think she's painting in trees that she's seen recently. *This* is helpful." Hank dashed out of the room, leaving Ben and Patricia to watch over Charlotte as she painted a landscape wildly different from the photo Eaton had provided.

Chapter 7

Charlotte prepared a palette and her canvas in silence, though her back already ached from sleeping on the cage floor and her range of motion was limited by the handcuffs. These shoes had zero support and the artificial lighting posed another challenge. Dark splotches and spatters decorated the area, bloodstains from abusing Mark in this very spot.

This didn't have to be her best work, but it had to be good enough to convince Eaton she'd tried.

"You refused to let me go so I would paint for you?" she asked, glancing at him from around the canvas.

He frowned. "You were in the wrong place at the wrong time. I decided to capitalize on the opportunity." He flicked his fingers, indicating she should get busy. "Be grateful I liked your work when I looked you up online."

She didn't have much confidence she could pull this off. He'd done nothing but ask her questions about the Rileys and though she'd kept her answers vague, she had the sense she wasn't telling him anything he didn't already know.

Being confined—literally—to this space and this canvas was bad enough. Creating a painting for the jerk holding them captive, threatening to hurt Mark if she didn't paint well, compounded the issue a thousand times over. Could she paint fast enough to please Eaton and slow enough to keep Mark safely in his cage for the entire day? He needed time to recuperate.

She wondered who monitored the cameras Eaton had installed, wondered if there was audio as well as visual. Did anyone edit the videos Eaton sent the general to torment him or was it all just a raw feed? She couldn't imagine the pain of watching a child endure the beatings Mark had taken. He played off the pain, but she could see his recovery took longer every night.

She hated being party to a system that brought pain to Ben and Patricia, though it would be worth it if she could use it to their advantage. "Where did you get the painting supplies?" she asked.

"I have means and men at my disposal," Eaton replied. "I assume the quality is sufficient to the task."

"Yes."

"Then shut up and paint."

Ignoring that, she studied the adorable face of his daughter, alight with joy as she held a bright pink flower in her hands. It was a lovely scene, Charlotte thought with some regret. As much as she despised whom she was painting for, she appreciated the time to paint at all. The tropical paradise in the photograph was lush and green with a soaring blue sky. The rich, verdant landscape surrounding the little girl bore little resemblance to the trees and path she'd seen on the walk here from the dock.

Still, there was some resemblance, in size and scope, with the tall trees that framed the photo. Enough to give the investigators Mark believed were searching for them a clue to their location. She used a blank space of the canvas and painted the leaves from trees she'd seen on the hike in from the dock. There had been stubby palms and swaying grasses and the ocean had been deep and clear under the dock.

Quickly she sketched out the path she'd walked, the plants and leaves she'd seen. Later she would add layers and depth to build the painting into what Eaton requested. She had no idea if the cameras caught any of her work or why Eaton would even give her this chance to put out a cry for help, but she did it anyway.

If he noticed and challenged her, she'd simply explain it away as a warm-up exercise. It hardly mattered. She didn't believe that he would set them free tomorrow, not by any reasonable definition anyway.

With no window, she had no idea how much time passed as she covered the quick beach scene here with the deeper blue-greens of the Hawaii landscape. She only knew her hands and neck had cramped and her feet were wishing for thick, warm sand rather than more of this unyielding floor.

"Could I walk a bit?" she asked, rolling her neck. "Just around the office would be helpful." Normally she'd take breaks for food, stretches or a long walk outside. She'd give her eyes and hands a break by reviewing inspiration boards or doing whatever she needed for the next burst.

From behind the desk, Eaton narrowed his gaze. "Is that part of your process?"

"Well, my process would be to go for a run or take a yoga break outside. Painting the outdoors isn't the same as breathing fresh air."

"No."

"Exactly. I didn't think you'd grant either of those requests."

"I won't take the cuffs off either."

"You do know the law of diminishing returns?"

"As well as I know you're running out of time," Eaton said, his gaze on his laptop.

She rocked back and forth on her feet, then twisted her shoulders side to side. Anything to get the blood moving. The girl in the picture had the sweetest expression and despite her aggravation with Eaton, Charlotte couldn't purposely botch that precious face. She wasn't particularly well known for her portraiture, but she didn't really have much of a choice.

His mention of the painting increasing in value hadn't escaped her notice. The prevailing joke among artists was that death was the best way to boost sales and gain fame. All she'd really wanted from fame was the means and reputation to eventually create a retreat that would give artists and other creatives a place to rejuvenate and recharge.

She peeked at Eaton again. What did he have planned? He wasn't going to let them walk out of here because he'd had a change of heart. He'd been too hard on Mark for her to believe that.

"Do you think you're in love with him?" Eaton asked, interrupting her speculation.

He'd asked her that question, or a variation of it, each time he'd had her brought in. The significance escaped her.

"I've loved Mark all my life." She gave the same honest answer as she had previously. If these were her last hours, she wouldn't hold back. "He's family." Though she kept her gaze locked on the canvas, she heard his chair scrape against the floor as he pushed back from his desk.

"He doesn't love you," Eaton said, his cold eyes stared at her from over the top edge of the canvas.

A bug under a microscope would have more confidence and definitely more space. Between his intimidation tactics and the cuffs changing the weight of her brush strokes, she was close to ruining the painting. There couldn't possibly be time to start over. She took half a step back.

"I've watched this family for years. Learned their patterns, strengths and weaknesses," Eaton bragged. "It's clear to me, and it should be clear to you, the Hanovers don't factor in their lives."

Then he hadn't done any deep research at all. The Hanovers and Rileys were inseparable in spirit even when they weren't in the same geographical area. Patricia and Sue Ellen had decided nothing would minimize their friendship and they'd built those values into the family dynamic.

One more reason Charlotte had never confessed to

her unrelenting crush on Mark. She wouldn't be the wedge that interrupted how well the families clicked or that made any of them feel awkward.

She lowered the brush so he didn't see her trembling. "Does that mean I'm free to go?" It was worth a try.

"No." He shifted a bit and she decided if she ever painted him, he'd be a snake, lurking and ready to poison any perceived happiness.

"The handcuffs are a hindrance," she said. "I'd like to honor your daughter by capturing the sparkle in her eyes. That's delicate work."

He came around to view the canvas from her angle. Watching him, she caught his first unguarded reaction to the painting. The meanness faded from his expression, softening as he took in the photo coming to life on the canvas.

A gratifying moment for any artist, to know the work makes an impact. Inwardly she sighed. If it was going to be her last painting, she should give it her best effort. Who knew taking pride in the work would be so frustrating?

He pulled a key from his pocket and released the cuffs. "Don't make me regret it."

"You won't." She shook out her hands and circled her wrists one direction and another, releasing the tension. "May I walk a bit?"

Eaton scowled. "Stay clear of the door and my desk."

Since he'd put the easel on the opposite end of the room, it wouldn't be a problem. She plucked the photograph from the clip at the edge of the canvas and paced the width of the office. Back and forth, letting her hands and mind rest. Using the wall for support, she stretched her back and legs too.

Eaton worked at his desk, ignoring her. Like the other times she'd been in here, she couldn't decide whether to be offended or relieved that he didn't see her as a threat.

Straightening, she came around to view the canvas from several paces away. Glancing between the photo and the canvas, she looked for a way to leave a clue that she'd painted this one under duress.

The only option that would possibly escape Eaton's notice was the foliage that wouldn't be found in Hawaii. She could leave in that live oak branch under the tropical canopy. And it really wouldn't matter unless Eaton sold the painting.

She studied the picture, creased and worn at the edges from being in his wallet.

Despite his blustering, he'd never sell this painting of his daughter.

She returned to the canvas and picked up her brush, determined to bring the girl's eyes to life before either the cuffs or reality paralyzed her. She'd stepped back again, almost satisfied when an outburst erupted from the other end of the building. The screech and scrape of metal dragging against metal hurt her ears.

Eaton was on his feet and out of the room in an instant. Was he having Mark tortured in the cage today?

Her eyes darted to Eaton's abandoned desk and then to the camera at the opposite corner from her easel. If Eaton was broadcasting the camera feed, someone was likely monitoring it.

Did she dare try to send out an SOS? After everything Mark had endured, she had to take the chance.

Another shout sounded from the direction of the cage room and she set aside her paint and brushes and scurried to the desk. She had no idea what she was looking for, only that she needed to find something helpful. He'd always kept the bulletin board behind his desk covered when she'd been in here. She pushed aside the rolling chalkboard and stepped back, aghast.

He had pictures of the Riley family organized almost like a police investigator, with facts and links and comments about each of the five siblings and Hank too.

Although it sure looked as if he'd hoped to kill Matt and Grace Ann, he'd clearly moved on when they survived, focused now on Mark. Beneath Mark's official navy headshot was a long list of potential attacks.

Disconcerting—fine, terrifying—but nothing she could use right now.

She reached for the bulletin board, intending to hold it up for a camera. It was secured to the metal wall. On an oath, she carefully untacked the plans for Mark and held them up to the camera, praying only Eaton monitored the broadcast. Since he was gone, she might stand a chance of this information getting through to the proper authorities.

Once the bulletin board was restored to its previous condition, she turned to the computer.

There had to be a way to send out a distress call of some sort.

Eaton, despite the bare bones set up, hadn't slacked on security for his laptop. She quickly discovered the device was password-protected and she had no idea what the code might be. She couldn't even see what he'd been working on before the noises drew him away.

Outside the door, voices were raised in anger. She could hear Quick-Punch Kid—the name Mark had given to one of the men—Eaton and Mark himself. If he was vocal, he couldn't be hurt too badly. It wasn't much comfort. She used the precious opening to search each of the drawers in Eaton's desk.

The voices swelled and she turned, caught in the harsh, cold gaze of Muscle. "What are you doing?" he asked.

His tone was too reasonable as he closed the door behind him. Locked it.

A fear bigger than anything she'd experienced so far gripped her joints as he advanced on her. She couldn't even stand up. So much for being an asset to Mark's escape plans. She was about to die.

A tear rolled down her cheek. She'd wrecked everything, doomed them both, since Mark was too honorable to leave her behind. Oh, she'd blown it.

"Stand up," Muscle ordered.

She managed it, barely.

"How did you get out of the cuffs?"

"Eaton took them off so I…" Survival instinct kicking in, she edged around the far end of the desk. "So I could paint without them." His eyes tracked her like a predator. She froze. The desk wasn't enough of a barrier and they both knew it.

"You're not painting."

"No." Her chin came up. Cowering only gave him more power. And pleasure. She could see the malicious intent in his gaze. "I needed more paint color. Your boss keeps the supplies there."

He shoved the desk aside and lunged for her and she

darted for the area where she'd been painting. Maybe he'd think twice about damaging the canvas Eaton had commissioned.

He was quicker than he looked and she found herself knocked face-first to the stained floor. She struggled to breathe and he easily flipped her to her back, pinning her under his massive body. The eager, sinister gleam in his eyes was enough to vaporize her moment of bravado. He flexed his pelvis and his evident erection made her stomach cramp.

This couldn't be happening. Could. Not. Recalling her self-defense classes, she aimed her forehead at his nose, missing when he moved out of reach. "You've got spirit." He chuckled. "I like that."

She resisted with every fiber of her being as he pushed her arms overhead. He clasped both her wrists in one unbreakable grip. The pose thrust her breasts higher. Wanting to squirm, she held as still as possible, unwilling to give him an ounce of satisfaction.

"You're hurting my hands."

"Don't care about your hands," Muscle said.

"You should." Eaton's voice carried a clear threat.

Relief coursed through her. Salvation shouldn't wear Eaton's face, but she'd take it. The moment Muscle released her, Charlotte scurried out of his reach, back to the easel.

The respite didn't last. "What did she do?"

Muscle pulled himself to his full height. "Found her snooping around your desk."

"I was looking for more paint. To capture your daughter's eye color," she spit out, glaring at Muscle.

"I told him that." She knew he could contradict her, but she relished planting doubt about him in Eaton's mind.

Eaton's dark eyes shifted to her. "I take it you were planning to punish her?"

Muscle stood tall, lips compressed, apparently smart enough not to answer that question.

"Go be useful and guard the dock," Eaton ordered.

Muscle's chin dipped once in the affirmative and he hustled out of the office, a little cowed in Charlotte's view.

As Eaton made way for the bigger man, Charlotte saw Quick-Punch Kid holding Mark, his handsome face a fixed blank mask.

"I'll kill you," Mark vowed, as Muscle walked by him.

"You're nothing but a little fish without your team." Muscle made a barking seal sound and then he was gone.

A chill slid down her back as Mark's gaze collided with hers.

Eaton walked over and slapped the cuffs on to her wrists. "Finish."

He turned on his heel, escorting Mark away with the other guard's help, and she feared she'd ruined everything.

Mark's fury wouldn't subside. Charlotte's face had been so pale, her blue eyes huge with fear, her hair a tangle from the scuffle. He prowled his cage, mentally tearing Muscle limb from limb. He could practically hear the man's dying breath.

Charlotte must hate him by now. He was the only

reason she'd been swept into this mess. His failure to outmaneuver the guards had given Muscle the opening to take advantage of her.

She'd been attacked, nearly raped, and he'd done nothing about it. All because Muscle was right—Mark couldn't get out of here without his team.

Patricia would get no argument from him now. He was as wrong for Charlotte as a man could be.

He couldn't get the scene out of his head. She'd been on the floor, utterly helpless beneath a man oozing violent intentions. He wouldn't ask forgiveness, but he'd feel marginally better once she told him she was okay, assuming she would even speak to him.

Mark dropped to the floor and started doing push-ups to burn off the sense of failure.

She would. Charlotte had a temper, but she didn't harbor grudges. Growing up, she'd always been willing to overlook his less-than-stellar moments. Hopefully that tendency would apply to this most recent error that ended with her pinned under a nasty excuse for a man.

She must have talked her way out of the handcuffs and used the opportunity to search Eaton's desk. She deserved a medal for that alone. Mark couldn't wait to learn if she'd found anything, unless Eaton kept them apart tonight.

He'd been so close to breaking out, taking advantage of just the smaller guard, when Eaton had stormed in to help Quick-Punch Kid subdue him.

Mark heard the bolt slide back on the door and popped to his feet. *Please let this be Charlotte.* He waited at the front of his cage, eager for a good look at her, a chance to see her accept his apology.

Unfortunately, Quick-Punch Kid walked into the cage room alone. That was a shock since the last time Mark had nearly overpowered him. "I can't decide if you've got an abundance of guts or a lack of brains," Mark observed.

Quick-Punch Kid didn't say a word. Eaton must have given him a lecture about being baited by the hostage.

"Tough getting a beatdown from the boss," Mark said with sympathy. "Does he issue demerits? What hoops do you have to jump through before he trusts you with a gun again?"

A bottle of water and a plate of real food, spaghetti with red sauce and a big meatball, were shoved at him. Mark did his best not to fall on the bounty like a starving dog. Quick-Punch Kid would like that too much. Then he noticed the lack of utensils.

Points to Eaton for always finding a way to disappoint.

"Carb loading? Is the annual Criminal Island marathon tomorrow?"

"Something like that," Quick-Punch Kid muttered. "Eat while you can, tough guy."

Mark took a small bite of the meatball, half-worried the food was drugged. "Did someone take food to Charlotte?"

Quick-Punch Kid refused to answer.

Feeling no immediate ill effects, Mark sloppily scooped up some noodles with his fingers. "Where's your pal?"

Quick-Punch Kid deliberately looked at the door.

Mark didn't much care about the mess he was making. Red sauce wouldn't be much different than the blood stains on his pants. His more immediate concern was whether or not he needed to save any of this for Charlotte.

"How'd you get roped into this gig?" he asked conversationally.

Quick-Punch Kid shook his head. "Just eat, man."

"You were more than happy to take shots at me yesterday and the days before, verbal and otherwise. What changed? You look like someone gave you an ice-cream cone and then knocked it out of your hand."

"Shut up, Riley, or I'm taking that food."

"Come in here and try it," Mark challenged.

On an exasperated sigh, Quick-Punch Kid walked out of the room. Mark slid the plate of food aside and though he would have drained the water, saved half of it as well, just in case.

The change in routine made him nervous. When Eaton was busy wearing him down, he couldn't pester Charlotte. Today though he'd taken her to the office, left Mark alone and ordered Quick-Punch Kid to remove the plywood divider from between their cages. They'd be able to see each other now, if Eaton would just let her come back.

Mark had been worried all day that Eaton would knock her around and dump her in the cell, forcing Mark to witness the damage he'd inflicted. A form of torture that would be a thousand times worse than taking a beating. He stood up to pace, remembering too late he was too tall for the cage. Aggravated, he sat down and looped his hands over his drawn-up knees.

There was a solution here, a way out—he just had to find it before it was too late.

He'd work on Quick-Punch Kid for a start—try to wear him down. He was a weak link, and maybe Mark could get him to see he was better off on the Riley side of the equation. If even the smallest doubt led to the man hesitating before striking a blow or pulling a trigger, it was worth the effort.

He'd given Charlotte some fast and dirty advice on surviving in the wild when what she'd really needed was a crash course in self-defense. Although very few moves, unpracticed, would've been effective against a man the size of Muscle.

He had to get them out of here. He rolled to his back and kicked the corrugated wall. They were probably on a barrier island based on what Charlotte had seen. He didn't hear voices or much activity once the men left this modified container. So they either returned to the boat or had a camp elsewhere. A camp made more sense. He hadn't once heard sounds of any boat or plane bringing in supplies and Charlotte had implied the walk from the dock was lengthy.

Which meant a big enough island that escape was worth the risk.

Cameras or not, he used his hands and feet, working to bend or unravel the links of the fencing, until—finally—he heard the lock open. Eaton nudged Charlotte into the room ahead of him. She looked weary and desperately unhappy and she kept her gaze on the floor as Eaton marched her along to her cage.

Obediently, she stepped inside when their captor opened the door. He set a plastic carryout bag on the floor just inside the door and then closed and locked the cage.

She turned his way and did a double take when she saw him rather than the plywood barrier. The new visibility didn't seem to please her.

"Charlotte?"

She shook her head and sat down, her back to him, as she poked at the food in the bag.

"You should eat," he said.

Her shoulders rose and fell. "Maybe later."

"I saved some of mine for you, just in case." He scooted closer, but she didn't turn around. "We can eat together."

He wanted to hold her and tell her it would be okay. She looked absolutely opposed to that sort of gesture, even if the fence hadn't been in the way. His heart raced as he considered the reasons for her silence. Had they hurt her?

She'd never been so cool and distant with him. For as long as he could remember, she'd greeted him with warm, occasionally shy smiles. The girl had always been different enough to make him curious and open enough to let him talk. He was at a loss for how to help now that she shut him out.

Asking if she was okay seemed like a woefully inadequate and superfluous start. Clearly she wasn't okay at all. In his mind, all he could see was her on the floor, upset and panicking with Muscle sprawled over her.

"Charlotte, I'm getting us out of here tonight," he promised.

She paused in the act of taking foil off a steaming plate of spaghetti. Just when he thought she'd turn and talk with him, she went back to her food.

Eaton had given *her* utensils. He withheld comment

and finished his food instead. As he drained the last of his water bottle, he took a good hard look at the fencing again.

Usually, when up against this kind of barrier, the team had bolt cutters. Once one link was clipped, it was easy to unravel. Nothing he could get his hands on in here was strong enough to unwind or cut through a link.

"What happened earlier?" She set aside her food and glanced at him over her shoulder. "Why was Eaton bringing you to the office?"

What lies had Eaton fed her? "I picked a fight with Quick-Punch Kid and almost got his gun."

"You did?"

She sounded impressed. "You don't have to sound so shocked," he teased. "I've been telling you I have skills."

"I've heard you," she said, sounding thoroughly defeated now.

Why wouldn't she look at him? "Charlotte, I was going crazy in here. He's never kept you that long. I heard the first scream and that was it. I almost got out. The idea of you suffering because—"

"I never screamed." She rubbed at her wrists. "Eaton didn't hurt me or touch me like that."

A red haze fell over his vision. "How did he touch you?"

"To remove the cuffs, that's all."

She faced him, inched closer. He wanted to hold hands as they'd done on nights prior, but she stayed out of his reach. "Who screamed? I never heard anything like that."

"I suppose that was my test today. He must have

piped in a soundtrack that I assumed was you being tortured. I'm not sure if it backfired on him or me."

He'd call it a win for getting under the guard's skin, but he hadn't made any progress on getting them out of here. "Charlotte, whatever happened, you can tell me about it."

"What you saw wasn't my best moment," she said, massaging the palms of her hands. "I'm not very good at snooping. Can we leave it at that?"

"Over here," he said, motioning for her to come back to the wall where her hand would fit through the gap in the fencing.

Her hand was so small in his and he was mindful of the pressure he applied to the tight spots along her fingers and particularly at the base of her thumb. She felt fragile. Precious. Muscle could have crushed her. "Did you sprain a wrist?" he asked, keeping his voice neutral.

"No. It's just the hours with a brush in hand and no real break."

"I know you were eager to sketch, but being forced to paint can't be the same thing."

"Yes and no. Creating is creating." She flinched.

He bent his head and brushed his lips to the tender spot. "Sorry."

"Don't be," she said on a sigh. "It feels great."

The compliment, delivered in her languid, almost mesmerized tone did things to his body that were a challenge to ignore. Instantly aroused, he barely managed to resist the urge to press a kiss to her palm and slide his tongue across her flesh to taste her. If—*when*—they got out of here, he could ask if she was interested in him that way. If she was willing to take on something that would have to be temporary. He hoped like hell she said yes, so he could discover other methods of drawing out that seductive sound.

He turned her hand over, running his thumbs between the tendons from the base of her fingers to her wrist. Her eyes closed and she practically purred. The long, even strokes meant to soothe her had him hard and aching, eager to learn what else she liked.

"Thanks." She pulled her hand out of his abruptly.

He reached for her other hand, but she scooted away. "I asked him to take off the cuffs so I could do some delicate work," she volunteered. "Then Muscle caught me snooping around the desk and..."

When her voice trailed off, it was like taking a kick to the chest. She'd been attacked, subjected to Muscle's brute force, and now she seemed reluctant to confide in him.

No one should have to go through that, but especially not Charlotte. She was everything light and good. She had a tremendous future as an artist and deserved to live out her dreams without this kind of trauma.

He returned to the corner where he'd been working on the chain and started wrestling it again.

"Mark, stop."

"We have to get out of here tonight." Now. Before anyone could hurt her again. He pried at the fencing, drawing strength from his anger. If he could get out, he'd find a way to pick the lock on her cage and go from there.

"Mark, listen to me."

He paused long enough to meet her gaze.

"We're being released in the morning."

"What?"

Her chin bobbed up and down. "I doubt it will be as simple as Eaton implied."

"What did he say?"

"Paint that canvas for him and we get out of here tomorrow." She hesitated, looking around and peering up at the corners. "I don't believe it will be a good thing."

"That's common sense." He could tell she'd found something else. Something that put deep fear in her gorgeous blue eyes. He hoped she hadn't found out that Eaton was going to let them be hunted, but that discovery would explain her reactions. "Eaton didn't bring us here for straightforward or easy."

"Clearly not."

Oh, how he wished she knew sign language or the coded phrases his team used that would give him a clue to her distress. As if on cue, the lights went out. With the plywood gone, he could see it was dark on the other side of the vent cut into the wall.

"Try to sleep," he told Charlotte. "I intend to employ *my* definition of freedom at the next opportunity."

"I'd like that," she said, her voice flat.

For a few minutes, the only sounds were Charlotte stretching out for the night, her breathing not as even as it had been on previous nights. A day without a beating left him restless. He imagined her lying next to him on a fluffy mattress in that five-star hotel and savored that delectable scenario until her voice came out of the darkness, teasing him.

"Mark, can I ask a favor?"

"Anything."

"When we *do* get out of here, will you kiss me? Please?"

Of all the things she might've asked, that one floored him. It was a challenge to hold back the enthusiastic response she deserved, but Eaton was eavesdropping. "I look forward to it," he said as casually as possible. Did she want to use him to erase the memory of Muscle's hands on her? Did he care? He could overanalyze the request or just be happy to have the opportunity.

One more motivation for survival.

He heard her moving around again, trying to get comfortable on the metal floor. She sounded much closer when she spoke again. "Do you mean that?" Her voice was so low he wasn't sure any mic could pick it up unless it was down here on the floor between them.

"Probably more than is wise for both of us," he replied.

"Thank you."

She was quiet after that, her breath steady, and he was grateful she'd fallen asleep. Like her, he didn't believe for a minute that Eaton would let them walk out of here. Based on the bastard's reaction when he'd seen her pinned to the floor under Muscle, Eaton's ultimate plan for Charlotte wasn't good at all.

Chapter 8

After the note she'd found in Eaton's desk drawer yesterday, Charlotte had only slept in fits and starts. Still, as the faint light filtering through the vent woke her, she knew she'd dreamed of Mark's kisses. Sitting up, she pressed her lips together gently as if she could preserve the dream kiss.

It hardly mattered what Eaton overheard or saw on the cameras now. According to what she'd found, their path was set. As if the universe concurred, she heard the engine of a small plane overhead.

"Too small for a rescue," Mark said, coming to his knees. He scowled at the ceiling. "Supplies?"

Her pulse skittered. She should tell him what she'd found and what she suspected. Before she could start, Quick-Punch Kid walked in. He unlocked her cage and led her out of the room.

He escorted her to the latrine. "Take a shower," he suggested. "And I recommend you use what Eaton brought in to look your best."

She glared at him and saw the pity in his gaze. He knew the plan. "Would you want to look good for a potential buyer?"

"Better to be seen as valued than disposable," he said. "Get going."

She quickly made the most of the facilities, fully aware it could be her last chance for some time. Or ever. Eaton had provided fragrant soap and shampoo and a deep conditioner, as well. A glimpse of heaven before they were tossed into hell. She kept the scrap of fabric she'd torn from the hem of her scrub top and used it to tie her hair into a ponytail.

More guilt surged through her as she brushed her teeth. She should have told Mark what she'd seen in the desk, given him time to prepare.

Quick-Punch Kid led her outside into a morning so bright she shied from the sunlight. He clamped her wrists in a heavy restraint. These cuffs had a solid bar that kept her hands about a foot apart and what appeared to be an electronic lock in the center. He tested the lock, then removed the other handcuffs.

"What are you doing?" Panic was a hot spark under her skin at the back of her neck.

He shook his head, completely unsympathetic. "Deal with it."

"No." The regular cuffs had been bad enough. She tugged one wrist and then the other, only to feel a small jolt of electricity that made her pinky fingers numb. "What's going on? Please, *please* take these off." She couldn't survive in or out of the cage with her hands in this contraption.

Muscle walked up from the direction of the dock and laughed. "Go on and get the other one," he said to Quick-Punch Kid. He aimed a Taser at her. "I'll keep her in line."

Being alone with Muscle again made her whole body quiver. She shifted her gaze slightly, keeping him in view, but deliberately focusing on the beautiful day. This was perfect weather for a picnic on the beach and here she was on what might be the last day of her life.

"You noticed the new cuffs have a sting?"

She cursed her knees for wobbling. She could *not* expect Mark to fight all of her battles or be her sole source of courage. Unpleasant as it was, she stared directly at Muscle and rolled her shoulders back. He wouldn't get the satisfaction of seeing her tremble or cower. Not today.

"I can drop you with the press of a button and do whatever I please." He tapped her temple. "You'd have to watch, trapped right there in your head."

The door opened and Mark appeared just ahead of Quick-Punch Kid. His electronic cuffs were already in place and he wore a small backpack. She had no idea how he would reach it. They'd given him clean scrubs, including a shirt this time, and slip-on shoes. His beard hid some of the bruising on his face and the shirt covered the damage Eaton's guards had done to his torso.

"You'll never touch her again," Mark said to Muscle.

"Shut up," Quick-Punch Kid responded. "He's all talk," he said to Charlotte. "He knows if he messes up the merchandise, he's a dead man."

As the horror of that statement slid through her, she watched Mark's expression go from fury to the blank mask she knew was even worse.

"Don't try anything, tough guy." Quick-Punch Kid shoved Mark to stand beside her, close enough that his shoulder bumped hers.

Just having him close gave Charlotte a boost of hope, though she still had no idea how they'd find a way out of what was coming.

"Merchandise?" Mark asked under his breath as the guard walked away.

"Eaton arranged for us to be hunted," she whispered. "I saw the note in his desk." She swallowed. "And the negotiated price."

"Why didn't you tell me?" His lips barely moved as he answered his own question. "You didn't want him to know you found out."

"I heard the plane this morning, but by then it was too late."

"Ah, Lottie." He rubbed his shoulder against hers. "That's a heavy burden to carry alone."

She sniffed back the tears that stung her eyes. Was that admiration she heard in his voice? "It certainly fixed any cash flow issues."

"Let's hope the check bounces," he replied. "It's not a shock to me. I heard him take the call and haggle over the price."

"And you didn't mention it either." She rolled her eyes.

"Didn't want to make things worse for you."

They were a pair, each of them too willing to protect the other.

A trio of men approached along the path she'd walked

from the dock. The man in the lead carried a rifle, with a handgun in a holster at his hip. He wore forest camouflage pants and boots, a khaki long-sleeved shirt and a vest that matched the pants. Take away the weapons and put him in business attire and he could be mistaken for an accomplished executive. The men flanking him were similarly dressed, but neither was visibly armed.

The man with the rifle stopped beside Muscle and smiled at her. She forced herself to be strong and not shy away.

"Miss Hanover. A pleasure to meet you at last."

"You know this guy?" Mark whispered.

She shook her head. "Only by name. Mr. Zettel reached out, asking me to paint one of his dreadful trophy kills."

"Your agent was dreadful, if you'll forgive me for saying so," Zettel said politely. "Before our host arrives, I'm compelled to offer you an alternative, Miss Hanover. I am here to hunt a SEAL. I have, in fact, paid dearly for the privilege."

She tipped her head. "Is that some sort of declaration of decency?"

"You must choose," Zettel continued. "Choose now to be hunted or spared."

There was no choice. She wasn't leaving Mark. He'd been a fixture in her life from day one. She was fully aware he wanted her out of harm's way, but Zettel was *not* what any sane person would consider a safe alternative.

"No, thank you." She'd rather be hunted than taken for a fool. Being *spared* wouldn't end well for her.

"I don't lose these games, Miss Hanover. Please take a moment to reconsider."

She pretended to indulge him. "If I choose to be spared, can I go home? You'll allow me to return to my family, resume my career and spend time with my friends too? Naturally, you'll have me sign a nondisclosure agreement or something similar to prevent any discussion about what's happened here. We wouldn't want to risk any tarnish on your reputation."

"Admittedly, your life would be different. You would remain in my company," Zettel said. "But you would be *alive*. You would be provided for and free to paint and travel. You will, in time, make new friends and, hopefully, a new family."

Her stomach twisted at the idea of bearing Zettel's children. She didn't know what would happen next, but anything was preferable to the life he offered. "No, thank you," she managed, her throat dry as sand.

Mark shifted as though he were bored, his shoulder brushing hers again. The unspoken support bolstered her courage.

Eaton came out of the office-prison, smiling. "Did you get your girl, Zettel?"

"No." His displeasure only fueled her will to survive whatever Eaton threw at them next.

"That's a pity. She's so talented. You should see the painting she did for me yesterday." His calculating gaze landed on Charlotte. "That's your final answer?" At her nod, he continued, "Not surprising, though it is unfortunate. I liked you, Miss Hanover. I'll console myself with the increased value of your final painting."

She silently vowed the painting she'd done for Eaton would not be her last. They would find a way to survive.

Eaton eyed his phone, then walked over and shifted Mark and Charlotte closer to the trees near the modified container. "Yes, perfect." He stepped back and did something with his phone. A moment later, he smiled as if he'd won the lottery. "We're live, gentleman." He tipped his head. "And lady."

Once more, Eaton had put them on display to continue tormenting Mark's dad. Apparently that was more important than exposing their location. Beside her, Mark twitched. He must be looking for the camera too. Eaton was talking, but Charlotte was too overcome to listen. Fury was scorching away her fears and for the first time, she felt absolutely capable of killing someone. If she'd had a gun, she would have aimed and fired and hit her target square in the chest. No regret, no guilt. Eaton and Zettel and their evil-minded cronies needed to die.

"Breathe." Mark said the word so quietly she thought she'd imagined it. "We're almost out of here."

This time she believed him.

Ben walked along the beach behind the house, periodically checking his cell phone to be sure he had a good signal. He did. Unfortunately no calls, texts or pictures were arriving on the device.

The live feed had been cut off shortly after Charlotte started painting. Hank's opinion of the clues she'd provided on the canvas had been backed up by the investigation team. Everyone was in agreement that Eaton was holding them on a barrier island south of Virginia.

That still left a great deal of coastline to cover. Ben and Patricia had returned home immediately to prep the sailboat for an extended cruise to help search. He wasn't leaving the fate of those kids to strangers—no matter how qualified or capable. The more eyes scouring the area for any sign of Eaton, Mark and Charlotte, the better.

Charlotte's parents would arrive this evening and the four of them would set out. Unlike previous trips, this time it wouldn't be as simple and pleasant as a long weekend with their best friends.

"Dad!"

Ben turned toward the shout and saw Luke coming down the steps from the deck. He carried a mug in each hand, but he didn't look happy about bringing out the coffee this morning. Matt, Grace Ann and Jolene were keeping tabs on the situation from their respective locations, all of them planning to gather here as soon as Mark and Charlotte were found.

"Mom wants me to tell you that staring at the ocean won't bring him back," Luke said.

"She should talk. The whole time Mark was in training, she'd watch the surf, shake her head and say a prayer."

"I did the same thing." Luke grinned. "Praying he'd scrub out."

At times like this, Ben was sure Mark went into the navy just to stir things up. "Don't let your mother hear you say that."

"I doubt she'd be shocked," Luke said. "Mark was all *SEALs rock, Deltas suck* when you were deployed.

The weeks while he was out of touch in training were so peaceful."

Ben sipped his coffee. "Your mother and I have always wanted each of you kids to achieve your own goals and dreams." He wrapped his cup in both hands. "Did we push too hard?"

Luke eyed him as if he'd sprouted a third eye. "Push us? Yes. Push us toward the army? No."

"That's good to hear."

"Yeah, well, four out of five kids made the smart choice," Luke joked. "That's a pretty good success rate. If one of us had to buck the system, it makes sense it was your favorite kid."

Ben arched an eyebrow. "You know your little sister is my favorite."

Luke nearly choked on his coffee. "Wow," he said, recovering. "I'd be offended by that if I didn't know about her psychology experiment in high school designed to favorably influence parents. Guess it finally paid off."

Ben couldn't quite manage the laughter over the old joke, consumed by a sudden image of his youngest girl caught in Eaton's net. They needed to put the man behind bars where he couldn't hurt anyone ever again.

"We'll get him, Dad," Luke said confidently. "Mark won't quit until Charlotte's home safe. His team is on standby, as is mine."

Eaton had been part of a team once, an excellent sniper Ben had counted on. "He's not the first soldier to snap under combat pressure," Ben mused.

"He's a disgrace to the uniform and the mission,"

Luke said. "You didn't send him off the rails. He did that on his own. Right mind or not, there are consequences."

"True," Ben agreed. "This feels all wrong with Eaton. It's unimaginable to be sure, but this entire ordeal has been too organized to blame on a broken mind."

"No one sane does what this guy has done to our family," Luke countered.

Ben stared out at the ocean, turned south as if he could see far enough to spot Mark and Charlotte. "However he's justifying his actions, his goal is to break me, to destroy our family."

"The Rileys stand together. We won't let him break any of us."

Ben was afraid Eaton was closer than ever with this game he was playing with Mark. The thought alone felt like a defeat. He had to stay strong. For all of them.

They finished their coffees and were headed back toward the house when his phone chimed. It was a text with a video attachment. Exchanging a wary look with Luke, he pressed the arrow to play the video.

The twenty-second clip showed Mark and Charlotte standing in front of a modified shipping container. They both wore hospital scrubs and slip-on shoes and it looked like Mark had a light pack on his back. They were confined by bulky handcuffs that appeared to have electronic locks in the center of the bars.

"You'll have an hour head start," Eaton's voice said from somewhere off camera. "The cuffs will open in five minutes. Evade the hunters for three days and you're both free. Good luck."

Mark and Charlotte hurried out of the frame and the camera followed their movement into the tree line.

"We have to get this to Hank right now," Ben said, as he forwarded the message. Then he and Luke raced for the house.

It was time for action.

Mark could indulge his temper later. Anger was a perk reserved for survivors. At the moment, all of his focus was on keeping them both alive. He'd watched Quick-Punch Kid fill the pack before settling it on his back. Several bottles of water and meal bars were more than he expected. If only the guard had included an inflatable raft and radio.

The hour's head start was almost fair, if Mark had been alone. Always harder to hide with multiple people, but he wasn't about to suggest he and Charlotte split up. Having the cuffs programmed to fall off at an appointed time wasn't as fair. He kept expecting the cuffs to zap one or both of them, but the hunter's money probably kept Eaton's urges under control.

He suspected the handcuffs, pack and clothes were tagged with trackers of some sort, yet Zettel had seemed all about a pure test of skill. Technology would go against his competitive nature.

Did the man hunting them have more favorable ethics than the man who'd kidnapped them? There was a curious thought. Philosophy was for survivors too, Mark decided, shifting to the west.

"You holding up?" he asked Charlotte, as they scrambled over a fallen tree.

"Hasn't it been five minutes?" she countered, shaking the cuffs.

"Probably. That's one reason I'm circling the starting point, so I'm sure we stay in range of the signal."

She shook her head and peered up at the blue sky peeking through the treetops. "I hadn't noticed we were circling." Her freckled nose wrinkled.

"That's not your job," he said, as they kept moving.

"What is my job?"

"I'm working on it." His fierce artist. He couldn't shake the possessiveness or protectiveness he felt for her. Sure, he'd want to protect anyone from Eaton, but this was new and specific. Something had shifted for him at the gallery, when he realized she was so much more than the neighbor he'd known as a kid.

In the days since, stuck in this impossible crisis, he'd really dialed in to both her and his gut instinct. Thinking about her was the sweet mental retreat he'd needed when he was pummeled by Eaton's men. Growing up, she'd always drawn him in. Not through any one moment or action, just by being herself. He'd always loved Charlotte; now he found himself almost willing to admit—to himself—that he'd fallen *in love* with her.

He couldn't say it; what woman would believe those words in this situation? It was a burden she didn't need. He wasn't even sure he could live up to what that meant. His first commitment was still to the navy and his team. Whether or not they had a future beyond one kiss and a sunset cruise, he could put his professional skills to use and get her off this island safely.

"Follow in my footsteps as closely as possible," he said. "It won't make a big difference, but every little advantage will help."

They zigzagged through the trees, loosely circling

the starting point. Once the cuffs unlocked, he could get more aggressive about their escape. He hadn't seen any sign of a camp beyond the container where they'd been held. The underbrush was as thick as the humidity and the live oak, pine and palm trees told him they weren't as far south as he'd first thought. Good news on both counts.

He moved around a fluffy pine sapling, careful not to bend the branches, and helped Charlotte do the same. "You didn't see anything in the office that resembled a map or location?"

"No. His computer was password-protected. I saw the board with all your faces and found the note with Zettel's name and sale price. And a couple of pictures similar to the one he was having me paint."

"I wish you hadn't kept that to yourself," he said, aching for her all over again.

"We were being observed," she began.

"I get it," he said, cutting off any explanation. "I can still wish." She had such a big heart and so much compassion. Despite her incredible inner strength, it felt grossly unfair for her to bear that information alone.

Suddenly a loud whistle sounded from their handcuffs. The shriek was surely magnified by their proximity to each other and likely the origin of the signal. No, Eaton wasn't playing fair at all.

The restraints fell away, and he and Charlotte were finally free. Or they would be in three days, unless Eaton changed the rules. Mark didn't plan on sticking to any rules other than his own, not when saving Charlotte was paramount. He picked up both sets of handcuffs and threw them, one at a time, in opposing directions.

Odds were slim that anyone would believe they'd split up, but it was worth a try.

He pressed a finger to his lips. She nodded once. From here until they found a hiding place, they had to stay quiet.

Standing out there while Zettel and Eaton postured had given him time to get his bearings. From Charlotte's description, he knew the ocean and dock were east of where they'd been held. The way most of the barrier islands were formed, he had a fair idea of the terrain they'd find to the south. The island had to be of a decent size or the hunt posed no challenge. He'd caught the disappointment in Zettel's eyes when Charlotte refused his offer. Though the hunter wanted her for himself, he'd also wanted an exciting hunt. Zettel doubtless believed Charlotte would slow Mark down and dull the thrill of tracking and killing a navy SEAL.

Mark would give them a chase, but they wouldn't live long enough to enjoy the memory.

He led Charlotte almost due west now, pausing occasionally to listen for Zettel or his trackers. They were still alone, but he didn't expect it to last much longer. Hearing moving water, he smiled to himself. A freshwater creek could be a great resource. It could also indicate the island was bigger than he'd hoped or even closer to the mainland.

He glanced over his shoulder. The trees provided decent cover. A person in the right camouflage would disappear a few yards in. Although the scrubs they wore were a drab olive, he knew they'd stand out to the men with the guns.

Zettel and Eaton were accomplished marksmen who

knew how to spot their prey. Mark and Charlotte needed to find not only a place to hide but some effective camouflage. He touched her knee where she crouched beside him and felt the now-familiar current of desire zip along his arm. "This way," he said soundlessly, moving only his lips.

They reached the creek and he dipped a hand in to smell and taste the water. Brackish and slow moving and no help if they ran out of the bottled water in the pack. The good news was that they were definitely on a barrier island. The mainland, and an escape route, might be within reach.

Provided they didn't encounter any aggressive or territorial wildlife along the way.

He shrugged out of the pack and stripped off the scrub top, stepping into the creek. Mud squished under his soft shoes. Dipping the top into the water, he pressed it under his feet, getting it good and muddy.

He rinsed out the worst of it and twisted the fabric in his hands, working the dark stains in.

Shaking it out, he liked the mottled result that would make it easier for them to blend into their surroundings.

He held out a hand for Charlotte's top.

Instead she waded into the creek on her own and slowly sat down in the muck. The water wasn't deep and she leaned forward, picking up mud and rubbing it into the scrub top. Her hands moved under the water and he assumed she was pushing the grime into her pants, as well.

When she stood up, the cotton clung to her, making it evident she wasn't wearing a bra. It made sense considering the dress she'd worn to the gallery. As she bent over to rinse the mud from her hands, he discovered he could see the outline of lacy panties.

This was the wrong moment for a bolt of lust to distract him, but his body had other ideas. He turned away to muddy up the backpack and hide his immediate and obvious response to her. They were both a mess when they came out of the creek, but the end result would work in their favor.

"What about my hair?" she asked.

His fingers itched to touch those wild curls and find out if they felt as warm as the rosy sunset they made him think of every time he looked at her. If he told her to, she'd muddy up all that glorious color. He couldn't do it. "Don't worry about it," he said. "We've done all we can."

Her lips canted to the side. "Give me one more second." He watched, caught somewhere between curiosity and regret, as she muted the light of her hair with mud and water. Her fingers deftly wove a braid through the long locks and she tied it off with a scrap of fabric.

"Better?"

She had a smudge of mud on her cheek, another on her chin. He couldn't explain why those imperfections drew him in or reminded him of the promise he'd made to her last night.

He wiped away the mark on her chin as he tipped up her face. He moved in slowly, watched her eyes go wide as his intent registered. He gave her room to change her mind, to say no. Instead her lips parted ever so slightly as he set his mouth gently to hers.

After holding her fingers each night, he'd anticipated the flash of heat and welcomed it. From the moment he'd seen her in the gallery, an island of beautiful calm surrounded by the sea of color and noise, he'd longed for a place where it was just the two of them. No distractions, no expectations.

One mistake out here with Zettel and it could all be over. If this was his only chance to keep his promise, he'd take it. He seized the moment, let it roll through him, and it was more than he'd known he could have. He breathed her in, finding her scent under the muck of the creek. Her fingers curled into his damp, muddy shirt and he wrapped an arm around her waist, pulling her close. She moaned as her body came flush to his and his tongue slipped into that soft heat to twine with hers.

What he hadn't expected was how fast and deep the first flash would burn through his system. All he could think was more, all, everything, right now. He cupped her face in his hands and forced himself to reel it in, to ease back. This wasn't the time or place to indulge in every vivid idea pounding through his bloodstream.

Safety was one hell of a motivation. Safety and that five-star hotel with clean linens and a big bed he and Charlotte had fantasized about while trapped in the cage. An hour ago, he'd been ready to sacrifice himself to save her. That option was still on the table, and odds were good it would come down to that. But now, after this taste of his glorious, fierce artist, he couldn't let the hunter win.

He rested his forehead to hers. They were both breathing hard. When he leaned back, he saw her flushed cheeks and dilated pupils and smiled. That kiss had rocked her world too.

There was something special between them. It would

be a travesty if they never had a chance to learn how great they could be together. Everything inside him laid claim to her, clamoring that she was his. Today, tomorrow, always.

The new awareness prickling through his system pushed his past failures aside, redefined the limits and decisions he'd made. It was as if one kiss with Charlotte reset his view of the future, but they had to survive the immediate danger before he could figure out what came next.

"We have to get going," he whispered.

"Mmm-hmm."

Neither of them moved. "I wanted to keep my promise," he said.

"I'd say you *um*…you definitely did that." Her gaze was fixed on his chest.

He grinned. She'd turned shy on him. "You know, in case something else happens." He nuzzled her cheek. "Did you know all of that was lurking under the surface?"

"N-no."

"Charlotte—" he tipped up her chin "—I'll make you another promise."

She stared at him, her blue eyes wide and waiting.

"That wasn't our last kiss."

Chapter 9

Wow. The man knew how to keep his word. It was Charlotte's only clear thought as she followed Mark, matching his footsteps as closely as possible. Not an easy feat considering that the whole world felt off-kilter and her lips tingled every time her mind strayed to that kiss.

Kissing Mark had fulfilled a fantasy she'd harbored deep in her heart for more than a decade, since the first time she and her friends had giggled over the mystery of kissing boys.

It had been worth the wait.

She wasn't motivated to think of other things. The immediate danger wasn't a pleasant diversion and so far there didn't seem to be much she could do to assist in Mark's escape plan. Far more enjoyable to trail after him, keeping her eyes on his broad shoulders and strong back while the anticipation mounted for their next kiss.

He stopped short and she almost ran into him on purpose just so she could touch him. She'd been too stunned and pleased and enthralled by the feel of his mouth covering hers to let her hands get in on the action.

What were the rules? They'd held hands every night when they'd been in the cages. Could she reach out and touch him whenever and however she wanted? A crazy new worry popped into her head. Did he expect her to make the next move? Probably best to pull herself together and focus on surviving this crisis than whether or not they'd just started a romantic relationship.

"Thank you for being here," she whispered, standing with him at the edge of the trees.

A marsh stretched out before them in all directions with no sign of civilization anywhere. The air smelled different and she couldn't hear the ocean at all anymore. Swathes of green-and-gold grasses were highlighted by the glint of sunlight on the water. It was a brilliant landscape full of wonders both seen and hidden, above and below the surface. She tried to commit it to memory so she could paint it once they were safe again.

"Can we cross it?" She'd never tried to cross a marsh on foot.

"I'm thinking." His rugged profile set in stern lines. He was listening and assessing, and though he had yet to suggest anything, she believed he would find a solution. That was a combination of her faith in his skills and expertise, as well as her lifelong affection for him.

She listened as well, trying to convince herself they'd found this place during a day sail and all she had to do was appreciate the wind in the trees and the birds calling back and forth. A great blue heron glided down into the marsh, settling near a wedge of grass to wait for an unsuspecting frog or fish.

Mark slipped the backpack off his shoulders and pulled out a water bottle for her. "Quick-Punch Kid packed this," he mused, showing her the contents.

About to take a sip, she sniffed the water first. It smelled normal enough. "Did he booby-trap it?"

"No, he made a point of opening a fresh case of both," Mark said.

"You're kidding."

"It was a shock to me too. Drink up." He opened a second bottle for himself. "It threw him when Muscle attacked you. I get the feeling this assignment hasn't been what he expected when he signed on."

"Please." At his quizzical look, she explained, "He was too well-trained to be a rent-a-cop and he was more than happy to use that training against you."

"Attacking women and hunting people for sport is a big leap from kidnapping or roughing me up."

"True." She thought about her interactions with the skinny guard. "If he has grown a conscience, maybe he'll notify the authorities."

"Personally, I'm hoping the live feed was enough for Hank and his team to find us." He gave a nod to the far side of the marsh. "We're on a barrier island. If we got through the marsh, we could swim for the coast."

"I have no problem wading through the marsh," she fibbed. This wasn't the time to get squeamish about snakes and other creatures that lurked in the thick grasses and dark water.

"I don't think so. We'd be sitting ducks." He laughed softly. "Big targets, easy to see. No, I'm trying to figure out how we make it *look* like we tried to cross the marsh."

"We could loop the pack around a clump of grass."

"I'm not ready to leave it behind," Mark said, brow furrowed in thought. "Eaton thinks he knows how I operate."

She recalled the bulletin board in the office. "He only sees you through the scope of your military service, if that helps." She closed her eyes and gave it more thought.

"You saw his notes on me?"

"Yes," she said, eyes still closed. "The bulletin board behind his desk had pictures and notes on all of you from Matt to Jolene. He even included Hank."

"The man's crazy if he thinks Dad will sit by while he tries to plow us all under."

She opened her eyes. "Agreed." She'd do everything possible to ensure Mark didn't become Eaton's first Riley kill. "I only had a minute or two to look, but I got the impression he wants to pit his skills against yours. When they dragged me along, it threw a wrench into the works."

"One he profited from." Mark massaged one palm with the opposite thumb. "If he wanted to go head-to-head with me, why sell that opportunity to Zettel?"

"Maybe it came down to cash flow."

"Maybe," he allowed. For several minutes, they listened to the sounds of the marsh together. "I'm not that good," Mark muttered, breaking the silence.

She knew he wasn't talking about kissing. "What do you mean?"

"I'm good at hiding a trail, but not the best. And with two of us together, they should be on us by now."

"Are you complaining that we haven't been found?"

"I guess I am." His gaze drifted over the marsh as a flock of egrets rose in a cloud of white and squawking calls. "Anyone in our situation would consider the marsh a viable escape route."

"Whatever you decide, I'm in," she said.

He turned to her and his thoughtful gaze sharpened, lingering on her lips. "That's great news."

She could see he wasn't referring to their escape. Her heart did a happy twirl in her chest. "Um. Yesterday, painting for Eaton, I changed up the trees from those in the picture to those I'd seen out here. If he did have a live feed going to your dad, maybe someone on the investigation caught those clues."

"That was really smart." He gave her a quick squeeze. "And brave."

She felt the heat rising into her cheeks at his praise. Why did he compliment her for the smallest things? Throughout high school and college, she'd been scolded by her peers for watching the world pass her by instead of diving in and participating. It wasn't entirely true, though she did like to watch and ponder. "Well, then I definitely hope that painting was a live performance."

"Me too, though it had to be hard on you." His smile warmed her straight through. "We can count on Hank." He caught her hand. "They're out there looking for us, Lottie. And you helped guide them in."

"We've done all we can, haven't we?"

"To help the search teams, yes," he answered.

"Thanks to you. Now, let's leave a clue here for Zettel and keep moving."

He reached for the hem of his pants and tore off a generous piece of the fabric. It was already muddy from the creek. "Be right back." He stayed low as he left the trees and waded into the marsh.

She could hear the muck of the marsh bottom sucking at his shoes. It was the only sound as he moved slowly and stealthily toward the first curve of tall grasses.

A rifle shot cracked through the air and another flock of water birds rose in a startled flurry.

"Go!" Mark shouted. Then he disappeared under the water. He couldn't mean that she should actually leave him out there alone against Eaton and Zettel. He surely didn't mean for her to try to navigate this island without him.

Moving as little as possible, she tucked the water bottles back into the pack and shrugged it over her shoulders. Mentally, she begged Mark to resurface. Staying low, she pressed her back to the nearest tree trunk, away from the sunlight flooding the marsh. The shadows were the safest place right now.

Where was Mark? She didn't hear any movement from the marsh. Holding her breath, she listened for any sound of the hunters.

She would *not* panic. She'd been kidnapped, handcuffed and kept in a cage for days. She would not allow terror to wreck whatever Mark had planned. If she got caught, it would make Mark's job of getting them off this island that much harder.

Where was he? She stayed in the low crouch, doing her best impersonation of a scrappy strawberry blond palmetto palm. He had to resurface for the sake of her sanity. Or if not her sanity, for the sake of more kisses.

A twig snapped behind her and she jumped, swallowing the startled cry.

"This way, Lottie."

His scrubs were soaked through and with the moss and grass stuck in his hair and clothing he resembled a B movie monster. He'd never looked better to her. She would have leaped into his arms if Zettel weren't out there looking for large sudden movements.

As they distanced themselves from the edge of the marsh, she realized he must have snapped that twig on purpose. He'd lost his shoes in the marsh and not one of his steps fell wrong or created any noise. She was the one most likely leaving a loud and visible trail as they moved toward the center of the island.

Mark didn't seem to care. He just kept pressing forward.

They came across the creek again and Mark paused to drink from a water bottle and rinse his hair.

His confidence that they were momentarily clear rubbed off on her. She stepped close and wrapped him in a big hug, resting her cheek against his damp chest, ignoring the muck as she breathed him in.

"I thought…" She couldn't say the rest, could only cling, grateful the worst hadn't happened. "I know you're trained and used to dangerous situations."

"Not quite like this," he admitted. His arms came around her, melting away a layer of fear. "I'm here. I won't leave you."

"Thank you." It was silly and felt like a woefully inadequate sentiment. "The rifle shot shouldn't have surprised me." She forced herself to back up and give him room.

"It is why we're out here," he agreed with a small grin.

"We need to find shoes for you."

He didn't seem to hear her, his gaze aimed at the trees. "It can wait. We'll keep moving," he said, his voice pitched low.

They headed out, in the same pattern as before with Mark in the lead and her trying to follow without leaving a trail. Thick patches of vegetation that hid their passing also made for slow going and tough hiking. When they stopped again for a water break, they rested against a live oak tree green with resurrection fern and dripping with Spanish moss. As he opened one of the meal bars and gave her half, it dawned on her.

"You," she said quietly. She broke off a piece of the bar so she wouldn't wolf it down.

"What about me?" Mark's gaze scoured the area they'd just traveled.

"You are the answer to that silly what-would-you-bring-to-a-deserted-island question. I'd bring you."

He turned all of that intense survival focus on her. "Gee, thanks. I'd rather you take me to a five-star resort."

"Obviously." A delicious little shiver of anticipation skated over her skin. Were they still going to do that? "But you have all the survival skills, and a great sense of humor. Plus, you smell good when you sweat."

His dark eyebrows arched toward his hairline. "You don't have to flatter me to keep my spirits up. We're out of those damn cages."

"But not quite out of danger." The conversations in the cage room had been introspective and emotional and still she had more to say. More he should know. That kiss had gone straight to her heart. "And it's not flattery, Mark. It's the truth."

She didn't want to dwell on worst-case scenarios, but if something went wrong, he should know what he meant to her. Except this wasn't the best time to confess her feelings. Even Mark, a man who knew she wasn't the grasping or clingy type, would run away if she said *I love you* after one kiss.

"I think this mess has altered your logic. Or you've had a heatstroke."

"In this shade?" She'd never known him to be so humble. "I don't think so."

"A humidity stroke?"

She covered her mouth before she gave away their position with a loud laugh. As it was, her shoulders shook so much she probably set the tree at her back swaying. "That's possible," she whispered, plucking her muddy top away from her skin.

Shaking his head, Mark tucked the empty water bottles and the wrapper from the meal bar inside the pack. Standing, he held out a hand. "Come on. We need to find shelter."

Mark glanced up at the midafternoon sky as thunder rumbled. He wouldn't mind a good drenching rainstorm to reduce visibility and make Zettel and his spotters miserable. If he and Charlotte could get through this first day and night, their chances improved exponentially.

Not that he expected Eaton to keep his word about letting them go. That was a problem for later. A problem that might not even come to pass. Hank and a rescue team were out there closing in on their position. Mark couldn't afford to believe anything else.

Charlotte was a trouper. She hiked, carefully and quietly, without complaint. Her strength and grit weren't a surprise. It took serious courage to put herself and her art on display for the world to judge. No, the real surprise was the tumult in his gut, twisting him inside out.

He told himself he'd feel this way no matter who was out here with him, but it was a lie. Charlotte was more. Her beauty and personality spoke to him, despite the mud and stress and lousy timing. Part of him wanted to park her somewhere as if she was a priceless treasure and just go nuclear on their enemies.

That option, aggressive and straightforward, tempted him. Even banged up, he knew he could get the drop on Zettel or anyone else. But he sensed that was what Eaton expected him to do. If he went on the offensive and one of the hunters or mercenaries got lucky enough to wound him, or worse, Charlotte would be at their mercy.

Her doggedly positive outlook under these dreadful circumstances was a huge help. She'd demonstrated remarkable ingenuity and pluck necessary to survive. Though he hated to admit it, he needed the tenderness and faith she kept pouring out for him. More kisses wouldn't hurt.

Despite her overwhelming relief when he'd returned from the marsh, she'd been careful with him, one of the toughest operators on the job. It was as if she'd had a map in her head of his bruises and wounds and found the one path that got her close without hurting him more.

He'd hugged her before. That embrace had been different in a thousand ways. Ways that moved him. Shaking it off, he kept searching the terrain for any sign that Zettel was flanking them.

Thunder rolled again. The sky was dark to the west. They needed to find some kind of shelter. With luck, the rain would last all day and they could hide until morning. The driest place would probably be on the ocean side of the island where the breeze kept the weather over land. Of course, the men hunting them would know that too. Someone had anticipated he'd move west and attempt to escape through the marsh to the mainland.

"How do you feel about rain?" he asked.

"I won't melt." Her bright smile was a beacon. "At this point, I could use the shower."

He grinned. There was an image he wouldn't soon forget. From a practical standpoint, she'd be cold, but he'd happily keep her warm. "If you get clean, you'll only have to go mudding again."

She shrugged. "Whatever it takes to get us out of here."

The dark clouds came in fast and the first fat raindrops started to fall. He led her under the shelter of the heavy sprawling branches of another live oak tree, doing his best to block her from the wind and rain as the storm came in.

"Do you remember our trip to Disneyland?" he asked. He'd been fifteen going on know-it-all and she'd just turned ten.

She shot him an arch look. "As if I could forget the way you and Luke snuck up on Jolene and me on Tom Sawyer Island."

"You screamed like little girls," he said, savoring the memory with pride.

"We *were* little girls." Her eyes filled with smug satisfaction. "I also recall that we got even in the Swiss Family Robinson Treehouse. Now that was a scream."

"You're right." He'd forgotten that part. "I jumped and knocked Luke into a post. His nose bled for days."

"Minutes," she corrected.

"His nose was still dripping blood when your mom bought him that pineapple ice-cream thing," Mark said with dark glee. "That was great."

"It was gross." She giggled now as she had then, the sound muffled by the patter of rain on the canopy of leaves. "I had to go buy him another one with my own money." Her knees pulled to her chest, she rocked into him and away again too quickly. "Still don't regret getting even."

"Mom was so mad at us that trip."

"Well, you were hellions," she said, a glint of humor lingering in her blue eyes.

"You and Jolene were easy targets on that trip."

She sobered. "I don't want to be an easy target out here." Her teeth were chattering, from cold or fear, he couldn't be sure. "I don't want to be a liability to you."

"You're not." He slipped his arm around her shoulders and pulled her close. "I don't know where you picked up that idea, but you're no burden." He tipped up her face, holding her gaze and giving her no room to doubt his words. "You're everything brave and good, Lottie. Remember that."

She licked her lips and need surged through his system. He let her lead this time, let her draw his head close for a kiss. He groaned, sinking into her, thoroughly lost.

The pop and hiss of a flare gun jerked him back to

attention. Twisting around, he saw the colorful shot of red smoke sailing right over their position. "Damn it."

There was no way they'd been spotted by chance. He could tell by the angle that the flare had been shot from a point perpendicular to their route, not by someone who'd trailed behind them or had come around to cut off their suspected route to the coast.

A shout carried through the rain and a response followed. Zettel wasn't wasting time on subtlety.

Mark urged Charlotte to the far side of the wide tree trunk. They didn't have much time to escape, but he was determined to find out how they were being tracked. Nothing obvious had been put into the pack when Quick-Punch Kid loaded the supplies. He supposed some new tracking tech could be on the scrubs, but the devices he knew of that could withstand the marsh and the creek were big enough to be noticed.

Cameras. Regardless of Zettel, this was Eaton's game and he loved nothing more than live video. He'd probably had the entire island covered in a closed-circuit network while planning this scheme.

Where was it? He crouched low, scanning their surroundings for something too straight or clean, or a telltale light that a device was active. *Come on, come on.* His gut told him he was right about this. He moved and caught the flicker of a red dot. Motion-activated recording. Clever.

Rounding the wide tree trunk, he clasped Charlotte's hand. The rain was coming down hard enough to mask their trail. They ran, somewhat blindly to the north and east. It didn't really matter, especially if Eaton's camera network did in fact cover the whole island.

Once again, he wished he had his team at his back. As a unit, they were unstoppable. Although they'd all had the same training, each of them had specific strengths. Mark wasn't the top guy on the team when it came to the tech stuff, but he was no slouch.

He pressed the pack into Charlotte's care. "Wait here."

"Mark, no."

He hesitated, hating the worry in her beautiful eyes. "Eaton posted motion-activated cameras around the island."

Her auburn eyebrows snapped into a scowl. She let loose a colorful, creative string of oaths that would've made his SEAL team blush.

"Agreed." He pressed a quick kiss to her lips. "I'm doubling back to take out the camera near that tree. Wait here."

She grabbed for his arm. "What do I do if…"

"Zettel doesn't actually want you dead. Work that to your advantage if he finds you before I get back. Remember, the cameras are motion-activated. Stay low and don't move."

"All right."

He crawled several yards away from her on his belly and then popped up, ready to lead Zettel and Eaton's cameras on a merry chase. All the while, his mind was on Charlotte, on the consistencies and contrasts of her. How could her lips taste so sweet while a tempest brewed in her big blue eyes?

"No one likes a cheater, Eaton," he murmured. He'd been inclined to take out the camera nearest her hiding place, but if he did that, it was as good as shooting off another flare. It was time to get unpredictable.

One of Zettel's men was loitering not far from the oak where they'd been hiding, his movements keeping that red dot on the camera lit. He didn't appear to be armed with anything more than the flare gun.

Mark's first instinct was to step up behind him and snap the man's neck: one less thug blocking his escape. If he did, the brutal act would be caught on the camera.

At Eaton's discretion, the video could be leaked and the world would see a trained navy SEAL killing a man standing around, minding his own business. The stain on the Riley name would be permanent and his father's reputation forever attached to the disaster. That kind of thing would leave the navy and SEAL program scrambling under the resulting media scrutiny, as well.

Thinking it through, he was 99 percent sure that was Eaton's goal out here. Bringing in the hunter only gave Mark more victims to destroy. No way would Mark play right into Eaton's hands.

Mark picked his way around, moving with the gusty storm, until he was behind the camera.

As Zettel's man continued to pace and watch, Mark pulled the plug connecting the device to the battery pack on the supporting stake. It was a clever design and now that he knew what to look for, it would be easier to locate more cameras and undermine the effort.

That still left the problem of Zettel's spotter.

He could sneak away, but he'd rather not. It was a golden opportunity to even the odds. Mark shoved the camera under some scrubby plants and took the stake in hand. Anger and indignation pushed him. He wanted to kill the man, but this guy had nothing to do with the kidnapping. He was nothing more than a pawn. A nasty pawn, working this hunt with Zettel, but maiming him and taking any helpful gear was the smarter move.

Standing tall, he cleared his throat. "Looking for me?"

The man spun around and his jaw dropped. It was the split-second advantage Mark needed. He charged as the other man scrambled for the flare gun. Applying pressure to the man's neck, Mark subdued his opponent before he could put up any resistance.

Mark let the man drop to the ground with a hard thud. "Ouch. That'll leave a mark." He searched the man's vest and pants for weapons or a radio and found only the flare gun and flares.

When he stripped off the man's boots, he found a good knife. He set the blade next to the flare gun and tried to get his bare feet into the man's boots. Too small. He'd take them anyway. The boots might fit Charlotte and would be an improvement over the flimsy shoes Eaton had given her.

Thinking of Charlotte, he considered his options. He couldn't leave the man to get up and walk back to camp for more gear. He'd be back on their trail in no time.

Mark didn't overthink it. Tucking the stake and flare gun into one of the boots, he picked up the knife and sliced the man's foot near his heel.

The pained screams and a smidge of guilt followed him for several minutes. When he was confident no one was tailing him, he returned to where he'd left Charlotte waiting.

This time he initiated the hug, taking all the warmth, comfort and relief she offered.

Chapter 10

Charlotte had been surprised Mark hadn't been stealthy when he returned to her hiding place. She'd been downright shocked when he dropped several items to the ground and pulled her into his strong arms. His heart pounded and his breath sawed in and out of his lungs. He might as well be her personal furnace in the chill of the heavy rain.

What had happened? She decided the details were irrelevant at this point. He was here and in one piece. Stepping back, she ran her hands lightly over him to check for injuries. He didn't seem to have a scratch, but his gaze was grim.

"I took one of Eaton's motion-activated cameras down," he said. "Got the spotter with the flare gun too. Any sign of trouble here?"

"Someone was close. I heard footsteps over that way," she said, pointing.

"To the west," Mark supplied with a quirk of his lips.

Without the sun, she had to take his word. "I was sure they'd see me, but then they turned back and hurried away."

"West again?"

"Mostly, yes. I think." She wrinkled her nose at her less than helpful answers. "It is raining pretty hard and I was trying not to get caught."

"Fair enough." He caressed her cheek, and his dimple flickered as he smiled. The expression was so tender butterflies soared through her belly. But he didn't kiss her again. "Try on the boots." He sat down and moved them toward her. "They're too small for me."

"Muscle's boots might fit you," she said, distracting herself from the idea of wearing a stranger's shoes. A stranger who'd cooperated with Zettel to hunt them.

"Got a good look at his feet, did you?"

"Actually, yeah. Sizing up people is part of the job." She routinely studied her environment as a puzzle, fitting together what she saw and how she would focus it on a canvas.

"When?"

The boots were a little too wide. "When what?" She set to work on the laces to see if she could improve the fit.

"When exactly did you size up Muscle?"

She peered up at him through the dripping rain. His jaw was set and his hands, tender a moment ago, were curled into fists now. "Are you jealous?"

"He had no right to touch you." Mark surged to his feet and paced away from her.

A bright red dot of color caught her attention. Another camera must have gone live. "Mark," she said.

"That one I'll kill," he muttered. "You're innocent. Off-limits."

She could see the rant brewing in the tight muscles flexing under the scrub top plastered to his skin. She didn't want to recall those terrible moments in Eaton's office and she certainly didn't want a burst of misplaced rage to bring Zettel and his men straight to them.

"Mark," she spoke through gritted teeth. "Stop. Moving."

He halted. She wondered that the rain, growing heavier again, didn't just steam off his shoulders. Mark's contempt for Muscle and the others was understandable. And despite the odds against them, being under his protection made her feel treasured and adored.

That kernel of romantic optimism that they might have a future, the secret dream she'd harbored for most of her life, was ready to explode like a fireworks finale on the Fourth of July. She had to keep it under wraps long enough to get off this island.

"There's a camera at my eleven o'clock," she said.

He stared at her and then turned. She watched him stalk straight over to the camera and dismantle it. With luck, that view would give Eaton a long-overdue moment of terror. Mark added the stake to the first one he'd secured through a loop on the pack. The camera he dropped at her feet.

"Stomp it."

She obliged, putting her borrowed boots to good use,

and was rewarded with a hot, lingering kiss that left her speechless. He picked up the smashed camera and walked away, toward the east side of the island. At least that was her best guess.

"Are you looking for the dock?" she asked after several minutes of his broody silence.

He grunted. "Might as well. Whoever didn't go out to help the spotter I wounded get back to camp is probably warm and dry, waiting out the weather on the boat."

Granted, he was the experienced part of their team, but she thought that sounded like an excellent reason to avoid the area. "And we're going to do what? Walk in and stage a mutiny?"

He stopped short and swiveled around to face her. "Boats have radios and charts. We can call for help, pinpoint our position or steal it outright."

Hope swelled; his confidence was her own personal rainbow in the gray, miserable day.

She'd painted rain-soaked cityscapes in Paris. Lightning storms in the Midwest. Foggy valleys in the Appalachian Mountains. Weather could be both treacherous and inspiring. She hadn't decided if she could do this weather justice. As a victim, she was too conflicted about the entire situation.

Despite Mark's presence, fear dogged her heels, enough that she wasn't sure she could find the beauty in all these layers of gray and green. On the flip side, with Mark right here and those kisses keeping her warm, she ran the risk of turning this hazy scene into a wondrous fantasy world. Neither portrayal was the whole truth.

"Why didn't you and Maria get married?"

He stubbed his bare toe on a root and she winced.

"I thought we were talking about stealing a boat," he said. "Why does it matter?"

They hadn't been talking about anything for several minutes. "I was curious. Our mothers are best friends," she replied. She'd tried her hardest not to hear about his dating life, but there were times, before she'd cut herself off for the show, that it was impossible to tune out. "You brought her out to Cape May and she was with you again at Labor Day the year before last."

He slid a look her way. "You weren't there."

No. She'd canceled when she'd heard he wouldn't be alone. "Mom mentioned it." She should drop it, but as she'd said, she was curious. The first kiss had changed everything for her. The fact that he didn't want to talk about Maria seemed important.

"We had different expectations," he said, his voice hard and tight.

Maria had hurt him, and Charlotte was filled with an outrageous urge to track her down and make her apologize. Everyone was so sure nothing really troubled Mark, but she'd learned early on, by watching him, that his humor was often a protective measure.

She didn't have time to ask for details. They'd reached a jagged line of wind-shaped palms leaning more than usual under the weight of the rain. On the other side of a ridge of tall grasses, a small cove welcomed the Atlantic. There was no dock in sight. Relief and disappointment warred for dominance.

"Guess we keep walking," she said. With the ocean in sight as a reference point, she had a better sense of direction. Based on where they'd been, she assumed the dock would be farther south.

But Mark didn't move. He pushed his toes into the sandy soil under his feet. "I meant to. Propose to Maria," he clarified, his gaze on the cove. "I shopped for diamonds and settings."

With her heart aching at the pain constricting his voice, Charlotte knew that given a canvas and time, she'd paint sorrow into the gray surrounding them. "What happened?"

He wiped the rain from his face. "Marriage isn't right for everyone."

"It's right for you," she blurted without thinking. With the right person. Of course, she wanted to believe she was that person, but even if she wasn't, Mark was built for commitment and a forever kind of partnership. The same core values held both of them upright as surely as bone and muscle. There was something more to the story, something she probably shouldn't poke at.

"What happened?" she asked again, despite her misgivings.

His gaze touched on her and then slid away. "We broke up."

Mark claimed to be the extroverted twin and he embraced the assumption that he was carefree, a slave to wanderlust. She'd watched him and loved him long enough to know better. She laced her hand through his and repeated her question one more time.

He didn't move, but his whole body seemed to slump, defeated. "She left me while I was deployed." He didn't turn from his study of the water. "I thought she was pregnant, but didn't ask before I left."

Charlotte's heart clutched at the pain in his eyes.

"I spent that whole operation grinning like a fool. I rushed home, ready to pop the question."

A hard shudder rippled through him and Charlotte held his hand, rode it out.

"Maria wasn't there," he continued. "I was so excited to go home. So damn sure she'd be showing. Eager to tell me." He cleared his throat. "And she… She was gone. Moved out. A few hundred phone calls and texts later, she finally agreed to meet with me."

Charlotte held her breath and prayed, for his sake, that she'd misunderstood what was coming next.

"She *was* pregnant when I left." Mark's big voice, all his normal vitality, faded on a shaky sigh. He'd had more life in the cage. "While I was gone, she got scared about being a single mom. In her mind, SEALs weren't good daddy material."

"She said that to you?" Charlotte couldn't suppress the indignation.

He squeezed her hand. "The divorce rate among Special Forces is pretty high."

Charlotte snorted. "She must've been pretty high if she couldn't see how *you* are different from a lousy statistic."

His lips twitched. "Ever the loyal one," he murmured. He finally dragged his gaze away from the ocean to look at her. His rough thumb wiped the rain from her cheek.

"That's right."

"Thanks for that." He seemed to pull himself together, though he still held tight to her hand. "Long story short, she ended the pregnancy. Ended the relationship. I just got the memo a few months too late."

"She…" Charlotte couldn't say it. It took several

seconds for her to absorb what he'd said. Her heart broke for him and the child he never met. "You never told anyone?"

"Where would I start?" he asked. "Hey, Mom, you're not having a grandkid after all." He slid his hand free and raked his hair back from his forehead, scattering raindrops. "At the time, sympathy wasn't what I needed."

Sympathy was exactly what he'd needed. He should have had support and love and the reassurance from his amazing family, and hers by extension, that the woman had been heartless, cruel and all wrong for him.

"Luke must have suspected something," she said.

"We were on opposite sides of the country at the time," Mark said. "The Continental Divide messes with the twin telepathy thing."

"Stop," she snapped, startling them both.

"Stop what?"

"Belittling what you went through." Her temper was running away from her and she couldn't quite catch it. "When we're out of here, I'm going to track down that woman and kick her butt for hurting you."

"My fierce artist." He laughed, the sound rather strangled. "You'd do it too."

"You bet I *will* do it," she said. "It's one more thing to look forward to." She was angry enough that if Muscle jumped out and attacked her now, she was sure she could take him down.

"I hate to disappoint you, but it's long over," Mark said. "I've moved on."

Right. He didn't speak about it like a man who'd moved on at all.

She was still fuming when he slipped an arm over her shoulder and kissed her temple.

"Thank you for listening," he said. "I didn't mean to dump that on you."

She thought of his words to her this morning. "You've carried that secret long enough all by yourself. Even with your amazing shoulders, it had to be getting heavy."

This time his soft chuckle sounded more amused and less pained. "Guess so. You won't mention it to anyone?"

She didn't want to keep something that big to herself, but it was his secret and therefore she would. "Not a word. It's not the kind of gossip artists are into," she promised.

Tears prickled in the backs of her eyes and she looked up at the sky. The breeze off the ocean kept the worst of the rain behind them. It was damp here, but they were no longer in the downpour. Out on the beach, it looked almost dry. And if they strolled out there to dry out and enjoy it, they'd be sitting ducks.

She plopped down and leaned back against a palm tree. "Do you think they've stopped for the day?" she asked.

"I imagine the injury I inflicted gave them something to consider. Why?"

"It's caught up with me," she admitted. "We can keep moving if that's best, but I wouldn't argue with just sitting here for a while."

"Wherever you are, it's a paradise," he agreed, dropping to sit beside her.

The quiet companionship was lovely, but she could

tell he was antsy, deliberating over their best next move. "You'd like to leave me here and just go handle things, wouldn't you?"

"Yes," he admitted.

"But you haven't."

"Those cameras changed the equation," he said. "Eaton loves a show and a SEAL on a rampage without any context would ruin me, Dad and put a significant dent in the program."

She hadn't thought of that, but it made sense in a sick way. She didn't know what to say, didn't have any helpful suggestions.

"Does death really increase the value of an artist's work?" he asked. "I hated that Eaton said that to you."

She nodded. "It's the law of scarcity. The painting I did for him won't be my last," she said. "And there are some pieces in my studio that I didn't think were ready for the show." She cocked her head, studied his striking profile. "Don't tell me you have one of my paintings."

"All right, I won't." She gawked and he chuckled. "Just hypothetically, how much would it be worth if you died?"

"Far more than it's worth now." Which painting had he bought and when? "Hey, maybe we should use the cameras and fake my death so we can all be rich."

"I'd give you a cut," Mark teased. "Of course, Eaton's rich enough thanks to Zettel's perverted hunting habit."

"True." She picked at the mud under her fingernails. "Even before Zettel, if you think about it. He had to have capital to set this up. Are snipers that well paid?"

Mark shook his head. "Eaton went into mercenary

work after he blew up his army career. He's made some powerful and ugly friends in the years since."

An understatement if ever she'd heard one.

"I think," Mark said, rolling to his feet, "with some scouting and planning, I can make this cove a safe place for tonight."

"If you disable the cameras we find, won't it be obvious we're here?"

"They're motion sensitive. If we block the lenses, they would come on when the wind blows, but they wouldn't show us moving."

"That's brilliant," she exclaimed, jumping up. "How can I help?"

He smiled. "We'll start with the closest camera and then I'll scan the cove for others. Then if there's enough light, we can see about finding the dock and a boat."

The encouraging plan gave her the second wind she desperately needed.

"Mark and Charlotte are being *hunted*?" Patricia didn't shout. She didn't panic. There were no tears. She spoke with the quiet, contained calm that was far more dangerous than any outburst.

Ben had been dreading this conversation from the moment the video clip had hit his phone. He and Luke had managed to get the information to Hank first, but as the day wore on and the plan came together, there was no keeping Patricia out of the equation.

He'd brought his wife into the office and prayed she wouldn't ask to see the video. It helped to know Hank, still working the investigation in Virginia, was on standby to answer any questions he wasn't comfortable with.

"Where are they?" she demanded.

If he knew that, they'd be having this talk on the boat and underway. "Based on the information from Charlotte's painting and the video clip Eaton sent this morning, Hank is narrowing it down. It is likely Eaton has them on a barrier island south of here."

"And when are we joining the search?" she asked.

"We'll leave in the morning."

She pursed her lips. "Sue Ellen and Ron are in town. I have our gear and food packed. We'll leave tonight." She stalked out of the office, giving him no chance to argue.

He didn't want to argue. Like her, he wanted to get out there and find the kids.

For the first time since Mark and Charlotte had disappeared, Ben hoped he and Patricia wouldn't be the first to find them. His wife would happily kill Eaton with her bare hands and then Ben wouldn't have a chance to beat the man senseless before the authorities locked him up for life.

Mark felt pretty accomplished by the time the storm blew over. It had rained inland all through the afternoon, which only made it easier to screen the two cameras he'd found.

They had a base camp, if woefully underequipped, but feeling safe in this protected corner of the island perked up Charlotte so much he didn't dare point out what it lacked in amenities. She made an adorable picture in her borrowed boots with her hair braided back and her muddied scrubs. He had to work not to stare.

Between the steady sound of the ocean rolling in and the quiet task of searching for the cameras, he'd shaken off the embarrassment of telling her about his ugly failings with Maria. Of all people to confide in, he wasn't sure why he'd unloaded on Charlotte.

Luke had pestered him a bit when he'd heard about the breakup. Mark had tried more than once, but he just couldn't bring himself to talk about it at the time. And, after several months had passed, bringing it up felt like wallowing. It was done, she was gone and no amount of picking it apart would change anything.

Blocking the cameras also gave him time to realize Charlotte was right. At the core, he was built for traditional family dynamics. A wife and kids, and that house he kept picturing in his head. He still had a few years in an intense career, but maybe someday that vision would come to pass.

This was a strange time and place for epiphanies.

He'd honestly thought Maria had been the one. Someone who could commit, love and compromise as they built a life together. Hurt by her rejection and devastated by the loss of a child he would never meet, he'd locked away those wounded pieces of himself and vowed never to let anyone in again. Charlotte made him want to reconsider, to break that vow and try one more time.

Did he have the guts for that?

As they split a meal bar, conserving their resources, he watched the sky. Dusk was falling and lead-colored clouds were breaking apart to the north. In a few hours, he could head out for some recon, maybe impair a few more spotters.

"You're thinking of leaving me here again, aren't you?" Charlotte asked.

"Yes," he replied. She'd see right through any attempt to lie.

"You have to stop doing that."

"Can't. Keeping you safe is my primary objective." Her lips tilted in a way that made him forget all about looking for an escape. He started to lean in to kiss her and pulled back.

He couldn't keep kissing her and expect to survive. Outwitting Eaton was enough of a challenge. With Zettel on the island, their odds of escape dwindled considerably.

"Don't go alone. I can help," she said. "Be a lookout or whatever."

"I'm sure you'd be an incredible lookout," he said. "I'm second-guessing the whole idea to find the dock right now."

"Why?"

"Ideally, I'd stay right here and forget about everything but you." She blushed and his blood heated. With a weapon and ammunition, it was a defensible position. Unfortunately they only had a flare gun, a knife and two ground stakes.

"You had a valid point earlier. If the boat is at the dock, everyone else is likely there too. No reason to have more than one guard at the office. Eaton must be using the boat as a staging point. How else would he have been able to pick up painting supplies or bring in the hot fresh food he tortured me with?"

"If Zettel did give up the hunt for today, I doubt he'd settle for a lousy outdoor camp when he could be warm and dry on the boat," she said. "He thinks he has all the time he needs. I'd rather not walk right into his rifle sight."

"I don't know the man, but I know the type. He isn't afraid to get his hands dirty or suffer for the sake of the hunt."

Her eyebrows flexed into a frown. "You realize that's not exactly comforting?"

"Wasn't meant to be," he said. "I said it mostly to remind myself what's at stake."

She pulled the tie from her hair and started untangling the mass of rose-gold waves with her fingers. The rain had washed away the mud she'd used to dull the color earlier. "I think we're better off sticking together."

"You don't approve of how I disabled the guard dog with the flare gun?"

"Of course I do."

She shook back her hair and then began weaving it into a fresh braid. It was all he could do not to help. He'd seen his sisters do the same countless times. Her too, but not like this. Not when all he could think about was how it would feel to unwind that braid again.

"You do what's right, no matter who or what you're up against," she said.

The all-encompassing confidence made him want to live up to her high opinion. "That's flattery," he teased. "You've only seen me at my worst. Ninety-nine percent of the good work I've done is classified."

She tied off the braid with the dirty scrap of fabric. Given a chance, he would dote on her and spoil her with the best of everything. But solid family values or not, he wasn't sure he was her guy. Not yet. There was still more he wanted to do with his career and his SEAL team. Could Charlotte be patient through that, or would she have second thoughts on lonely nights like Maria?

Charlotte wasn't Maria, but it would be worse to make the wrong moves with her. A mistake between him and Charlotte would have repercussions through both of their families. Did they have anything in common beyond a talent for kissing and a mutual belief that he could do anything? She was built to create and develop and celebrate life. He was trained to kill. She deserved a man who would be home for her every night, a man who could give her a real relationship.

What had she planned for her career? He knew about the art therapy, and the year in her studio, but what was next? He caught himself before he asked. The idea that her work or her heart would carry her out of his reach was a hard pressure in his chest.

He had to be overreacting. Pain, stress, lack of sleep and the emotional conversation about Maria's choices were obviously impairing his judgment. Feelings weren't his strong suit. Better to focus on what he did right.

"Are you fishing for compliments?" She tossed her braid over her shoulder.

"What?" It took him a second to pull his thoughts back in order. "No."

"I've seen you play just about every sport either casually or competitively. I know what you can do. And I watched you repeatedly draw Eaton's attention from me."

"Yeah, that worked so well," he grumbled.

"Worked well enough that we're both still alive," she said. For a quiet girl, she suddenly had a lot to say. "I know you took every beating Eaton dished out, all the while thinking about how you'd save me."

"That's a no-brainer. You're precious—"

"So are *you*, Mark."

Shocked by her declaration, he gaped at her.

"Yes, I said it. You're precious to me and plenty of other people. Looking for the dock on your own is too risky. We don't have a way to communicate if one of us gets hurt or found," she said. "Leaving me sitting here fretting over you won't do either of us any good."

And there was his answer about the future. Leaving her sitting at home fretting while he was deployed would drain her wonderful, vibrant and creative spirit. He wasn't the guy for her.

"If we go together, we could just as easily be caught together." He felt obligated to point out the obvious.

She spread her hands wide. "So far, we've made together work in our favor."

He knew when to compromise. "All right. Let's go." He caught the flash of victory in her blue eyes before he ticked off the ground rules. She listened attentively, promising to follow his directions and bolt if he told her to go. He carried the pack, though they left half of the remaining water and meal bars hidden at the camp. Better odds for her survival if they did get separated.

"The general plan is to follow the coastline to the dock," he explained. "That way all you have to do is retrace the route if there's trouble."

Her lips pursed. "Relax. I'll only send you back if absolutely necessary."

"And what if you're the one who has to retreat?" she asked.

He supposed such a scenario was possible, but the idea made him queasy. "I'll do it," he promised.

They left the cove in silence, both of them on high alert for any sound that didn't belong in the maritime forest or the sloping beaches where the island met the ocean. He made note of the first camera they found on their route, but he didn't block it. It was aimed inland and they were able to maneuver around it.

"Do you think he has someone watching the beach?" she asked in a whisper.

She never ceased to impress him, though it was odd to hear her voice the question that was at the forefront of his mind. "It would be the best way to keep an eye on these open stretches. I looked for camera gear in the trees around the cove. Either the person who staked the cameras on this side is afraid of heights or the breeze off the ocean renders them useless."

They walked on and he resisted the urge to take her hand and pretend they were just two people out for a stroll.

At the first sound of voices, he stopped moving and tucked Charlotte behind him. The speakers were too far away for him to pick up particular words, but there was definitely more than one person. Under the voices, he heard the break of soft rollers coming in from the ocean and the random squeak of plastic bumpers designed to protect boat hulls from a dock. He crouched low, signaling Charlotte to wait. Inching forward, he crept to the edge of the trees to see who was there.

Mark had to give Eaton a gold star for organization

and planning. The dock was sheltered from open water on one side by a sandbar. He'd used the island topography to great advantage. The odds of being noticed from anyone out on the ocean were slim and day travelers cruising between the mainland and island would never see it.

Eaton had guards posted at both ends of the dock and Mark smiled. The man had prepared for an assault from the water. So he *was* smart enough to respect Mark's training.

The boat tied up now wasn't the glamorous yacht he'd expected to see. Maybe Zettel would prefer camping to the cramped and worn cabin cruiser that would benefit from some serious maintenance and a fresh paint job.

Looking back, he motioned Charlotte forward. She soaked up details like a sponge. "Is that the boat you arrived on?"

"Yes."

His body came to attention as she stretched out beside him, brushing against his leg, hip and side. Her cheek was close enough to kiss and if he leaned in just an inch or two, he could bury his nose in her hair.

"We won't get on that boat tonight," he whispered, focusing on their immediate crisis. They'd wasted time and energy on this hike after all.

"What about the modified container? If everyone's here, we could send an SOS through the cameras there."

"I'm not convinced everyone is here," he replied. "That's Muscle at the ocean end of the dock. I've never seen the guy closest to us, have you?"

She paused, studying the scene. "An extra from Zettel's team?"

"Possibly." Eaton seemed to have a steady supply of mercenaries ready and willing to cash his checks. "The spotter I wounded needs a doctor. They wouldn't have been able to get him out by plane during the storm."

"I never heard the plane leave after Zettel arrived."

He'd been thinking the same thing. "But where did they land? There must be a clearing on this side of the island."

"Or it's a seaplane. Either way, he'll have it heavily guarded." She wriggled, her hip bumping his. "The supplies must be on the boat," she said. "They weren't in the container where we were held."

"Then we must be close to a good-sized city for Eaton's men to keep things stocked. In a small town, that crew would stand out too much."

She nodded her agreement. Resting her chin on her stacked hands, she watched the activity on the dock. "I have this urge to ask you to go all covert ops and take that vessel."

He smothered his laughter in his arm. "The kiss was that bad that you'd send me on a suicide mission?"

She turned her head and met his gaze. He was instantly lost in those blue depths, deeper in the fading light. "I would never want anything bad to happen to you."

"Same," he said. He forced his gaze back to the dock and watched for a few more minutes. Was there anything he could do tonight without getting captured, killed or putting Charlotte in grave danger?

"What I wouldn't give for binoculars." He eyed the

worn footpath from the dock, across the dunes and into the trees. The trek wasn't a total loss. He now had a mental map of this segment of the island, but could only guess as to the full length, breadth and location. Having actual coordinates would mean a faster rescue if they could snag a radio or phone.

As far as Mark had seen, Eaton didn't trust anyone else with the radio. That posed a problem for Mark, who wanted to steal it, but it made things challenging for Eaton, as well. His men couldn't call for backup or to clarify orders if they got in a bind. Mark intended to put them all in a bind in the days ahead.

His pulse settled as a loose plan took shape in his mind. Before he and Charlotte retreated, he'd give Eaton something to think about overnight.

"I'm taking the flare gun," he said, reaching into the pack she wore. "You start back—" He stopped talking as someone approached.

"I want the cameras disabled," Zettel was saying.

"No," Eaton replied. "If you want a fair hunt, don't look at the feed or read the movement reports."

Charlotte trembled and Mark rested his hand between her shoulder blades, keeping her still, offering reassurance.

"That's impossible," Zettel roared. "Your men gossip like schoolgirls."

He pointed to the camera stake nearby. It wasn't facing them or the bullets would be flying by now.

Mark embraced the familiar battle calm, shifting into fighting mode. At his side, he felt another tremor ripple through Charlotte. What he wouldn't give to have her anywhere else right now. He pressed his leg to hers in silent reassurance. She stilled.

The light was nearly gone and the men were little more than loud shadows among the thick brush and trees.

"You never said anything about watching the hunt," Zettel bit out in a tone bordering on petulant. "I can track the man without this junk you've tacked up everywhere."

One of the shadows bent and struggled with something. Leaves rustled and Eaton swore.

"Put back my equipment, Zettel. If you don't like the parameters here, get out of the game."

"I wanted a hunt, not a shooting gallery. I have a reputation."

"So do what you came to do," Eaton said. "Enjoy your hunt, make the kills and no one will be alive to speak ill of you or your reputation."

"You have a reputation too," Zettel countered, his voice full of threats. "I should have listened to the naysayers before wiring the money."

"If you're unhappy, leave."

"I am unhappy with the *cameras*."

"Will you continue to disable them?" Eaton asked.

Mark cringed. That was a trick question if he'd ever heard one. Although it was nice to know Zettel was interfering with Eaton's observation tactics, this wasn't going to end well. Eaton was addicted to the power high and looking for another hit. No way would he allow Zettel to mess with his ultimate plan for vengeance against the general.

Mark had a flare loaded in the chamber and the hammer cocked. He aimed the flare gun at the men, prepared to offer a temporary end to the argument.

"I paid for a fair hu—"

Two quick gunshots cut Zettel's words short before Mark could fire the flare. The man slumped to the ground. Eaton used the radio and snapped out orders. Mark wondered who would answer. He'd never seen a radio on Quick-Punch Kid or Muscle.

The answer became evident as a man stepped out of the boat's bridge and shouted to the man posted at the near end of the dock. Mark and Charlotte had to get out of here before they were spotted. He signaled her to back up slowly, keeping to the darkness created by the trees' shadows.

Every foot of distance gave Mark options and Charlotte a chance. Another few yards and they could make it out unnoticed.

Eaton was muttering at Zettel's lifeless body when his radio crackled. He toggled the switch. "Say again?"

Mark knew they'd been spotted. Zettel must not have disabled the camera when he pulled up the stake and when it fell, the field of view must have changed.

Mark shot the flare, aiming for Eaton's feet. The signal projectile wasn't known for accuracy and it floated and tumbled through the air in a shower of sparks and a trail of smoke. A split second later, it flared as designed and simultaneously lit up the area. The red plume burned and skittered across the ground, creating a bank of foggy smoke.

Eaton's night vision would be compromised and the sizzling flare made enough noise to cover their escape. Mark urged Charlotte up and into a run. "Go! Go!" Yes, their rapid retreat meant they'd leave a trail. They might even get picked up by a second camera, but he'd blow up that metaphorical bridge when he got there.

One gunshot, then two more sounded. Fired from the dock, based on the sound. None of the bullets landed close enough to worry him.

"Keep going." They were almost out of range.

Charlotte tripped and went down, sprawling across the ground before he could do anything to keep her upright or cushion her fall. He helped her up. "Go straight to the cove," he said. "Don't argue," he added. "I'll hide our trail and then I'm right behind you."

Chapter 11

Charlotte didn't want to leave him, but did. She'd promised to run if he told her to, though it made her legs heavy and her heart ache. What if Eaton caught him again? The beatings and lack of food and care had taken their toll on Mark.

She tripped over a root, hauled herself up and kept going. What if, by some miracle, she survived and had to tell his parents he didn't make it?

She ran harder, scolding herself for doubting his skills. They were in this together and they'd get out of it together. She had to trust him to stay alive just as he trusted her to find her way back to the cove. As long as she kept the water on the right, she couldn't miss it.

He must have known where they were when he sent her on, because she reached the cove sooner than expected. She bent over, hands braced on her knees, breathing as deeply and quietly as possible.

Trusting him to come back to her was different than trusting him as a person. Fear did that. She had to be stronger than the fear. Instead of pacing and wringing her hands, she sat down and waited, listening for any movement.

Her mind fought back, racing in wild, panicked circles.

Zettel was dead. The man was awful. The world was surely safer without him. So why did her hands shake and her eyes fill with tears? It was dumb to grieve a man who would've killed Mark at the first opportunity. A man who'd wanted to own her.

She hugged her knees to her chest and tucked her head to muffle the scream she knew she couldn't suppress much longer. Where was Mark? If she hadn't fallen, they wouldn't have lost precious seconds. Now Mark was out there putting himself at risk to hide their trail.

Charlotte was inept out here and it could cost them their lives. This wasn't roughing it for a weekend with the family, even with a Riley present. This was life and death and she was ill-equipped to manage it.

Mark had given her survival tips, but she had no confidence that she'd get through this without him. At the sound of footsteps nearby, she crouched low, out of sight, her entire body braced for trouble.

"It's me, Lottie."

Mark's low whisper brought an enormous wave of relief. Her knees nearly gave out as she leaped up and rushed into his arms. He smelled like safety and every bright hope she'd ever had. If she could have, she would have held him forever. Mind-blowing kisses or not, that would lift clingy to an all-new level.

"I'm so sorry." Her voice cracked and she stepped away from him. "For tripping," she finished.

"Don't apologize, honey." His lips brushed over her temple, her hair. "They won't find us tonight, even if they make time to come looking."

She nodded at that, before she remembered he couldn't see her. The moon was almost full, but heavy cloud cover moving across the sky made the low light unpredictable. "Okay."

"That was quite a tumble," he said. "Are you hurting anywhere?" His hands rested lightly on her shoulders, his thumbs gliding along the slope of her throat as if he could see her best with his touch.

She couldn't answer. His hands were soothing and electrifying in turns. She wasn't even sure how she was still breathing. He enticed and tempted even as he reassured.

"Charlotte, are you hurt?"

"N-no."

She would be if she didn't pull herself together. She wanted Mark. She'd lost count of the nights she'd dreamed of being in his arms, savoring his kisses and more. How could life be so cruel as to give her a few of her sweetest dreams amid this dreadful nightmare? Art had taught her beauty and pain walked hand in hand, that light and shadow must coexist for the work to have depth and purpose.

She wanted him, even though wanting felt so self-ish when she wasn't sure if his feelings went any deeper than the surprising physical attraction. Wanting in silence hadn't gotten her anywhere. In the days since they'd been kidnapped, she'd been plagued with thoughts about the worst-case scenarios.

If this was her last night, she wouldn't leave anything unsaid, though speaking up scared her almost as much as Eaton himself. "We're safe tonight?" she asked.

"Yes. There's no trail to find and Eaton is putting out fires, literally and figuratively, since he shot Zettel. You went down hard. Tell me where it hurts."

She rubbed a hand over her heart where all the aching had settled. "Feels like I only scraped my palms and knees."

His hands coasted over her shoulders, sliding the straps of the pack down and away. She'd forgotten it was there. He'd thrust it at her when he'd told her to go ahead of him. He dropped the pack and it landed with a muted thud on the sandy ground. He continued to trace her arms all the way to her hands. He turned her palms up and bent his head close.

She had no idea what he thought he could see in the darkness. Her fingers curled in protectively. "It's nothing."

"It's everything." His voice was soft and rough, like velvet. He stroked his thumbs across her palms to open her hands.

Her breath caught, not from pain but anticipation. Every nerve ending surged toward that point of contact, eager for more of his touch. They could have been anywhere in the world and it wouldn't have mattered. This was her fantasy, her sweetest, most impossible dream, coming to life in the darkness.

"These are your tools," he murmured. "A treasure." His lips brushed her palm. "Precious."

This time when her fingers curled, it was to caress his scruffy bearded cheek. She relished the texture, the whiskers a delicious rasp against her skin.

He leaned into her touch and dropped to his knees in front of her.

"Mark?" The move was so unexpected she worried he'd been injured. "What's wrong?" His arms came around her waist and he pressed his face to her midriff. "Are you hurt?"

"No." He cleared his throat. "I'm so damn relieved you're okay." He gave her a squeeze. "We need to rest. Eaton will come on strong tomorrow."

Rest? She'd been anticipating another kiss, her body primed and ready. She ran her hands over his hair, the back of his neck. His arms banded even more tightly around her. She stroked his shoulders. He was a feast for her hands, all these sculpted swells and angles. Knowing him all her life, her mind filled in the details her eyes couldn't see well in the dark.

"I need—" She bit back the words. They weren't the last two people on earth. Hank and his investigators had clues. They would be rescued. Together. She had no business begging for more than he wanted to give.

"That need is just adrenaline," he murmured, easing back to sit down.

She dropped down beside him. "Oh, it's more," she admitted, though it would be best to turn this back to friendly territory. She thought of the woman who'd left him. Was Charlotte doing Mark any favors if she pushed for a connection he wasn't ready to make?

No.

Even if her body was brimming with desire, his body had been put through the wringer for days. He needed the rest. "Do you think it's safe to go down to the water?" she asked.

"Why?"

"I thought a moonlight swim might feel good."

He cocked his head, his expression too shadowed to read. "More five-star resort fantasies?"

"Something like that," she said, as if she extended this sort of invitation all the time.

He rolled to his feet and reached back to help her up. "I'm game. We can do some reconnoitering."

They walked down to the water, side by side, without touching. The world seemed so still, only the movement of the clouds overhead and the waves lapping at the sand made the moment real.

She saw Mark gazing intently up and down the coastline, to evaluate their surroundings. He'd get a better view once they were in the water, so this little respite would refresh and provide them with information.

She sat down to take off the boots and Mark stripped out of the scrubs and waded into the water, wearing only knit boxers. What she wouldn't give to share this moment on a sunny day to enjoy the view of him. At least the low light camouflaged the worst of his bruises. The sand squished under her toes as she wriggled out of the pants but when she reached for the hem of her top, Mark balked.

"What are you doing?"

"I'd planned to swim."

"But you—" He cleared his throat. "You don't have a swimsuit."

She swallowed her surprise and a flash of annoyance. "That didn't stop you." She tossed the top back on the sand and walked into the water.

"Charlotte." He groaned and ducked under the water. Coming up again, he scrubbed at his face.

She submerged herself for the sake of his newfound modesty. "When did you get so sensitive?"

"I'm not." The clouds parted and the moonlight spilled over them. "It's just…it's you."

What did that mean? This was the perfect time to confess her crush, to tell him he'd always been loved, he just didn't know it. "I get it. Go on and swim. Relax. The water must feel good."

"It does," he admitted, lying back to float. "We're safe here. I don't see anything indicating trouble. We can grab a few moments to relax. We need it."

She waded deep, scolding herself for expecting too much. She willed her thoughts away from what wouldn't happen tonight, trying to think of how she would resume her old life. That's how it felt. Old. Before. She already knew these days had changed her irrevocably, would change how she painted, how she interpreted the world. Recovering from this ordeal would show up on the canvas, but her artist retreat seemed more important than ever.

"Charlotte?" Mark floated closer to her. "When you were getting muddy in the creek, I thought I'd lose my mind wanting to touch you."

She stared at him. How had he kept *that* to himself?

Then again, she'd been holding on to a pretty big secret herself.

"If we were at the five-star resort, how would this play out?" he asked.

Returning to the diversion they'd used before made it easier. "You'd kiss me."

The words were barely past her lips when he laid claim to her mouth. Nothing gentle or easy this time, just pent-up need and desire. His tongue stroked across hers and she ached for more. Drawing her body flush against his, he boosted her up. The new angle put her in charge. She wrapped her legs around his hips and gasped at the feel of his erection at her core.

That alone was enough to take her right to the edge. She was shocked the thin layers of fabric between them didn't simply dissolve.

He arched her back and trailed kisses down her throat, lower to her breasts until he was circling her nipple with his tongue, drawing the tight bud into his mouth. "You're glorious," he said against her skin.

He made her *feel* glorious.

She reveled in the sensual onslaught, as he teased and pleasured her body. Careful of his injuries, she sought out the caresses that made him groan with desire as the night ocean flowed around them. She wanted him inside her but he held back, bringing her to a peak with his hands and the most astonishing kisses.

After her second climax, she dropped her forehead to his shoulder. She wanted to take him deep inside, to feel him filling her, but she suspected the past sorrow haunted him. Following her intuition, she wrapped her hand around his erection, refusing to be distracted or diverted this time. His hips flexed into her touch as she stroked him until he found his release.

She touched her nose to his and feathered kisses across his lips. He held her close and leaned back, letting the waves nudge them toward the shore. Neither one of them spoke until they were back in the shelter he'd fashioned for them earlier.

"Would you just hold my hand?" she asked. "Until we fall asleep?"

"Sure." His husky reply scraped over her senses and gave her chills. This close to him, she couldn't hide the shiver.

"Cold?" he asked, curling his body around her and pillowing her head with his arm.

"Not exactly." She was still on fire, for him. It felt amazing, and absolutely right, to lie here with him. Maybe it was the endorphin rush, but she was done holding back. "I want to make love to you."

"I think we've crossed enough lines burning off the adrenaline tonight," he said.

"That wasn't just adrenaline." She took a deep breath. He'd bared his soul; it was her turn. "I've had a crush on you for more than half my life," she began. "I might never have told you, but if something happens tomorrow or the day after…well, I don't want to carry regrets. I love you, Mark. I've felt that way long enough to know my heart will always be yours first whether we're friends or lovers, in the same room or on opposite sides of the world."

He didn't reply. She waited, but he didn't say a word. If his body hadn't gone so still, she might have thought he'd fallen asleep.

She pressed her lips together and closed her eyes tight so she wouldn't cry. No regrets. Things might be difficult and awkward, assuming they survived tomorrow, but it was better for him to know.

Mark told himself he was hallucinating. She did *not* just say what he thought he'd heard.

She *loved* him?

He couldn't make that fit. Attraction, healthy desire between two consenting adults was understandable. But love? No way. She wouldn't have kept *that* bottled up all this time.

It had to be the situation. He was all wrong for her, with a chronic sarcasm habit, and he took pride in his job on a team of warriors. He gently shifted her in his arms, wishing for better light to see her eyes.

"You're mad," she whispered.

He kissed her, helpless to do anything else. "Shell-shocked is a better word." He focused on what made sense. Physical pleasure and needs. He wanted to make love too, but they weren't actually in a five-star resort. He wouldn't take that risk out here without protection or the basics, like a bed.

"This isn't a living-in-the-moment thing." Her voice drifted around him, as soft as a fog bank. "I've held back my true feelings for you for too long. You deserve to know."

"Lottie." His lips found hers again. "You..." He didn't want to offend her, but he couldn't accept this, couldn't encourage something that was wrong for her. "You're everything light and joyful. I'm too much of everything you don't need."

"That's not how I see it. You're warm and kind under all the skills and distance you need for your career. You're one of the most balanced people I know," she said. "Every artist knows light needs the dark to really shine."

"You can't mean it," he insisted.

"I do. I've traveled, dated, been in relationships. No one else is you."

"Luke is practically me," he joked, hiding behind the humor while he sorted out this pressure building in his chest.

She didn't laugh. Her only response was to trail a finger over his lips. She rolled over and snuggled her back to his chest. "You were right. We need to rest."

He wrapped himself around her, sheltering her, but he didn't sleep. That hard emptiness he'd been dealing with since Maria's betrayal seemed smaller. Letting Lottie in wasn't soothing. His heart kicked, resisting the risk and danger that came along with the pleasure and comfort he found in her arms.

What if Lottie suddenly came to her senses one day and walked away? That would destroy him, not to mention the strain it would create for two generations of friendships.

And what if, as she so deftly avoided mentioning, they died tomorrow?

Tomorrow he had to get aggressive and proactive. Once they were safely out of here, they could talk rationally about whatever she thought she felt for him. He felt her body relax and while she slept, he kept watch and made plans.

Hours later, as the first glow of sunlight appeared

on the horizon, Mark was up and alert. He dealt with the necessities and then woke Charlotte with some soft kisses. Blinking, she stared up at him, then looked around as if trying to decide which part of the morning was her imagination and which was real.

"Yes, we're still stuck." He handed her a bottle of water and a meal bar. "But I have a plan."

She sat up, brushing at the salt that lingered on her arms after last night's swim. "Did you sleep?"

"I did more plotting than sleeping," he admitted. "But I'm ready to go." She was adorably kissable first thing in the morning, so he indulged himself. Her big blue eyes were full of affection and it humbled him.

He wasn't sure if she'd be aloof or distant today since he hadn't given her loving words in return last night. It wasn't as if she could just go her own way out here. Not safely. Just before dawn, he realized he should've told her he loved her too. But he couldn't say it now when they were under such ridiculous pressure.

When he gave her the words, he wanted them both to be sure he meant it.

She returned from taking care of herself, seemingly enamored with the view of the sun rising over the ocean. As she ate her meal bar, he heard her chuckle. "At the gallery show, all I wanted was a quiet sunrise on the beach," she explained.

"Happy to oblige," he teased.

"Really?"

"Hey, we built this hideout," he said. "I'm not letting Eaton take any credit for the good things."

"I can get on board with that."

His delight with her reply was muted when a seaplane engine whirred from somewhere nearby. A few minutes later, they saw it fly over their position. He waited, worried that would be Eaton doing an aerial search, but the sound faded and didn't return. "That must've been Zettel's men with the body."

"Evens the numbers, I hope." She glared at her water bottle. "Will the five-star resort have coffee?"

"Definitely." He was missing the hit of caffeine too "They'd lose a star and be disqualified from our fantasy if there's no coffee."

"Something to look forward to," she said, without much conviction.

He understood the doubts she must be feeling, but he was confident enough for both of them that today they would turn the tables on Eaton. "Make sure your laces are tied and double-knotted," he said. "We're going to be on the move."

She brightened, her eyebrows arching. "You have a plan."

"We'll take the boat today." He'd thought about it in great detail through the night. After hearing the plane leave, he felt even better. With Zettel dead and his men gone, Mark expected Eaton to send out every man he had to scour the island for them. "Barring that, we'll take the radio."

She stared up at him. "Correct me if I'm wrong, but that means going after Eaton directly," she said.

"It does," Mark replied. "It's high time he realized who he invited to this fight."

She rolled to her feet and the smile she gave him was unexpected. Radiant. Caught off guard, he didn't know quite what to say. Thankfully, she did.

"Lead the way."

He'd never been quite so inclined to kiss a teammate before a mission. The woman had facets and layers he'd never get enough of. That would be a new danger to assess once they got out of here.

"First stop, the container where they held us," he said, as they set out. "I want to look for any supplies or weapons we can use against them."

Two ground stakes and a knife would be tough going against a renowned sniper who could pick them off from hundreds of yards away. The terrain was the only thing working in their favor. In addition to weapons, Mark wanted to find a workable pair of shoes and some real food.

He set a brisk pace, pleased that Charlotte kept up. After yesterday, he had a good feel for the pattern of the camera network Eaton had planted. Today, he had no intention of avoiding or disabling all of them.

Every guard sent to intercept him and Charlotte meant less protection at the locations he planned to attack. Only a few minutes after purposely ignoring a camera, Mark heard someone closing in behind them.

At his hand signal, Charlotte ducked behind the wide trunk of a live oak tree, leaving him free to handle the threat. He pulled the knife and waited for the man on their tail to charge.

The fight was over before it began. The grossly unprepared guard came straight at Mark and within seconds Mark slammed him into the ground, knocking the wind out of the man. He stared up at the sky, gasping like a landed fish.

Using the guard's Taser, Mark incapacitated him

and cuffed him to the nearest tree. This guard's boots were too small for him, as well. Were his feet really that big? Irritated and hungry, he roused the guard. "Where are we?"

The man shrugged and Mark shook him hard. "Tell me."

"G-Georgia coast."

Progress at last. "How many of you are out here?" he demanded.

The guard shook his head. "Dunno."

Mark raised his fist and the guard mumbled a reply, his words nearly unintelligible thanks to the jolt of the Taser. "How many?" Mark repeated. "I know about Eaton, the big guy and his skinny friend." He ticked off the opposition on his fingers. "How many more?"

"Th-thr-three," the man managed at last.

"Counting you?"

The man nodded.

Satisfied, Mark used the man's sock as a gag and then flung his boots into the brush.

"Us against six?" Charlotte asked, emerging from her hiding place.

Mark nodded. "Five now." And he wanted to save Muscle for last. Not because he was afraid of the fight. No, he wanted to take his time with that nasty brute.

They made it to what passed for a headquarters without further trouble. As he'd expected, Eaton had abandoned the office and cage room, leaving the doors unlocked. Sensing a trap, Mark didn't go inside. He didn't care about the bulletin board. If Eaton and his laptop or radio were here, the man would be gloating and throwing out challenges by now.

Someone had tried to disguise a path leading from the container where they'd been held into the trees, but they found it. Cautiously, they followed the trail to an established campsite. Two hammocks were still strung up between trees. A box of trash, a cooler and a small locker were all that was left. No weapons, food or boots.

Charlotte turned in a circle. "You think they're coming back or did they leave in a hurry?"

"Probably left in a hurry," he said. "No reason to stay out here during the storm when they had the boat."

"There's a soda here," Charlotte said, rooting through the cooler. "Do you want to share some caffeine?"

"Yes, please." He didn't care that it was lukewarm, the carbonation felt great on his sore throat. The only items in the locker were a black T-shirt and a pair of flip-flops. He shoved his weary feet into the sandals and decided some protection was better than none.

The hair on the back of his neck lifted and although he couldn't spot the threat immediately, he obeyed his instincts. "Let's get to the dock." They were too exposed out here in the clearing.

Mark hiked along, Charlotte just behind him, his flip-flops slapping against his feet.

"Why aren't you worried about the noise today?"

"Because every one of us on the island knows the score," he replied. "Eaton has the matchup he wants, a SEAL with a code of honor and a family friend to protect. He wants to goad me into becoming a killer and catch me in action on one of these cameras."

"But you're not doing that."

"You and I know that, but he won't stop trying." The only man he wanted to kill was Eaton, to ensure Charlotte and his family could be safe from now on. That didn't mean he'd do it on camera. Or kill him at all. He did work from a code and had no plans to take lethal action unless it became a matter of survival. "I'd rather see Eaton prosecuted and jailed for the rest of his life."

He veered away from the established paths, staying within the shelter of the trees as they neared the dock.

Charlotte grabbed his arm. "Where's the boat?"

"I'm guessing it's anchored out of sight. Makes sense to send it away so we can't steal it."

"You aren't worried he expected us to come here?"

"No," Mark replied. "I'm disappointed, but it's simple logic." Surely by now Hank or his dad had enough information to narrow down a search area. The investigators would pore over every pixel from every image available. "We just have to hang on until the rescue party arrives."

"Then that's what we'll do." Charlotte's grip eased and she rubbed his arm. People were looking for them. He had to keep believing it, keep reminding her to believe, despite the lack of evidence.

Charlotte tensed as the guard patrolling the empty dock turned toward them, his gaze skimming over their position in a standard watch cycle. He was another one of the new guys. He had a pistol in a holster on one hip and a radio on the other.

Eaton wanted clear communication today. Good.

That left one new face still unaccounted for, likely someone watching the camera feeds and reporting their movements to Eaton. Didn't matter. Nothing short of a nuclear strike would derail his plans to get Charlotte safely off this island.

No boat posed a problem. What did he need to do to bring that boat back into the dock?

"Mark?"

"I'm thinking." No boat meant no easy access to a long-range radio. It was time to get aggressive. Hard to believe Eaton was fool enough to strand himself out here with a highly trained navy weapon.

"Eaton isn't the type to work without an exit strategy," he said. "There must be another boat or a specific rendezvous time." He watched the guard continue pacing his watch.

Mark wanted that radio. Was it a trap? "We're off the Georgia coast," he said, thinking out loud. "We have one boat and one new guy unaccounted for. Eaton and the two guards we know are still around somewhere." He shook his head. "We need to find an advantage."

"You're the real advantage," Charlotte said.

He took his eyes off the guard long enough to admire the soft curve of her cheek. Despite the stress, the tangled hair and smudges of ocean salt and island grime, her beauty struck him. Her consistent demonstrations of resilience and grit were even more attractive.

She caught him staring, arched an eyebrow. "What?"

The answer was a list way too long to enumerate here and now. "*We* are the advantage," he said. "Us, together. They underestimate you. We also have surprise, will and sneakiness on our side."

She held his gaze, one eyebrow arched as if she was waiting for the punch line.

There wasn't one. Together they could do this. "They don't expect us to split up," Mark said, jerking his mind back to the issue at hand. "I want you to stay right here and watch the dock. I'm going to draw the guard away."

"And reduce the odds."

"Exactly." He caught her chin lightly and kissed her. Creeping away, he moved with the breeze until he was ready to be seen.

He looked back, pleased that he had to work to spy Charlotte, though he knew where she was hiding. She'd adapted quickly to the survival game and he hated that he hadn't been able to spare her this craziness.

Despite it all, she kept her fight and inner glow. That was her real strength. She'd given him so much through this ordeal. Her engaging conversations had carried him through the worst of some painful beatings. Kissing her was a new adventure in desire every time their lips touched. And last night, her words had undone him. He'd been so tempted to make love to her, even without any protection, just to show her everything he didn't dare say out loud.

She'd made being kidnapped by a madman almost a good thing.

When they got out of this, he expected her to come to her senses. Knowing that, he kept the mushy, needy words locked down tight. His career would definitely kill the sweet family-filled future his heart wanted to promise her.

Charlotte deserved better. A man who would be there for her, put down roots and build a life without darting away to carry out lethal actions around the globe. He still had a few years of tactical operations and combat missions ahead of him. He'd seen worry and doubt ruin marriages, not to mention the mess he'd made with

Maria. He'd watched men give up choice assignments
and take administrative paths to please their wives. He
didn't want to be the source of her worry and he didn't
want to push paper, so where did that leave them?

First things first, he thought, as the guard turned
his way again.

Mark stumbled forward and let out a cry as if he was
in pain. The poor sap fell for it, rushing up the dock, gun
aimed at Mark's chest, shouting into his radio.

Mark raised his hands, swallowed his pride and
begged the guard not to shoot.

"Stop moving." The guard kept his gun level with
Mark's chest. "The boss wants you alive. On your knees.
Keep your hands up." The barrel of the weapon remained trained on the same spot, center mass, as Mark
complied.

"Do you have any water?" Mark had noticed the top
of a water bottle poking up from one of the pockets on
the leg of the man's cargo pants.

"Not for you."

"Please," Mark begged, adding a dry hacking cough
for good measure. "Please. I'm so thirsty."

The man stared a moment and then handed over the
bottle. It hadn't even been opened yet. He didn't know
it, but that small kindness just saved his life.

Mark sipped greedily, watching the guard search the
surrounding area. "Thank you. What's your name?"

"John Doe," the guard replied.

"Right." Did Eaton give his hired muscle a training manual? "I'll call you J.D.," Mark said, wiping his
mouth with the back of his hand. "Whatever he's paying you, I'll double it if you help me get out of here."

J.D. sneered. "I've been paid, thanks. And there's a bonus waiting when we're done. Get up."

Mark made a production out of standing up, judging how to make a clean grab for the radio. "Come on, I don't even know why I'm here. Your boss is playing a really sick game."

"Shut up, Riley."

Being addressed by his name caught him off guard. J.D. jabbed him in the chest with the barrel of his gun and Mark stumbled back. "Turn around and let's move."

"Can't we sit out here?" Mark asked.

"Not your call, is it?" This time the gun caught him in the shoulder, twisting his torso and jabbing a particularly sore spot. "Move."

"You know who I am, so you know the navy will want me back. Name your price, J.D. Be rich by this time next week."

The guard snorted, but Mark could tell he was thinking it over. "Man, anything you want, I'll give you. Just get me out of here alive."

The guard jerked his head back toward the dock. "Are you blind? The boat's gone. We're all stuck on this glorified sandbar until further notice. Now, where'd you stash your pretty friend?" J.D.'s gaze searched the immediate vicinity for Charlotte.

"We got separated," Mark lied. "She's probably dead by now."

"Nah. They told me you were some kind of hero." J.D. circled his finger in Mark's face. "I think she's close. Call her out and I'll let you both go. Give you a good head start before the boss uses you for target practice."

Mark wasn't about to expose Charlotte to any further harassment or pain. "I told you, I don't know where she is. She was rambling about getting to the creek and…"

The guard toggled his radio, asking for orders that didn't come. He shoved Mark forward. "I'll just take you back and dump you in a cage."

Mark dragged his feet and stumbled away from the dock and closer to Charlotte's hiding place. He had the terrain memorized, knew exactly where he wanted to make his move once they were past her.

The path between the dock and the cage room meandered around the bigger trees. At a sharp bend, Mark spun around and grabbed the gun. He jerked J.D. face-first into the tree trunk and followed up with a driving blow of his elbow into the guard's sternum.

Done correctly, the move would shock an opponent's heart and incapacitate them. Either Mark missed or hadn't put enough force behind the blow. J.D. fell hard but didn't stay down. They wrestled for control of the gun in a life-and-death game of tug-of-war. In peak condition, it wouldn't have been a fight at all, but the abuse and stress had dulled Mark's edge.

J.D. twisted around and swept Mark's legs out from under him. Mark scrambled to get some distance, only to be caught around the ankle. He landed a kick to J.D.'s shoulder and even without a boot, the guard howled in pain. The other guards would descend on them in a hurry, but this wasn't where he wanted to make his last stand.

Riding a burst of adrenaline, Mark jumped to his feet and went for the gun again, but J.D. wrenched it out of his hands. Mark plowed a foot into one of J.D.'s knees, but the kick lacked enough power to do any real damage. He picked up a rock, determined to put this guard down permanently, when a scream lanced through the air.

Charlotte.

Mark reacted. He dropped the rock and then grabbed the guard's ankle, twisted his leg awkwardly around a tree. J.D. screamed. Too bad. Mark had to be sure the man couldn't follow him.

He grabbed the gun and the radio that had been broken in the fight. Heedless of his bare feet, he raced toward Charlotte's cry.

Chapter 12

Swinging upside down, tethered to a high limb by her ankle, Charlotte cursed every useless tear dripping into her hair. Furious she'd been caught, angrier still that she'd screamed, she tried again and again to reach the knotted rope around her ankle. Calling herself names, she thought she might as well have sent Eaton or anyone else on the island an engraved invitation to her demise.

Following Mark's instructions, she'd been watching the water beyond the dock for any activity while listening for Eaton and the others closing in on him from the island. The only voices had been Mark's and the guard he nicknamed J.D. She hadn't heard any radio response to the guard's calls. Since the night they'd been kidnapped, she'd seen firsthand a wide range of Mark's skills and tolerances. His acting skills impressed her as much as all of the others as he manipulated the guard, luring him away from the dock.

He'd told her to stay put and watch. She'd meant to do only that. But when she noticed the stack of crates near the trees on the other side of the path, she couldn't help but take a closer look. The promise of bottled water and the potential of finding a weapon was a draw she couldn't resist.

She'd walked right into a trap. And because she'd screamed, she knew Mark would do his best to get to her. They might both be caught again. Recalling the cages and the brutality Mark endured, guilt swamped her. She didn't want any more of his blood on her hands. She resolved to get herself out of this snare. Mark couldn't be expected to do everything for her, not even out here.

The pack thumped against her back as she twisted, trying to get a hand on one of the stakes to cut herself down. A bloodcurdling scream sailed through the air and Charlotte froze. Praying that hadn't been Mark, she jackknifed at the waist in another effort to escape. It wasn't enough. She swore under her breath. Anything to give release to the frustration.

"Easy there, love."

She twisted around to see Mark step into her upside-down view. "I'm sorry." She flung a hand toward the crates. "Water and a gun… They're probably empty," she grumbled.

"I get it. Would've done the same." He walked a circle around her predicament while she swung like a sack of potatoes. He was barefoot again and she wanted to cry. He must have tossed the flip-flops in order to run to her aid. Guilt was a rash of sharp prickles under her skin while he searched for a secondary trip wire.

"I'm sorry," she muttered again. "How'd things go with J.D.?"

"He won't be taking any long walks for a while." Mark set the gun down and pulled the knife out of the backpack. "The effort wasn't a total loss."

"Yay," she cheered with fake enthusiasm. "Is anyone else headed this way?"

"Not so far," he replied.

"You should go," she said. "Hide until they come for me."

"Not a good play."

She disagreed completely. He could hide and pick off whoever came for her.

He gazed above her at the rope. "Let me make sure cutting you down doesn't trigger some other trap. How's your head?" he asked.

It took a second to follow the conversational leap. "Aches." In fact, her vision was starting to blur. "Hazy."

"Sure, sure."

"I should have spent more time on abs at the gym."

"Your abs are fine," he said, laughing a little. "I saw them just last night."

Stopping directly under her, the snare kept his face just out of kissing range. But she could touch him, so that was a bonus. She ran her fingertips across his beard, swaying a little with the motion, unless that was only an effect of her blurred vision. "Are there two of you?"

"You wish." His lips twitched.

"Don't you dare laugh," she ordered.

"Lottie, you put the cute in life-and-death situations."

"That doesn't even make sense," she said.

"It doesn't." He seemed to say it more to himself than to her. His gaze tracked up the length of her body to the rope again and presumably to where the line was anchored. "I bet you'd do just about anything for this knife right now."

"Stop teasing and get me down." She was terrified Eaton would catch them both and the nightmare would start over again. "Better yet, just leave me here and capture Eaton when he shows up." Had she said that? Becoming bait wasn't the worst idea. She'd finally be an asset rather than a burden.

"You've suggested that."

"I did?" It was getting harder to think clearly. "Did you like the idea?"

"No," he replied. "I'm not leaving you like this."

"Think about it," she urged, twisting to try to keep him in sight.

"Hush."

He went perfectly still. Or she thought he did. It was hard to tell when a breeze caught the tree and set her in motion again. The pounding of blood in her ears made it harder to hear anything else. Was it too late for Mark to set a countertrap?

"Hide." She waved her hands for him to run, but as she twisted around, she couldn't see Mark at all.

In the distance, she heard Eaton barking out orders. It was impossible for her to determine if he was talking to someone directly or using the radio Mark wanted so badly. She couldn't make out his words, though that didn't matter to her as much as making sure Mark got away safely.

Fighting the tunnel vision and pressure from hanging upside down, she vowed to fight back, stall or otherwise impede Eaton's plan. She'd do whatever was necessary to give Mark a chance to escape.

Suddenly the ground surged up to meet her and a big drab olive shadow blocked her vision. Mark's leg, she realized slowly. He'd added his weight to the snare line. She could touch the ground with her fingertips, but she wasn't free.

"Almost done. Protect your head and neck," he whispered. "Going down," he continued like an elevator operator.

She did her best, willing him to hurry. In a moment, her body dropped and she curled in on herself as she hit the ground. What were a few more bruises among friends?

Before she could stand, Mark was at her side, cutting away the rope knotted around her ankle. He helped her up, giving her a steady anchor point as her blood flow resumed a normal healthy pattern away from her head. Her vision still fuzzy, she had no idea where he was taking her until the blast of sunshine caught her in the face. She winced and shied away.

"Keep going, you're doing great," Mark encouraged. "They probably know by now that I have the guard's gun and radio. It will give them something to think about."

Believing him took less energy than arguing and it was far more pleasant to think she really wasn't the problem child out here.

She heard a shout behind them and this time the

sound was clear, close and furious. Either her hearing had improved or Eaton was practically on top of them.

"I'm sorry, sweetheart," Mark said.

She could smell the brackish water of the creek and knew what he intended. "Beats death by madman," she quipped, following him into the murky water. Once more the creek bought them precious seconds.

When Mark gave the all clear, she climbed to the opposite bank, grateful they had several hours of sunshine to dry their soggy clothes.

"Why didn't you just kill Eaton back there?"

"I thought about it," he admitted. He used his hands to squeeze the water from her hair.

His gaze turned possessive as he studied her face. Suddenly, the sunlight wasn't the source of the heat coursing through her system. It was a wonder her clothing didn't instantly steam dry. When his thumbs glided over her cheekbones, she thought she'd melt from the tenderness in his touch. "You were fading," he said. "Besides, if I'd missed, you would have been hurt."

"You don't miss."

His lips kicked to one side. "Your confidence notwithstanding, I couldn't take that kind of chance with you."

"But—"

"No buts, Charlotte. When we get off this island, you *will* be in one piece." He kissed her, a sweet, gentle assurance for both of them. "You'll be able, mind and body, to return to the life you've made for yourself. Anything less is a failure in my eyes."

"Mark…" She couldn't articulate everything his words and hands and lips stirred up inside her. Not when he touched her with so much love while at the same time he spoke of going their separate ways when this ordeal was behind them. It hurt that he seemed so determined to walk away from the connection and passion she felt growing between them.

Love was patient, she reminded herself. And love didn't look anything like she thought it might or should. Her infatuation with him had only been the first spark. What she felt now was something so different and deep. It was a fresh and unexpected view of the man she thought she'd known. She started to try again, but she could tell by his narrowed gaze that he'd snapped back into survival-guide mode.

"We need to dry out and find a safe place for the night."

"It's not even noon yet." She tipped her head back, trying to peer at the sun's position in the sky.

She trudged after him, feeling another stab of guilt that he was barefoot again. As much as she'd previously protested the option, she was more and more convinced that he should park her somewhere and just finish this on his own. When he looked at her, he couldn't see anything more than an obligation. A pretty one, by his words, but still an extra person he had to keep track of. She was making his survival harder. Maybe now that they had a gun he would implement the stash-the-inept-girl plan. She could defend a secure position with a loaded weapon.

"Promise me something?" She wanted several promises from him, but this time the most important one was about making sure he'd take care of himself.

"Whatever you need," he replied without looking back at her.

"When we get out of here, promise me you'll get a pedicure and then never go barefoot again."

"That sounds…"

"Delightful?" she supplied when he was lost for words. "Luxurious? The right thing to do for your poor, abused feet?"

He turned, a grin spreading across his face and the dimple flashing in his cheek. "Horrific. Besides, according to those cheesy romantic movies my sisters watched, walking barefoot on the beach beats paying someone to exfoliate. Plenty of room to do that right here."

She remembered a line like that from a movie she and Jolene had watched on one of their boisterous dual-family vacations. "But you have to follow up the exfoliation with hydration and preferably shoes," she said.

"One step at a time," he teased.

When he looked at her that way, those silly youthful fantasies of Mark sweeping into her life like those teenage heroes filled her head and carried her away to a sweet place without cages, guns and men bent on violent revenge.

Until a chunk of the tree on the other side of Mark's head exploded.

Mark gathered Charlotte into his arms and took them both to the ground, his body covering hers.

All this time, Eaton had let others do the dirty work. Finally the man was pulling the trigger himself. Of course, that was little comfort considering he was a world-class sniper, willing to take the hard shots.

They were too far from the creek now for that escape route. Putting himself between the gunfire and Charlotte, he pushed her along ahead of him, deeper into the trees. In this area, it was impossible not to leave a trail through the ferns and fallen leaves and needles of scrub pines.

Sure enough, bullets followed their movement, biting into the bark here and there. The man was missing on purpose. The movement they made scrambling through the trees might as well be a beacon to a shooter of Eaton's skills.

Charlotte's body jerked with every shot and Mark's temper rose in response. She didn't deserve this. No one did, but especially not a woman so full of talent and light. The world needed the hope and beauty she could offer.

Mark's mind worked through what he knew of the island. Based on the angle of the first shot and those following them now, Eaton was trying to herd them into the marsh where they'd be completely exposed. The trees were their only defense and at the same time telegraphed their movements too well.

Spying a gap created by a tree recently felled by a storm, he nudged Charlotte over the rotting log and into momentary safety. "You okay?" he whispered.

Her blue eyes were round with fear and full of worry. "I'm not wounded if that's what you mean."

"It is." Mark paused, listening for any evidence that Eaton's men were trying to flank them. "He's pushing us to the marsh."

Her hands gripped his tightly. "I don't want to hide in that water."

"I know, sweetheart." A bullet whizzed overhead, punching through a small limb. Mark covered Charlotte, letting the debris rain down across his back. He barely felt it, his mind shifting to operator mode while his body catalogued her long legs and soft curves tucked under him.

"He's guessing now," Mark said. "Do you know where we are?"

"Hell," she replied in a weary whisper.

He chuckled. "Close enough. I meant specifically."

She closed her eyes for a moment and then looked up at the sky and the trees overhead. He knew she was mentally retracing their route away from the dock.

Another bullet grazed a tree nearby. Charlotte tensed and trembled. If they'd been on the move, Eaton would have guessed their position with distressing accuracy. It also confirmed Mark's theory that the man wanted to push them to the marshes.

"The marshes are on the west side. So we must be heading in that general direction," Charlotte said, her voice pitched low. "These are live oaks and they grow thicker inland."

"You're brilliant." He smiled, more pleased than he cared to admit. "Can you get back to our camp at the cove from here?"

She nodded, her gaze drifting to his lips. Yeah, he had a long list of things he wished they'd done last night too.

"You'll need to move north and east," he said, trying to focus on saving them.

Sitting up a little, she glanced around, getting her bearings. "I can do it."

"Good. Go back there and hide behind that screen of palm leaves we made." He pressed the gun into her hands. He knew she could shoot and was familiar with a weapon like this.

"What about you? You'll need this."

He shook his head. "I'll be fine." He pulled out the radio. "I might be able to get a signal. Either way, I'll stroke Eaton's ego and let him drive *us* toward the marshes."

Her long fingers curled around his, gripping hard. "Please don't do that. It's too open."

"Shh." He cupped her cheek, giving her all the tenderness he could offer. Once they parted, he had to be ruthlessly focused on taking out the enemy. "Alone, I can get him where he wants us and come back to you."

"What about the others?"

"Dwindling numbers," he reminded her. "Someone is with the boat. It will be months before the guard from the dock can do anything after I tore up his leg."

"That still leaves Muscle and Quick-Punch Kid helping Eaton. They're rested and you've been physically punished for days. What if they're armed?"

Mark hated the fear in her eyes. Fear for him. A prickle of unease slid along his skin. He didn't know what to do with it. Did she want him thinking about failing her?

"This is what I do, baby," he said, mustering every drop of arrogance and bravado he had left. "I need you to take the gun and wait this out at the cove."

Her gaze narrowed and her full lips thinned. He held

on to that annoyance, leaned into it. This was survival. "Wait until he's following me, and then go."

"Sure."

He gazed into that lovely face, regretting his tactic immediately. He didn't want her harboring any doubt about how much he cared. Stealing a fast kiss for luck, reassurance or both, he popped up and started running.

When bullets followed him, he grinned like the fool he was.

Charlotte gazed up at the star-studded sky overhead and couldn't help thinking the island at night would be a beautiful place to unwind. Especially if she could re-move the terrors seeking them out and add spa-quality bathrooms and a well-planned picnic basket complete with good wine.

She was ridiculously proud of herself for finding the cove without getting lost. She hadn't even had a heart attack while she worried and waited for Mark to return to the cove. The occasional gunshots had done more than rattle her. She was sure her stylist would find her hair had turned gray after this.

When Mark had returned to the cove at twilight, he'd been a muddy mess, and full of himself for sending Eaton on a wild chase. His only regret had been that he hadn't been able to get the radio working to ask for help. She'd launched herself into his arms when that dimple had winked at her, not caring if he'd thought she was a worrywart. She hadn't been able to help it. He wasn't just her best hope of getting out of here alive. He held her heart and always would.

No amount of that brusque-and-brave-warrior routine could change that.

After going for a swim and downing a meal bar, he'd stretched out beside her, but he wasn't asleep yet. She'd promised to keep watch, but she didn't think he could actually shut down. He'd done everything short of building a raft to escape. Knowing him, he'd probably thought of it and rejected the idea because it would make them easy targets as they floated out to sea.

She continued to watch the sky, debating how best to get all those layers of darkness to sink into the canvas and reach back out again. In the sky at full dark, she saw the immense, limitless beauty. "I'll paint this sky when we're home," she murmured. To purge the dread and reclaim the good, she would paint this sky.

"You *want* to remember this place?"

"Why would I want to forget your bravery and courage?" she countered. She'd never forget his kiss or his touch, the exquisite pleasure he'd given her. She surely wouldn't forget the way he kept putting her safety and well-being above his own. "You've taught me tactics and directions and other things I didn't know I wanted to learn."

"You wouldn't need to learn any of it if I hadn't followed you into the alley."

The idea of him out here, coping with Eaton alone, sent a fresh spike of icy fear down her spine. "Sounds like it's my turn to remind you that someone is looking for us. We need to stay positive."

"But will they find us in time? I'm sorry." He sat up a little, his silhouette blotting out a chunk of the sky and filling her creative mind with more ideas for another series of nightscapes. "I can't help wondering that if someone was coming to help, they'd be here by now."

"We took out the cameras, with good reason," she added hastily. The less Eaton could use against the general, the better.

"We have to end this," Mark said. "I can't ask you to deal with this for one more day."

"It would be over by now if the boat had been there," Charlotte reminded him. "We'll make it." She flopped to her back once more. The deep velvet-black sky, dotted with stars, winked overhead through the swaying palms as the wind picked up.

The breeze through the palm fronds was constant, just like the steady beat of the ocean against the shore or her boundless love for the man beside her. She turned her head, admiring Mark's strong profile. This man was a constant, as well. Take away the guns and the madman and there were worse things than being stranded on an island with a sexy, affectionate man.

"Charlotte?" he asked, turning to her. "You with me?"

Always. In any time or place, she was his. Following the welcome distraction, her artist's memory filled in the details of his face that the shadows blurred. "I'm with you," she replied. She might not be survival trained like he was, but even she recognized they wouldn't last out here indefinitely. "Are we planning our five-star resort or a way off the island?"

He didn't laugh. Instead he rolled to his side, facing her, almost nose to nose. "I'm thinking we need to surrender. It would draw Eaton in and we could negotiate to get you out of here."

"No." He had to discard this plan immediately. "I am *not* leaving this island without you." Her heart thumped in her chest at the thought of returning to civilization without him.

"Even if it's the only way to save your life?" He trailed a finger along her jaw.

She reached up, covering his hand, holding the touch close as though she could absorb still more of his courage through her skin. It stung a little, acknowledging how much she must be holding him back, though she'd done her best to keep up. "If we go to the dock and surrender, he'll kill you from a hundred yards out and not bother to ask me questions later. He's not going to give me up just because you want him to." At his sigh, she added, "You know I'm right."

"It's still four against two, Lottie, and the one radio I stole was busted."

"We'll make another plan, Mark."

He rolled to his back again and he was quiet for so long she thought he'd fallen asleep.

"Eaton intends to survive at all costs," he said.

"Obviously." She reached for his hand, laced her fingers through his. "So do we. We have a gun, a knife and two stakes. I think the odds are in our favor."

"I like your ruthless side."

She heard that sexy, unrepentant grin in his voice. "Thanks. Now, without a boat, how do we make tomorrow our last day in paradise?"

"He isn't leaving until I'm dead or until I break and kill a bunch of people on camera. Can you think of a way to fake either of those scenarios?"

She knew he didn't expect her to have an answer,

but still she tried to come up with something. "What about the flare gun?"

"Who would we signal?" he asked.

"I'm thinking about what Eaton would do if we set the dock or part of the island on fire. It's not ideal, but I think our lives outrank nature in this scenario."

"Tell me more," he urged.

"Well, if we successfully set something on fire, it might be seen from a boat out on the water."

"That's a plus for as long as the fire burns," he said.

"You mentioned Eaton had an exit strategy. He obviously won't let anyone else kill you. Today while he thought we were together, no one came anywhere near me."

"If Muscle was helping Eaton hunt me, he was in stealth mode," Mark said, propping up on an elbow. "Quick-Punch Kid is the only other person I saw."

"Maybe Muscle took the cabin cruiser in for supplies or reinforcements. And where would that leave the third man on the new team?"

Mark was nodding now. "Guarding a second boat, maybe? It would be easy to hide something like a rigid-hull inflatable in another cove on the eastern side."

"Surplus military issue, no doubt," she said, peeved. Eaton was such a scumbag.

"No doubt." He leaned over and kissed her. "Talking it out helps."

She was immensely pleased with the praise. "So how do we win?"

"We stick together this time," Mark replied, subdued again.

Guilt swirled through her mind like a wisp of smoke,

leaving a bitter scent of failure behind. No matter what he said, her misstep in that trap today had cost them a good chance to gain any real advantage. Though he was kind enough not to blame her outright, she blamed herself.

He pressed a kiss to her palm, the gesture equally comforting and stimulating. She scooted into his embrace, momentarily forgetting the threats and consequences currently out of sight.

As his lips slanted over hers, she surrendered to the marvelous distraction of being in his arms. When he eased back, she was breathless, her pulse thundering in her ears. She laid a palm over his chest and felt his heart racing, as well. It was wonderful to be wanted by the man she loved, even if he continued to hold back. Maybe that five-star resort would be where she broke through the last of his shell.

"About that plan," he said after several long minutes.

She smothered a giggle. It wasn't at all where her mind had been. "Yes?"

"We'll wing it. You're practically a SEAL now anyway."

She curled into him, smothering her laughter over such an enormous exaggeration. His breathing settled as his amusement faded, but she knew he wouldn't sleep deeply. A part of him had kept watch from the minute they'd been kidnapped. She wished there was something she could say or do to convince him to really sleep.

That too might have to wait for the resort.

"Charlotte?" He stroked her hair back over her ear in a motion that never failed to knock her out. "Sleep while you can."

She took a long, measured breath and let it out, repeating the process a few times, but her mind was restless. However this ended, did she dare hope for some kind of romantic future?

What would that even look like? Would they go back to Virginia and start dating until he deployed again?

If they took Eaton down, she assumed Mark would be free to get back on the regular rotation with his SEAL team. Where he belonged, based on how well he'd endured these past days. She couldn't deny that.

Regret was a cold vise around her heart. In the light of a normal day, would Mark be able to look at her and not think about these days of torture and abuse? What kind of Special Forces operator would build a life with a woman so closely tied to his worst memories?

Sure, they were physically compatible, obviously, but that wasn't the kind of foundation for the relationship she wanted anyway. He hadn't given her any indication of his feelings for her, not even echoing the loving words she'd given to him. Which was absolutely fine. She appreciated that Mark didn't plant false hope when it mattered most.

His actions showed how much he cared. Caring would have to be enough for her.

She *loved* him. Not a fleeting trial-by-fire sort of affection either. No, she loved him enough that she wouldn't say it out loud again. When they were rescued and back in the real world, she'd walk away from him with her dignity so he wouldn't feel forced to push her away.

As she'd told him, her heart would always be his.

Despite the fear and terror of the ordeal, new paintings were already filling her mind and she focused her thoughts on what she wanted to create. Small and cramped canvases to challenge the audience. Open soaring views tethered to nothing but hopes and dreams. Those would likely challenge even more people. A direct encounter with death changed a person. There was no going back to the woman and artist she'd been a week ago.

If only she had the courage and skills to slip away and take out Eaton while Mark dozed.

She didn't.

She was an artist, stranded with the man she'd dreamed about for over a decade, and she had no tangible skills or recourse to help them survive.

Chapter 13

Early the next morning, before the sun was much more than a glow at the edge of the ocean, Mark roused Charlotte so they could move out. He regretted his decision to take another run at the boat almost immediately. The stress and chaos of Eaton's antics had taken a toll on Charlotte. She was trying valiantly to keep up with him, running on sheer adrenaline and desperation.

Holding her in his arms last night, the words had been on his heart. *I love you.* He couldn't push them past his lips. Not yet. If they got off the island, there would be time to make it up to her. If they didn't, there wasn't any point in declaring feelings he couldn't back up with actions.

And, as much as he prided himself on his bravery and self-confidence, he had no idea how she'd react.

Would she even want to waste another minute with him after this?

He didn't hold out much hope.

Creative problem solving was a hallmark of his career, yet he'd failed her in a spectacular manner when it had mattered most, back in the alley before things had really gone south.

They kept to the thickest part of the tree line and found the dock empty again as the sun inched over the horizon. While Charlotte stood watch, he carefully gathered up dried palms, stuffing them into an empty crate. He carried the crate to the dock and using the flare gun, he set the mass on fire. With a little luck, the fire would burn a good long time. At the very least, it should create a smoke plume and potentially catch a search party's attention.

Or the attention of the boat, bringing it closer to shore where they could more easily try to commandeer it.

Mark was kneeling at the edge of the trees with Charlotte when he heard raised voices. South of the dock, on a small crescent beach, he spotted Eaton and Quick-Punch Kid.

Eaton was the only one with a radio.

They wouldn't get that radio as long as Eaton continued breathing. The man was armed and motivated by a vast, inexorable sense of vengeance. Worse, he'd shown a remarkable lack of remorse over his actions.

Mark had no doubt that should Eaton get the chance, he'd kill Mark and Charlotte and never look back to this island. He started to give the hand signals for how he wanted to advance and realized he didn't have the team. Only Charlotte.

She'd held up, but she didn't magically know the code and signals. "I'll take out Eaton," he said, his voice barely audible as he eyed the best way forward. "Quick-Punch Kid will try and intervene, but he isn't armed, and there might be a limit to how involved he wants to be."

"I can handle him." Her voice was intense, ready. She had the gun in her hands and he had the knife ready. "I'll keep him distracted," she promised.

"Shoot him if you have to." Mark was relieved he didn't have to ask her to distract Muscle, though he had no doubt she'd happily find a reason to put a bullet in the big man. He kissed her. Fast and quick. Not a last kiss, more of a promise there would be more once the work was done.

"You do that with your SEAL team?" she teased.

"They wish," he quipped.

She clamped her lips together, her eyes dancing with laughter. In that moment, he was suddenly sure everything would work out.

He picked up a rock, hefted it in his hand and waited for the right time to strike. He hurled it, pleased when it struck Quick-Punch Kid solidly on the side of the head. The man stumbled and fell forward to his hands and knees.

Eaton turned back and Mark charged forward from the dappled shadows of the trees, the knife in his grip. He used the downed man as a springboard and launched himself into Eaton, knocking the man to the ground before he could fire. His weapon flew across the sand toward the surf.

Mark drove a knee into Eaton's gut, once, twice and a third time. The man gasped for air while Mark scrambled to get the radio off Eaton's belt. He couldn't manage it with one hand and Eaton knew it.

Eaton twisted around, landing an elbow to Mark's jaw that sent him reeling. He dropped the knife. That never would've happened before being caged and tortured and manipulated by the threats to Charlotte. Excuses didn't make a SEAL strong; adversity did. Mark blocked the next punch and bucked his hips, rolling Eaton over and finally pinning the man to the shifting sand.

Protective concern tempted him to glance over his shoulder and check on Charlotte's progress. He had to trust she could manage on her own. Eaton was too dangerous and would capitalize on the smallest opening. Distraction equaled disaster here. Mark would *not* let him land another blow. Would *not* give him another minute to exploit Charlotte or inflict emotional abuse on his family.

He dug his knees into Eaton's sides, squeezing his rib cage and impeding his breathing. Eaton wedged his body into the loose sand to get relief. It was enough to throw Mark off balance and he rolled away and up onto his feet. Eaton reached the knife before he did.

Holding the man's attention, Mark moved to put his body between Eaton and the rest of the island. If Charlotte had failed, he was now vulnerable to a sneak attack from Quick-Punch Kid. Mark didn't peek over his shoulder, he kept his eyes on Eaton.

The older man's face was red from sunburn or exertion or a combination of the two. Didn't matter. Winning this fight for Charlotte's life mattered.

"You think you're special, Riley?" Eaton taunted.

Mark ignored his taunting. The sly gleam in Eaton's eyes was enough proof that they both understood the stakes here. Only one of them would walk away from this beach.

Mark stalked closer to his prey, not giving a damn who currently had control of the knife.

Eaton lunged, Mark spun, felt his shirt give as the blade sliced through the thin fabric and his skin. The sting and burn were only more motivation. Using his momentum, he caught Eaton around the hips and threw him back toward the encroaching surf, farther away from Charlotte.

Eaton struggled to break Mark's hold and his rusty hand-to-hand combat skills made it clear why he liked to stay behind a gun. If the man hadn't had the knife, Mark wouldn't have any injuries worth mentioning as they grappled for dominance of the weapon.

The surf was sucking at the sand under their feet, challenging his balance as the water foamed up around his ankles. His hands, slippery with blood, made it hard to get a good grip. At last Mark succeeded and tossed the radio up toward Charlotte as he fell to his knees.

Eaton, yammering on with nonsensical threats and insults, let loose a violent scream of frustration as Charlotte sent out the Mayday call, just as he'd instructed her earlier.

She'd survive. It was like taking his first breath after a long dive. One way or another, she would get off this blighted island and resume the life she was meant to have, the work she was meant to give.

Eaton turned, knife raised high over his head as if he was auditioning for a remake of Hitchcock's *Psycho*. Charlotte screamed. Mark focused.

Dodging to the side, he used Eaton's power against him, driving the blade deep into the man's thigh. Shocked, mouth open, eyes glazed with pain, Eaton fell forward into the surf.

Gripping fistfuls of Eaton's shirt, Mark hauled him deeper into the water. The whole way, the man continued tossing out dire threats against all Rileys. Despite everything he'd done, with Charlotte watching from the beach, Mark might have been compelled to grant mercy if Eaton had asked. Thankfully he didn't.

Mark walked out farther, still dragging the man who'd put his family through so much fear and grief in recent months. The surf swirled around Mark's knees, buoying more of Eaton's body. The ocean was Mark's element, soothing and centering, even as the salt water illuminated every open wound.

Though Eaton thrashed, Mark held on, dragging him deeper. The man tugged to free the weapon from his leg. Blood tinted the water—his or Eaton's, Mark didn't care. He started shouting more nonsense and threats. Mark shoved his head under the water and waited. Eaton came up sputtering and cursing.

With both hands, Mark shoved him hard in the chest. Eaton stumbled backward as the surf moved over the sand. For the first time in days, Mark was grateful for the thin scrubs and his bare feet. Eaton's heavy boots and clothing were waterlogged, making it impossible for him to fight the ocean's pull.

Now, it would be man versus nature. Mark watched with detached curiosity to see who won.

Eaton flailed in the next wave and went under the surface.

Mark kept his eyes on the spot as the surf flowed out from under him and he let the rollers buoy him onto the beach, away from the blood trail flowing out of Eaton.

The man's head didn't clear the water again.

Nature had won this battle.

He hoped a shark wouldn't be injured by the knife in the man's leg.

Watching Mark in the gently rolling surf, Charlotte held her position just out of reach of the groggy Quick-Punch Kid. She'd trussed him up, using the cord of his survival bracelet to bind his hands together behind his back. She'd cinched his ankles together with his belt. He didn't put up much of a fight, either due to the head injury or simply the realization that he couldn't get out of this, she wasn't sure. He was too heavy for her to move him to a shady spot. She assumed after the coast guard arrived, sunburn would be the least of his worries.

She had control of the gun now, as well as the radio. While Mark had wrestled Eaton, she'd considered shooting their tormentor, but held back, afraid she'd hit Mark by accident.

Her hero, she thought, her heart swelling with pride and love as Mark rode the waves back to shore. Alone. Gripping one item in each hand, she held her ground, waiting for a signal from Mark that it was safe. She assumed Eaton was dead. Remorse didn't even flit through her mind.

She focused instead on Mark. He exhibited an ease in the water she'd always admired. She took a halting step toward the water. A swim might do them both some good, but she'd prefer to find a place where Eaton's body wasn't lurking under the waves.

Suddenly it was as if everything caught up with her. Her knees felt stiff, her feet sore and her entire body begged for a warm soaking bath, fragrant soaps and a head-to-toe massage. Her hands ached with the stress of staying out of Mark's fight with Eaton. Her pulse pinged oddly and her stomach clenched as if she might be sick. After everything they'd endured, this seemed like the wrong time for her body to stop cooperating. Shouldn't they be celebrating?

Forcing herself forward on wobbling knees, she went down to the tide line to meet Mark, staying clear of the bloody ruts in the sand. "Mark? Are you okay?"

"I am now."

Now she could see his shirt had been sliced and blood seeped from a long thin cut across his shoulder blade. That would leave a big scar across those perfect muscles as it healed. She didn't mind the potential imperfection. No, she struggled against the idea of another woman seeing it years from now. They'd faced impossible odds and survived. They had a shared history of sorts as family friends and they'd certainly explored a passion that had both startled them and saved them during the crisis.

She'd told Mark she loved him, but still she couldn't seem to find the courage to ask for what she really wanted. Forever had been a clear and tangible end point when Eaton was in control. Now it seemed like a wisp of something she couldn't grasp.

Life and freedom. They had both now. The wide-open possibilities of the future created a new kind of fear in her heart. Fear that these were her last moments with Mark. Her breath caught as the incoming tide swirled between her toes.

The urgent need to tell him what she hoped for most faded much as the foam skittered away to rejoin the ocean. He'd been through enough, saving them both. She wouldn't take the risk that he might see her feelings as yet another burden.

Offering only comfort, she rested her hand on the top of his shoulder, well away from the injury. "This needs stitches."

"If you say so. You can see it better than I can." He tilted his head up, blocking the sun with a hand. "You're shaking like a leaf."

"Dumb time to lose it, I know," she said.

His long fingers circled her wrist and a new shiver went through her at the touch. He tugged her down beside him in the sand and pried the radio from her grasp. "And the gun," he said, holding his palm open.

"Is he dead?"

"Unless he had oxygen tanks tethered right where I dropped him."

After what she'd seen, she wouldn't put it past him. "You're not serious?"

"No. Logically, he's fish food." Mark cocked his head, his gaze on the soft rollers rising and breaking.

"Although I wouldn't have minded watching a shark frenzy in this particular instance."

"He didn't deserve the fanfare," she said.

Mark chuckled. "I do like this bloodthirsty side of you."

Relief and need overwhelmed her. She climbed into his lap, straddling his thighs. Gently, gently, knowing he was sore and there were likely plenty of injuries she couldn't see, she took his face into her hands.

She was about as useless as could be with survival and fighting, but she knew how to bare her soul, to open that window and give back the beauty she saw in the world. With every heartbeat, she willed him to accept everything she offered, whether or not he could reciprocate.

Right now, she only wanted him to feel this astounding awareness that life was new again, all options open. Where there had been terror and fear, she would have him embrace hope and love.

When her mouth met his, when his hands cruised up and over her hips and stroked heat up the length of her spine, she started to believe the worst was done. Fresh need spiked her system and bright energy sparkled along her skin at every place their bodies touched.

"I called for help," she said as his lips and tongue glided down her throat. "On the emergency frequency."

"I heard. I knew you could do it." His voice rumbled against her skin and she trembled. "How long do we have?"

"I don't know." She didn't care. Her hips rocked against his arousal. Yes, adrenaline was a contributor here, but it wasn't the only factor. She needed all the physical affirmation she could get that they'd made it.

His hands stilled her hips, holding fast when she tried to move.

"You didn't get an answer to the Mayday?"

"I did." His grip eased. "The coast guard answered. I told them what we know of our position." She dropped her head to his shoulder and just breathed in the scent of him. If this was all he could give, she'd savor it. "I described the cabin cruiser and Muscle."

"What did they say?" he asked. "Exactly."

"Someone saw smoke from the fire we set. Help was coming since this is supposed to be an uninhabited island." She would paint the feelings of this moment and their ordeal for years to come. All the ugliness they'd endured and the glorious passion they'd shared was imprinted on her mind, body and soul. Already she knew her brush would touch the canvas differently. She could hardly wait to explore the new facets this experience revealed.

"Anything else?"

Tears burned behind her closed eyelids. She could cry later. When she was home and Mark was gone, out of her day-to-day life. "I don't know. You were fighting and I...I..." She just couldn't put her deepest fear into words. Not even with Eaton gone.

Mark had said she was light and joy and he was too dark, too jaded for her. Should she try again to explain the essential compatibility of light and shadow? As her first professor in Paris had said at the end of her time there, this interlude is at an end, but the memories would carry her as she reached for new stars.

For once it would be nice if the journey toward new stars didn't feel so lonely.

"*Shh,* it's all good." Mark smoothed a hand over her hair. "You're amazing. Just amazing, Lottie." He shifted her to sit beside him again and then seemed to melt into the warm, damp sand. "Let's just breathe here for a minute."

"You need water. First aid."

"Later. Just be here with me."

She stared into his face, still handsome under the mosaic of cuts and bruises Eaton had dished out. "You're the most beautiful man I've ever seen."

"Now I know you've had a heatstroke." His lips twitched in a faint echo of the teasing smirk he used to flash all the time. His eyes flew open, alert and ready once more. "Or hit your head. Did Quick-Punch Kid hurt you?"

"Easy," she soothed him this time. "I'm fine." Especially now that she knew he was mostly okay. "You're the one still bleeding."

He'd taken the brunt of Eaton's vengeance since that first moment in the alley behind the gallery. It seemed a lifetime ago.

"A scratch," he insisted.

"If you're sure."

He reached up and cupped her neck, bringing her face close for a kiss. She lost herself in the gentle affection and now-familiar heat of desire. Until she recognized the bone-deep weariness that echoed her own.

Lifting her head, she bumped her nose to his, then rolled to her back. Her hand found his and they stared up at the impossibly blue sky. "We'll rest and breathe until the coast guard arrives."

It was the best plan they'd made in recent days.

Hours or minutes passed. Quick-Punch Kid shouted and was summarily ignored. The shadows from the trees shifted as the sun moved higher into the sky. And the two of them rested, breathing it all in until at last the radio crackled to life and the commanding voice of General Riley asked for confirmation of their position.

Mark handled that call while Charlotte tried not to cry.

At the unmistakable sound of a helicopter rotor, she sat up and waved at the orange coast guard rescue helicopter overhead. A few minutes later a coast guard cutter came into view, trailed closely by the Rileys' sailboat. Her emotions simply overflowed and she was laughing and crying with relief and joy as Mark pulled her to her feet and held her close, keeping her steady.

Rescued! They could finally rest easy, completely safe for the first time in far too long.

If only she didn't feel as if her first steps toward rescue and freedom meant walking away from loving Mark.

Chapter 14

Mark watched Charlotte's parents hustle her away, toward a guest cabin on the ship where she could clean up and a doctor would tend to any wounds. With each bit of distance, the ordeal they'd survived pressed heavier on his shoulders. He thought it would have been the opposite.

When she was out of sight, his breath just stalled in his chest. This wasn't how things were supposed to end. He didn't want to be apart from her; he'd grown too close during their ordeal. Why now, when she was out of reach, did he finally have the courage to give her the words? As if tethered by some invisible bond, he lurched after her.

His dad clapped him on the shoulder, steered him down a passage and into another room. "Clean up. Let the medic deal with the mess you're in while we talk."

He didn't want to talk. Not to his parents and not about the man he'd hauled into the ocean to die. He wanted Charlotte all to himself for a month in Fiji. Even in his mind, he sounded petulant.

Alone in the shower, he indulged in a fantasy of Charlotte in a skimpy bikini the same color as her eyes, reclining next to an infinity pool. She'd give him that slow smile and joke that any shot at fame had been wrecked by the rescue.

His hand trembled as he reached for the soap dispenser. If she was here with him, where she belonged, she'd take his trembling hand in hers and steady him. The woman was a rock. Through it all, she'd been his touchstone, his focal point. Keeping him grounded and boosting his determination.

He wondered if she felt as lost without him.

Clean up now. Break down later. He showered off the days of grime, watching blood and dirt and sand swirl around and down the drain. He toweled off, regretting the streaks of blood his wounds left on the white terry cloth towel. He avoided the mirror as he brushed his teeth. There was no need for a visual to know where the bruises were. He trimmed his beard, careful around the tender spots on his jaw. His ribs would ache for another week at least.

With the towel wrapped around his waist, he stepped out of the bathroom. His father and a medic were waiting in the cabin.

"Feel any better?" his dad asked.

"Ask me again after you give me a beer."

Ben laughed. The medic directed him to a chair and

worked swiftly, taking a quick inventory of his wounds and treating each in turn.

"You did well, son."

Well. Not the word he'd put to it. He'd killed a man, a former soldier, on American soil. He couldn't work up an ounce of sympathy for John Eaton. However the man had started his military career, he'd lost his way and turned into a monster.

"How'd you get to us so quickly?"

"Your mom insisted we leave a half day earlier than Hank suggested. We were cruising up and down the shoreline, looking for likely hiding places when the coast guard arrived and organized the full search."

"Eaton chose a good one." Mark winced as the medic prodded the knife wound that creased his shoulder blade. "It didn't hurt that bad in the shower."

The medic game him an unconvinced hum. "Needs stitches." Of course it did; Charlotte had told him so.

"Is that really necessary?" Mark argued. "Won't glue do it?"

"Too deep," the medic replied.

Mark grunted his assent.

"Hank moved on the compound Eaton built in Arizona," his father said. "We should have an update in a few minutes."

"We're a long way from Arizona."

Ben agreed with a slow nod. "Each layer we pull back proves the man had quite a reach."

Footsteps in the hallway rushed closer, followed by a rapid knocking on the cabin door. "Ben? Mark?"

Mark caught the worry in his father's gaze as he opened the door to Patricia. "He's fine," Ben said.

"Good." She peered around Ben. "You're good?" At Mark's nod, she looked back to her husband. "It's Hank."

Mark jerked at the pain in her voice and the medic grumbled as the movement tugged on the stitches he was trying to finish.

"Easy," the medic said.

"Wrap it up," Mark ordered. His mother hadn't uttered another word, collapsing into his father's embrace. The rare display of emotion and despair rattled him.

"What happened?" Ben asked, holding her close.

"He was shot." The words were muffled in Ben's chest.

Mark's stomach twisted.

"I don't know how badly yet." She leaned back a little and fanned her face. "He didn't make the call. One of the other investigators did."

Ben glanced at Mark over her head.

"Go," Mark said. "I'll find you as soon as this is done."

It seemed to take forever for the medic to wrap things up. When the young man started to give him directions on wound care and pain relief, Mark shooed him out of the cabin.

Dressing swiftly in shorts, a loose T-shirt and the deck shoes his mother had brought along, he bounded up to the cutter's bridge to find his parents and get the facts on Hank. His heart rate steadied when he recognized Hank's voice, tight with pain and temper, on the other end of the radio.

"It will take us weeks to sort through this material," Hank was saying.

Mark went to flank his mom, who was still leaning heavily on his dad.

Their bond was remarkable. Whether they were standing side by side or with half a world between them, their unity was a tangible force. Mark had taken their commitment to each other and to family for granted growing up. It was only after being out on his own that he'd realized not only the treasure of his parents' bond but the beauty of it.

He'd given up on finding a woman worth the effort and commitment, until he'd looked at Charlotte differently. Until, in the middle of the unimaginable, she'd given him a priceless gift. Now he couldn't shake the idea that she could be that partner for him.

Distracted with thoughts of how he might become the man she needed, he only caught bits and pieces of Hank's report on Eaton's compound.

"In the meantime," Hank continued, "Luke, Jolene and I can't let down our guard."

"Wait. Why?" Mark asked.

"Mark?"

"Yeah, it's me."

"How are you doing?" Hank asked. "Looked a little grim there for a while."

"Chicks dig scars," Mark joked, dodging a glare from his mother. He leaned closer to the speaker. "Better now that Eaton's dead. Why would you still be on guard?"

"Thanks for handling that, by the way," Hank replied. "I guess SEALs get the win this time around."

Mark laughed. "Always."

"We'll see," Hank replied. "I'm hoping your success there will be enough."

"Why wouldn't it be?" Mark queried.

Patricia gripped Mark's hand, careful of the scrapes on his knuckles. "Eaton put a bounty on Luke, Jolene and Hank too," she said.

"What the hell? No one will follow through if he's too dead to pay them, right?"

"I'm sure you're right," Hank said. He coughed a little. "But I don't want to assume anything just yet. You'll understand when you see what I'm looking at."

"Fine." Mark believed him, though he wasn't eager to take a deeper look at anything else they gathered on the scumbag. "Have someone else take over, all right? And let a medic take a look at you. Mom's eyes are bugging out over here."

"I beg your pardon," Patricia said.

Her tone earned a pained laugh from both Mark and Hank, while Ben managed to keep a straight face, assuring her Mark was exaggerating.

"It's not that serious, I promise," Hank said.

"Come on. She won't believe you until she sees you with her own eyes."

"I know." Hank managed to sound greatly inconvenienced. "I'll be back as soon as possible."

The update over, Mark walked out on deck, hoping to find Charlotte, but apparently she was still being treated below. She was safe now. That was the important point. They would see each other at family events and he could always ask his mom about her.

"How are you really feeling?" Patricia asked, joining him at the rail.

Inadequate and guilty. "Sore," he answered instead. He noticed the look in her eye. He had to give her something close to the truth or she'd press him harder. He didn't want to face any of the tough questions about being caged, beaten and hunted.

Neither his confidence nor skill would change the fact that Charlotte had been exposed to outrageous danger and trauma.

"Do you want me to go check on her?" Patricia asked.

"No." It would take time for her to recover from their ordeal. "She'll come up when she's ready."

"You love her."

Mark stared out at the island they'd escaped. Eaton had been a monster, no doubt there. Quick-Punch Kid and the man Mark had cuffed to a tree were in custody. The coast guard expected to apprehend Muscle and the injured man presumed to be on the boat with him in due time. All of that should make Mark feel better.

He didn't. No matter the jokes Charlotte had cracked about dying increasing her value as an artist, he'd let her down. Deliberately he shifted his gaze to his parents' sailboat, bobbing in the swells aft of the coast guard cutter. "How long until you and Dad head back?" he asked.

She sighed at his diversion. They both understood she wasn't fooled and he wasn't ready to share.

"Sue Ellen and Ron and your father and I agreed it was best to stay here with you and Charlotte through the morning at the very least."

"In case one of us falls to pieces? It won't be her," he said.

She cocked an eyebrow. "You're in a safe place," she said. "It's not the worst idea to relax and enjoy it. What Eaton did—"

He didn't need his mother to run that down. "I'm good, Mom." He stared out at the island. From this vantage point all he could see was the beauty. In his mind though, he kept reliving the horror through Charlotte's eyes. "He didn't beat us."

"Rileys are a tough lot."

Mark agreed with her. Rileys were tough and as she'd so recently pointed out, far too jaded for an artist with mermaid hair and a gift for finding the beauty in everything. Including him.

"Come in out of the sun," Patricia said. "You need to hydrate."

"Mom." He shook his head, cutting her off. "It was only a week."

"A week in hell from what we saw."

He winced at her choice of words. Charlotte had felt the same way. "I'm all right. I know the drill. I'll have water even though I want a beer. And I'll get something to eat in a bit."

Just as soon as he was sure his stomach would tolerate real food. He understood his physical limitations. He was having a harder time accepting the boundless and unfamiliar emotions that being with Charlotte had dredged up.

He walked toward the stern of the cutter, letting the breeze from the ocean blow over him. Could he live without her?

Of course.

Did he want to?

No. Unfortunately he was certain she'd be better off without him underfoot, forcing her to consider the less beautiful side of life. That was the crux.

Eaton might be out of the picture, but the end of one crisis didn't change Mark's career path. His office wasn't in a sleek high-rise with normal hours and holidays off. He didn't wear a suit—he wore body armor and carried weapons as needed.

"Mark?"

Charlotte's voice interrupted his internal reality check. He turned, thankful she was alone.

She'd washed her hair and left it loose. That damp strawberry blond cloud flowed in waves past her shoulders. *Mermaid hair*, he thought again, half expecting her to dive into the water and disappear with a flash of a glimmering tail.

"How are you feeling?" they asked each other in unison.

"You first," he said, gripping the rail. If he moved, it would be to wrap her in his arms. If she rejected the advance, it would be the catalyst of a breakdown his mother was braced for.

Charlotte swallowed, her lips twitching to one side.

His body jerked, wanting desperately to bury his nose in her hair and breathe in the love and peace she'd once offered. Instead he held his ground. He could handle whatever rejection or blame she dished out.

He deserved that and so much more.

Charlotte wanted to burrow close, but he stood there so stiff and aloof. He looked clean and fresh and strong as if the scrapes and bruises she could see weren't real. And whatever soap he'd used smelled so tantalizing she had to work to keep her distance.

"I'm tired," she admitted, answering his question at last. "In a weird I-don't-want-to-sleep way."

"I get that. It will pass."

His guarded expression bothered her. Though he smiled, it didn't quite reach his eyes. "How many stitches did you need?"

"Maybe a dozen. I was too annoyed with the ham-fisted medic to keep track."

She wanted to turn him around, lift his shirt and see for herself. She had a ridiculous urge to inventory his wounds as she kissed each one. But this wasn't the man who teased and joked and showed her tenderness while saving her from certain death on a deserted island. This was the guy no one could get close to. He was the warrior again, eager to be done with the niceties and get back to work.

Would he push her away if she admitted she needed a hug? His hug. She shouldn't ask this man for just one more minute of listening to his steady, reassuring heartbeat under her ear. Fighting tears, she turned her face to the breeze and did her best to breathe through it. Pain would fade.

"Charlotte?"

"Hmm?"

"I asked if you needed stitches."

"Oh." She hadn't heard him, so lost in her own agony. "No. Nothing worse than a scrape." She tugged a strand of hair away from her cheek. "You." Her breath caught. "Thank you for taking the brunt of—" What did you call the ordeal they'd survived? "—everything out there," she finished.

"I'm sorry you were caught up in Eaton's vendetta against my family."

Looking at him, she could almost see the shiny new walls he'd rebuilt to protect himself. Though he would say he was protecting her from him. Hadn't he learned anything about her?

She wasn't half as fragile as he thought. Being an artist was no picnic. Something deep inside her clicked. She couldn't let him off that easy. He might turn her aside, but she wasn't going without a fight.

"I love you, Mark. Whatever else is going on in your head or heart, I hope you can hear that much."

"Charlotte."

She knew that tone. "Careful," she said, holding up a finger. "Don't give me lines about survival and stress-induced confusion. My feelings for you were clear before this mess, during the mess and they remain crystal clear now. It would be nice to know how you're feeling."

She felt her heart crack when he hesitated. Her pulse seemed to slow down, reverberating in her ears.

"Charlotte, it isn't that simple."

The fight of a moment ago faded out of her. "It is, actually." She'd been so sure he'd seen her as an independent, separate woman. Not an extended family member, more than a friend or a damsel in distress. "This isn't an ultimatum or a challenge. It's just love." She stepped closer and stood on tiptoe to kiss his cheek. "And it's all for you. Be well, Mark."

He needs more time, a small voice in her head whispered through her mind as she walked away. After all, he hadn't been crushing on *her* half his life. Even so, waiting for him to come around felt weak and pathetic.

"Charlotte."

"What?"

"I am in love with you." He rubbed his sternum as if the admission caused him physical pain. How was that any better than saying nothing? "The part of me that wants what's best for you isn't so impressed by what I feel."

He looked so confused she almost relented. "Shouldn't you be more concerned with *my* opinion of what's best for me?"

"Probably." His lips twitched. "Definitely."

She stepped close to him again and eased his hand from the railing, lacing her fingers through his. She lifted their joined hands to her lips and kissed his battered knuckles. The smallest of his injuries, those scrapes signified so much more to her. His determination, his fight, his courage. His ability to coax the best from her in the worst circumstances. Tears welled in her eyes.

"Thank you for never giving up on me," she said.

He drew her close, finally, his body warm and solid as his arms surrounded her. He was her perpetual safe place. "I could say the same to you," he murmured into her hair.

"Please don't let this be the end." She couldn't regret the small plea. Her entire reason for seeking him out before he slipped away was to be honest and open and leave no room for misunderstandings.

"Being a military wife is enough of a challenge. Being married to a SEAL takes it to another level. You'll resent me for leaving, always at the worst times, and just when you're comfortable in an area, the navy will send us to a new base."

Was that a proposal? Did he hear what he was saying? "Your parents and mine have both managed military careers," she pointed out.

"You're not them. You're special. Precious."

Her temper flared. "Be very careful with your next words, Mark Riley."

"You're an artist. You need good light and time and a cheering section."

She eased back, just enough to get his attention and keep her focus. "Love is its own kind of light," she said. "Trust, commitment and joy add color to the world and to my work. Which piece of that do you think I'm lacking?"

"None of it." He pushed his hand through his hair. "I'm in love with you, Charlotte."

"And I love you too. Doesn't that put us ahead of the game from the start?"

He shook his head and a swell of sympathy washed over her. "Then what are you afraid of?" she asked gently.

"I'm terrified of the day you walk out on me, fed up with the life I sucked you into."

Her heart ached anew. "That's not giving either one of us much credit." She stroked his windblown hair back from his forehead. "We're better than that and much better together. Look what we accomplished with a few bottles of water and a flare gun."

His brown eyes filled with grief and doubt rather than laughter as she'd hoped. "You need to be able to realize your dreams, Charlotte. Galleries, showings and healthy, beautiful inspiration. I've been too scared to ask what you want next."

"Mark, you are my inspiration. Long before we wound up on that island." She laid a hand over his heart. "Choosing to make a life with you isn't any risk in my mind. The thought of weaving my future with yours only fills me with confidence. Your goals or mine, we can reach them together."

"Are you proposing to me?" he asked, incredulous.

"Why not? I have to say I think it's better than the antiproposal you made a few minutes ago."

He frowned. "You'd really want to be my wife?"

"I've stated my case," she said. "My heart's yours, Mark Riley. It's been yours for so long that together or apart won't change things."

He heard the combined voices of their parents approaching and leaned over to the aft rail. "Do you trust me?"

She did, despite the wicked spark in his eye. "You know I do."

He clasped her hand and led her down a narrow stairwell. "Go, go," he said quietly. He hurried toward the lifeboat and helped her into it.

She smothered a giggle as she realized what he was doing. "You're stealing your dad's sailboat?"

"And you are my accomplice." He winked and gave her a quick kiss. "I warned you that life with me would be trouble."

At the sailboat, he helped her up the ladder, and tied the lifeboat to the line so the coast guard could reel it in.

"How will our parents get home?"

"They're smart. Let them solve their own problems.

You and I need some time alone, to recover from our ordeal."

She looked around. "Are you sure the two of us can handle this?" she asked, a little overwhelmed by the unfurled sails, the tall mast and the various lines.

"A SEAL and his future bride can handle anything."

She liked the sound of that.

He started the motor quickly and put some distance between them and the cutter before turning back and coming alongside.

"Are you stealing my boat?" his father called out in his booming command voice.

"Yes, General, I am," Mark shouted. "We'll meet you at the house in a few days. Maybe a week."

"Take your R&R," Charlotte's dad said with a laugh.

"But don't you dare elope!" her mother added.

"Yes, sir. Ma'am."

Charlotte blew kisses to their parents as her future husband sailed away, leaving laughter in their wake.

Hours later, with the sun setting over the Florida Keys, offshore and alone, they finally made love and gave each other the words and touches that mattered most. It was better than any of her fantasies.

Afterward, brimming with happiness, she snuggled under a blanket, her back to Mark's chest as they shared a bottle of good wine under the stars. Loving him, telling him, was the best thing she'd done with her life.

"I'll resign if you want," he said abruptly.

She twisted around, startled that he'd brought this up again. "Why would I want you to leave a career you love? You wouldn't ask that of me."

"Your career doesn't put you in the crosshairs," he pointed out.

She arched an eyebrow.

"Well, hopefully not ever again," he allowed.

"I'll make you a promise," she began, pleased when his eyes sparkled. "Whatever comes our way, we'll go on as we've started. There isn't any challenge we can't overcome together."

"As long as we celebrate every joy the same way," he said.

"Now you're getting it." She kissed him tenderly, her heart full to bursting. Despite everything she'd imagined, it was even more wonderful to feel her lifelong crush blooming into a lasting love.

* * * * *

Don't miss previous titles in Regan Black's
The Riley Code miniseries:

His Soldier Under Siege
A Soldier's Honor

Available now from
Harlequin Romantic Suspense!

#2119 COLTON 911: THE SECRET NETWORK
Colton 911: Chicago
by Marie Ferrarella

When a child is found at a crime scene, social worker January Colton's main goal is to protect the girl now in her care. Detective Sean Stafford is no stranger to protecting children, but he needs to know what she saw. As January and Sean work together to keep Maya safe, they find their opposite personalities create a spark they never expected.

#2120 COLTON'S DANGEROUS LIAISON
The Coltons of Grave Gulch
by Regan Black

Struggling to resolve a baffling betrayal within her department, police chief Melissa Colton must team up with Antonio Ruiz, a handsome hotel owner with a tragic past. Can she keep her heart protected in the process?

#2121 THE WIDOW'S BODYGUARD
by Karen Whiddon

Jesse Wyman is charged with protecting a high-profile widow from the men who killed her husband. He may have fallen in love with Eva Rowson while previously undercover in her father's motorcycle gang, and his secrets could ruin any chance they might have at a future.

#2122 HIGH-STAKES BOUNTY HUNTER
by Melinda Di Lorenzo

For six years, Elle Charger has managed to keep Katie away from the girl's father, but now the vicious man has caught up to them and has kidnapped Katie. Elle's only hope is Noah Loblaw, a bounty hunter who has his own haunted history.

"Get down," he shouted. "It's a drone."

Eva had seen enough movies to know what drones
could do. Jumping aside, she dropped to the floor and
crawled toward the door, glad of her dark room. If the
thing was armed, she wanted to make herself the smallest
target possible. Luckily, her window was closed. She
figured if it crashed into the glass, the drone would come
apart.

By the time she reached her closed bedroom door, the
thing hovered right outside her window, its bright light
illuminating most of her room. She dived for the door
just as the drone tapped against the glass, lightly and
precisely enough to tell her whoever controlled it was
very good at the job.

She'd just turned the knob when the drone exploded,
blowing out her window and sending shards of glass like
deadly weapons into her room.

"Eva!" Jesse's voice, yelling out her name. She focused on that, despite the stabbing pain in her leg. Somehow, she managed to pull the door open and half fell into the hallway, one hand against her leg.

Heart pounding, she scrambled away from her doorway, dimly registering the trail of blood she left in her wake.

"Are you all right?" Reaching her, Jesse scooped her up in his muscular arms and hauled her farther down the hall. Outside, she could hear men yelling. One of the voices sounded like her father's.

"Is everyone else okay?" she asked, concerned.

"As far as I know," Jesse answered. "Though I haven't been outside yet to assess the situation. What happened?"

"It was a drone rigged with explosives." Briefly she closed her eyes. When she reopened them, she found his face mere inches from hers. "Someone aimed it right at my window."

Fury warred with concern in his dark eyes. He focused intently on her. "There's a lot of blood. Where are you hurt?"

Hurt. Odd how being with him made everything else fade into insignificance. In his arms, she finally felt safe.

Don't miss
The Widow's Bodyguard
by Karen Whiddon, available January 2021
wherever Harlequin Romantic Suspense books
and ebooks are sold.

Harlequin.com

HRSEXP1220